BRIDGERS 4: THE MIND OF MANY

STAN C. SMITH

*To those who take what they are given
and make it into what they want.*

THE MIND OF MANY

Every person here is capable and has a set of skills. Everyone here is badass in one way or another.

INFINITY FOWLER

1

ST6

SEPTEMBER 4 - 6:03 AM

INFINITY FOWLER STARED at herself in the mirror as an earthquake rattled the entire SafeTrek bridging facility. She reacted only by bending her knees slightly for stability. The tremors had become so frequent that she barely noticed them anymore. Besides, her mind was elsewhere—she was now in her last hour on this version of Earth. Within minutes, she'd be leaving all this destruction and horror behind. But she couldn't stop thinking about the fact that eight billion other people didn't have that option. They would all die, along with every other living thing on the planet.

She ran her fingertips over three scars on her belly, each about an inch long. Knife wounds, from thirteen years ago. Eddy Chastain had stabbed her three times over a goddamn t-shirt. She was proud of most of her scars—and she had a lot of them—but these three were troubling. For the first time, she was bothered by the fact that Eddy Chastain had given her a wound that may have stolen her ability to have children. It didn't comfort her much to know that, if the bastard was still alive, he was about to die along with everyone else.

Her hand moved up past her breasts to the large tattoo in the center of her chest. It was of a bird—a painted bunting—inked in blue, red, and green, although the colors had faded. Each time she bridged to an alternate world, a little more of the ink was stripped away. But today's bridge would be her last.

She stared at the tattoo. Passerina. That was the bird's genus name. And it was Infinity's birth name, given to her by her parents. Infinity's chest heaved, surprising her. What the hell? It was a sob. Why would she be crying now?

As a kid, she had hated her parents. She'd left home at fourteen and never returned. Not because her mom or dad had beat her. They hadn't. Besides, she could have endured just about any physical abuse, even at that age. And they hadn't verbally abused her either. Verbal abuse would have required that they cared, at least a little. Instead, they had been completely, unconditionally indifferent. It was as if Infinity—Passerina—had become invisible once she was old enough to dress herself and get ready for school. Her parents would get up, go to work, and come home. Occasionally, the three of them would sit and eat together, but even then her mom and dad would hardly talk to each other, let alone to their daughter.

She pulled her gaze from her bird tattoo and looked into her own eyes. They were slightly teary. Where were her parents now? The world was coming to an end and she hadn't even tried to locate them. She didn't even know whether they were still alive. Even if she had found them, what could she have said? *"Hey you guys, it's me. Remember that last thing I said to you when I left, that I hoped you'd both die in pain? Well, you're about to, along with everyone else on the planet, and it's partly my fault."*

Her chest heaved again, and she turned away from the mirror. These thoughts were a waste of time. She had less than an hour left, and she didn't want to miss seeing her last sunrise on this world.

She turned to the black shorts and racerback sports bra she'd selected, her favorite fightwear outfit. It was strange to think that this would be her last time wearing them. After pulling them on, she left her bunkroom.

The mostly-empty halls of the SafeTrek facility were deceptively quiet. Infinity knew that just outside the building were thousands of refugees hoping against all odds to be selected for an outgoing bridging colony. During the last few days, the scene outside had become increasingly chaotic and violent, as food and other necessary items dwindled. As many as two thousand National Guardsmen had been brought in to protect the facility and provide resources to the refugees, but at least a quarter of the guardsmen had defected since being brought in. Infinity didn't blame them—most had families.

Her bare feet nearly silent on the tile floor, she made her way to the back of the facility and entered the stairwell leading to the roof. After climbing three flights, she emerged into the open air. The sun wasn't up yet, but the eastern sky's orange glow illuminated the roof enough for her to see that her hopes of quietly watching this last sunrise with Desmond were in vain. Desmond Weaver, her bridging partner and now her lover, was there waiting for her, but he wasn't alone. Beside him was Armando Doyle, Infinity's boss and the CEO of SafeTrek. Also present were Lenny Stiles and Xavier Cahill, Desmond's friends who, with Desmond's help, had managed to secure their own spots with the outgoing colony—colony ST6. And at least thirty

National Guardsmen were also on the roof, stationed around the perimeter, monitoring the ground below.

What the hell was going on?

"A slight change of plans," Armando said as Infinity approached.

She frowned and glanced at Desmond.

"Don't worry," Desmond said. "We're still going out with group one at seven."

Infinity exhaled, relieved. "Then what's the problem?"

Armando pointed to the northwest. "Not a problem, exactly, but we're expecting one more refugee to arrive within the next few minutes. Hayley Millwright."

She stared at him. "As in *President* Hayley Millwright?"

"How's that for a zip-banging head rush?" Lenny said. "The president of the United States is going to be in our colony. My hopes for becoming colony leader have been crushed."

Armando actually chuckled at this before saying, "President Millwright has requested to join group thirty-six, the last group to bridge out."

Infinity tried to wrap her head around this. Apparently the federal government expected colony ST6 to be the last colony to bridge out, the last hope to save a small portion of the human species.

"She'll be arriving in a chopper soon," Desmond said. "So, um, do you still want to watch the sunrise together?"

Infinity looked around at all the guardsmen and sighed. "Damn right I do." She stepped to Desmond's side and took his hand. They both turned and gazed at the orange horizon. She squeezed his hand tightly, feeling its warmth. He was the one thing in this world she would not be willing to leave behind.

Desmond then spoke to her by sending his thoughts through his arm, across the place where their skin touched, up her arm, and into her mind. "I can't believe we're actually leaving this world forever. Are you ready for this?"

She glanced at him. On their most recent bridging excursion he had obtained the ability to project his thoughts telepathically to any person he was touching, and apparently this somewhat creepy ability hadn't diminished, even after having bridged back to his own world. Infinity had refused the serum that would have given her this ability, which meant she couldn't reply to his question without speaking aloud. Instead, she just squeezed his hand more tightly. She didn't know how to answer the question anyway.

She and the others stared out at the orange and navy blue sky in silence. From the sea of thousands of camping refugees below, she could hear faint conversations, crying children, and the clinking of cookware and other equipment. Later, as more of the refugees awoke, arguments would begin, eventually escalating into fights, protesters would chant against SafeTrek's seemingly callous colonist selection process, and desperate campers would attempt to infiltrate the ranks of the 718 refugees chosen for colony ST6. The lucky refugees of ST6 had been separated from the others using hastily-constructed fencing, and they were protected by hundreds of vigilant National Guardsmen, but the sheer number of campers streaming into the area was concerning. Infinity shuddered at the thought of what might happen if those people somehow learned that ST6 was almost certain to be the last outgoing colony.

Armando sighed as if he were content simply to stare at the sunrise, but then he said, "I don't suppose any of you have heard the story of how bridging got its name?"

Infinity turned to him. She had been bridging for Armando for over four years, but he had never mentioned this.

Armando continued. "Most people think it was simply

derived from the fact that the technology allows one to bridge to alternate universes. But not so. I was the first to muster the funds for an operational bridging center, so I had the privilege of coming up with a suitable name for the process." He paused, as if thinking. "I'm a scholar of the great explorers throughout history, including a man by the name of Jim Bridger. Bridger considered himself a native Missourian, by the way, but he explored much of the western United States between 1820 and 1850. He saw sights that no man of European descent had ever seen before. A fascinating, larger-than-life character by any measure. So I decided pioneers using this new technology should be called bridgers, and the process should be called bridging."

"Well, that was kind of random," Lenny said. "Interesting, but random."

Infinity gazed at Armando. She had gradually come to think of him as the father she had always wished she'd had, and she was grateful he'd decided to bridge out with colony ST6. But at this moment he looked more frazzled than she'd ever seen him. His eyes were sunken from lack of sleep. His characteristic bowtie was missing, and his white shirt was untucked. His disheveled, thinning hair made him look like a mad scientist. His back was stiff, as if he were in pain. For his sake, she hoped the upcoming bridging process would be relatively smooth. She was pretty sure he'd never actually bridged before.

"Uh, you guys. What is that?" It was Xavier. He was pointing north.

The tip of the sun was just now coming up over the eastern horizon, and the sky to the north was illuminated with a deep blue hue. A massive black cloud was growing there. No, not just growing—it was churning and heaving like a living thing. Tiny flashes of lightning twinkled constantly, like fireflies, revealing how immense the storm was.

As Infinity stared, it became obvious that the dark mass was rotating.

"God almighty," Armando said.

Lenny whistled. "That's one big-ass tornado."

"It can't be a tornado," Armando said. "It's at least ten miles wide. The largest tornado ever recorded was only two and a half."

The cloud's rotation was picking up speed, throwing up a smaller cloud of tiny specks. Infinity squinted. At least some of the specks were uprooted trees.

"Look at that," Xavier said, pointing west. "More of them."

Two more black clouds were forming, each at least as large as the first, and one was already visibly rotating. Armando had been wrong—these things weren't ten miles wide. They were at least fifteen.

The building lurched, forcing the guardsmen to move back from the edge to keep from falling off the roof. The building had heaved upward at least six inches. This was immediately followed by several smaller tremors. A swell of cries arose from the camped refugees below.

Xavier was still watching the storms in the distance. "They're either getting larger, or they're coming this way!"

He was right. The two churning clouds to the west were definitely moving toward SafeTrek. And now they were throwing up just as much debris as the storm to the north.

"When is Millwright's chopper supposed to arrive?" Infinity asked Armando.

"Should be here any time," he replied, not taking his eyes off the approaching storms. "The chopper's coming from Kansas City."

Infinity turned to the northwest and scanned the sky, which now had taken on a strange contrast of orange and green hues. Surely the pilot would have turned back at the sight of these freak twisters. But the storms had popped up so quickly.

Suddenly she spotted the chopper, a miniature black toy to the north of one of the twisters coming from the west. The chopper was headed straight for SafeTrek, but the massive tornado was approaching the facility at a surprising pace, threatening to force the aircraft off course.

"This doesn't look good," Armando said, having spotted the helicopter. "What is that pilot thinking?"

Desmond said, "He's thinking about saving the president's life. Bridging out with ST6 is her only chance."

Infinity pulled her eyes from the chopper to look at the tornado nearest to SafeTrek. Its size and violence made her stomach lurch. Swirling around its base were hundreds of uprooted trees and other objects that might have been houses and vehicles. No human-made structure in its path—not even the SafeTrek building—could survive its fury. The roof beneath her feet began to shake from another ground tremor. A low roar was building in volume, from the earthquake, the approaching storm, or both.

"Go faster!" Lenny cried, staring at the president's chopper.

The helicopter was approaching fast but struggling to hold a straight course, pitching back and forth from the turbulence. The swirling black cloud appeared to be almost touching the chopper, but this could easily have been an optical illusion due to the tornado's size.

Infinity glanced at the other two twisters. The one to the southwest appeared to be fizzling out, and the one to the north was moving east, staying at a safe distance. The third one was still getting closer, although it appeared to be shifting northward. It was a dark, menacing wall, thousands of feet tall.

Even if the twister continued angling north, it would only miss SafeTrek by a mile or so. Could the building survive?

The chopper started descending, thrown to the left and then the right. Fortunately, it was a large, heavy aircraft—otherwise it wouldn't have had much of a chance.

Desmond shouted something, but his words were lost in the deafening roar. He pointed, and Infinity saw—the twister's debris field was about to envelope the chopper. As she watched, a tree that was nearly as long as the helicopter narrowly missed smashing into it.

"Go, goddammit!" Infinity shouted. The chopper was seconds away from SafeTrek, perhaps a quarter of a mile.

As debris started hitting SafeTrek's roof, the guardsmen headed for the door to the stairs, herding the civilians with them. Infinity paused just inside the door as the last of the guardsmen filed in past her. She shielded her eyes and turned back to look. The chopper was attempting to land, but it was being buffeted wildly. An airborne tree limb suddenly struck the tail rotor and the chopper started to spin. The pilot dropped the chopper the last ten feet with what little control he still had, and the massive aircraft jostled to a rough stop near the roof's edge.

Infinity stepped aside as the guardsmen poured back out of the stairwell and ran to the chopper, hunkering low to avoid flying debris. She glimpsed two heads of wildly-blowing blonde hair amidst the ten or so people emerging from the helicopter— President Millwright and her daughter. The guardsmen surrounded the new arrivals and hustled them back toward the stairs, shielding them with their own bodies.

Infinity held the door open, struggling to keep it still, as the mass of people pushed through to the stairs. Before shutting the door, she looked back once more, just in time to see the massive green and white helicopter tumble over the side of the roof and disappear.

She descended the stairs, following the others. She could hear them shouting to each other, but the clatter of debris pelting the stairwell housing and metal door behind her was too loud for her to make out what they were saying.

Infinity had just turned the corner to start down the second flight when she heard the door to the ground floor below being opened. This was followed by more shouting, and then gunfire from somewhere within the building. What the hell? Who was shooting? The only scenario she could imagine was that the refugees from outside had somehow broken through the front doors seeking shelter from the storm, in which case the guardsmen may have panicked and opened fire.

She emerged from the stairwell to a scene of chaos. The guardsmen, surrounding the president and her entourage, were moving steadily down the hall, firing at someone Infinity couldn't see.

"What the hell are they shooting at?" Infinity shouted as she caught up with Desmond, Lenny, Xavier, and Armando immediately behind the mass of guardsmen.

Desmond shook his head, indicating he had no idea. But they didn't have to wonder for long. As they continued following the armed men through the hallway, they soon found themselves stepping over the bodies of several civilians.

"Stop shooting!" Infinity screamed. "These people are not a threat!"

But her words were lost in the chaos. The president's body-guards and some of the guardsmen continued shooting people who couldn't or wouldn't get out of their way.

The hallway opened up to the expansive area that included

the cafeteria, lounge, and entryways that led to other halls that led to offices, bunk rooms, the bridging chamber, and the quarantine lab. The entire space was filled with people, most of them cowering in fear from the advancing armed men.

"Hold your fire!" a woman's voice shouted through all the other noise. "For God's sake, stop shooting!"

The voice belonged to President Hayley Millwright. Infinity seldom watched the news, but she had heard that voice plenty of times when passing by the TV in the lounge.

The large room became relatively quiet, and for the first time, Infinity realized the floor was vibrating, either from another earthquake or from the massive storm outside. She scanned the crowd. Hundreds of refugees—perhaps thousands—were crammed into the space, along with National Guardsmen who had apparently been working outside when the tornado had formed.

"Clear the way!" a guardsmen shouted. "We're coming through, even if we have to walk over your dead bodies."

Infinity nudged Desmond. "I have to do something." She pushed her way through the throng until she was beside President Millwright's knot of protectors. "Listen!" she shouted to the crowd. "I know we're all frightened, but—"

"Frightened, my ass!" a man in civilian clothes shouted. "Do you have any idea how many people are dying out there in that storm? And you folks are in here safe and sound, ready to bridge away from this hellhole." The man put a hand on the shoulder of a frightened-looking kid about ten years old. "I brought my boy all the way here from Des Moines, and even if you won't let me go, I'm begging you to take him. You're one of them bridgers, aren't you?"

Infinity shook her head. "I am, but I don't get to decide who goes."

A woman in the crowd pointed and said, "That's President Millwright! If anyone can decide, she can. Mrs. Millwright, we don't want to die any more than you do. You've got to help us!"

Infinity turned to Millwright. Instead of cowering behind the bodyguards and soldiers, the president stood up straight and stepped forward. Millwright's husband and daughter were with her. Both were wide-eyed, but they stood as tall and dignified as the president. Millwright's daughter—Infinity couldn't remember her name—was like a twenty-something version of her mom. Both women looked disheveled, their blonde hair having been blasted by the wind so that they looked completely different than they normally did on television.

"I hear what you're saying, and I understand," Millwright announced. "I came to this place not because *I* insisted on it, but because my advisors convinced me to come. They believe my presence within the next outgoing colony could be valuable, both to the colonists themselves and to the occupants of the world we bridge to. And so I agreed. And I'm confident that each member of the colony was selected based on their ability to contribute significantly." She paused expertly, and everyone became silent in order to hear what she was about to say.

"So I have a proposal," she went on. "If you can bring some order to this mob, and if you can form an orderly line, I'll have a team of people interview each and every one of you. You convince them that you would be valuable to the colony—more valuable than any one person already assigned to the colony—and they will put you in that person's place. If not in this colony, then perhaps in the next. Can you think of any procedure more fair than that?"

The room was silent, other than the wind that was still raging outside.

"This is bullshit!" said the man from Des Moines. "Why

should my son be left to die just because he's not a doctor or a politician? Does that make him less important? Is he less important than your husband or daughter? And we know damn well there won't be no more colonies going out. This building could collapse any minute!"

As if in response, the floor suddenly lurched, throwing people off their feet and prompting a chorus of screams. The lights blinked off for a moment and then flickered back on.

"To hell with you!" the man cried, staggering to his feet. He then rushed toward the president as if he intended to attack her.

Before the guardsmen could shoot the man, Infinity clotheslined him and took him to the ground. She locked her legs around his chest and clamped her right arm around his neck, immobilizing him.

"Unless you all want to be slaughtered," she shouted at the refugees, "you need to back off and consider President Millwright's offer!"

Abruptly, the floor heaved again, this time sending light fixtures and pieces of concrete from the ceiling crashing into the crowd. A wave of panicked screams came from the direction of the building's front door. These were more than screams of fear —they had the horrific and unmistakable tenor of pain and death. Infinity realized what was happening. The thousands of refugees still outside were forcing their way in, probably trampling and crushing people in the process, pushing a wave of tremendous force toward the center of the building. The advancing pressure of bodies would reach this central room within seconds.

Infinity released the man and jumped to her feet. "Get Millwright to the bridging chamber, now!" she shouted, pointing down the hall to her right.

And then the heaving wave of humanity flowed into the

open space of the large room. Screaming refugees and guardsmen were forced into the room like twigs carried by a flooded river.

"Clear the way!" one of the president's bodyguards shouted. But it was no use—the space was too tightly packed.

Somewhere nearby an automatic weapon fired a two-second burst, which only intensified the panic and screams. More gunfire quickly drowned out the voices. Dozens of guardsmen were spraying the ceiling with bullets in a deafening attempt to clear a path to the bridging chamber. Several of the men began shooting into the crowd, adding splattering blood and falling bodies to the mayhem.

Refugees began climbing over each other to get out of the way, creating a tangle of limbs and body parts. Miraculously, an opening began to form. The guardsmen pushed through, pulling the Millwrights with them.

"Follow them!" Infinity yelled at Desmond.

Desmond, Armando, Lenny, and Xavier huddled against the pack of Millwright's protectors, following them, with Infinity bringing up the rear.

Seconds later they passed through the airlock into the quarantine lab adjacent to the bridging chamber. Lab techs slammed the two airlock hatches shut behind them and secured the locks.

In the center of the lab stood fifteen of the first twenty refugees to be bridged out with colony ST6. Beside the refugees was Reece Eagleton, the regional FEMA Administrator who was in charge of overseeing SafeTrek's attempts to save the human species.

"What the hell's happening out there?" Eagleton demanded.

"A better question might be, what *isn't* happening," Armando replied. "The mother of all tornadoes nearly took out the building."

"Unauthorized refugees breached the facility," one of the guardsmen added. "We had to inflict some casualties to get through with President Millwright."

Eagleton looked at Millwright. "Welcome, Madam President. Don't fret over the extreme measures taken to get you here. Those people out there are going to perish soon anyway. The important thing is—"

"Shut up, Reece!" Millwright said. "All of you just shut up!" She rubbed her face with her hands. "I know exactly what's happening out there, and I don't need to hear you talking about those people as if they were acceptable losses. Have some respect!" She stared at her fingers, which were trembling, and then balled them into fists.

Infinity didn't know much about Millwright, but her opinion of the woman had just risen a few notches.

Millwright's husband and daughter remained silent but moved closer together as the president looked around with burning intensity. "I don't know if you people have heard, but SafeTrek is the last of the seven bridging facilities still standing." She nodded toward the airlock hatch. "I just told those people out there we would allow them to make a case for being included in the colony. Assuming your machinery is functional, would it be feasible to bridge some of them out?"

After several seconds of uncomfortable silence, Armando said, "I can't say how feasible that is, but my gut tells me we need to start bridging now, before it's too late. Madam President, I want to shift you and your family to group one." He glanced at his watch. "And group one should have bridged four minutes ago."

"We had discussed being included in the last group going out, group thirty-six," Millwright said.

Armando shook his head. "I don't think you should wait."

One of the guardsmen chosen to be part of group one stepped forward. "It would be my honor to shift my spot to a later group to make room for you, Madam President."

Another guardsman stepped forward, this one a rough-looking woman. "And I'll shift my spot for your husband or daughter, ma'am."

"And I'll step aside as well," another uniformed man said.

"We'll shift these three to group two, Madam President," Armando quickly said. "They'll show up at the destination world one hour after you and the rest of group one arrive there."

The building began shaking again, and faint screams arose from the mob of refugees beyond the airlock.

Armando stepped toward the bridging chamber and gestured toward the hatch. "Please, everyone, this way. Hurry!"

Millwright sighed, obviously reluctant. "Thank you," she said to the three guardsmen who had volunteered their spots. The president, her husband, and her daughter were then ushered through the airlock. They were followed by two history professors, a man and woman, selected as arbitrators between the refugees and the residents of the destination world. But since colony ST6 was headed for a world that had diverged from Earth's timeline only twenty years ago, the historians' job was expected to be easy. Following the professors were four doctors. Three of these, all women, were SafeTrek med techs, including Infinity's favorite, Poppy Safran. The fourth was a man from Saint Louis who happened to have no family to prevent him from volunteering.

Infinity, Desmond, Lenny, and Xavier entered the chamber next. Infinity and Desmond were the official bridgers for the colony. Lenny and Xavier had bridged only once before, but Armando and Eagleton, with a bit of convincing, had agreed that

Lenny and Xavier's experience, as well as their biological expertise, would be valuable.

Armando and his assistant, Celia Pickett, entered next. Infinity had recently convinced Armando to join colony ST6, and he had insisted on Celia joining the group as well. Between the two of them, Armando and Celia possessed more knowledge about bridging technology than anyone on Earth. That knowledge would almost certainly be useful to the people of the destination world, if for no other reason than to prevent them from destroying their own version of Earth the way this version had been destroyed. But Infinity's reasons for wanting Armando to join the colony were of a more personal nature. He was a dear friend.

Finally, five guardsmen entered, now down from eight since three had volunteered to bridge with the next group.

This was the first group of twenty. If the bridging device continued to function, thirty-five more groups would follow, one group per hour. These were the limits imposed by bridging technology, although no one knew why. The technology had actually come from an alien civilization in the form of encoded instructions sent through space via a radio signal. Only 20 people per group. Any more than that and the device would simply not function. It took about sixty minutes to prepare the device to bridge another group, and the device would keep a connection to a specific destination world open for only thirty-six hours. After that, the connection would be severed forever. Again, no one knew why. Or how.

Infinity and Desmond stood facing the other eighteen refugees, and Infinity instructed them to spread out with about a foot of space between them.

"You can leave your clothes on, or you can take them off,"

Desmond said. "Either way, you'll arrive at the destination world naked. And without your hair."

Everyone remained still except for Armando and Celia, who both removed their shirts. Their motions were rather stiff, and Infinity immediately saw why. Both of them had fresh tattoos covering their entire backs. The skin bordering the ink lines was red and covered with glistening ointment. It was obvious what the tattoos were. Each of their backs was covered with the entire set of nine hundred symbols constituting the "key" to bridging technology. A grid, thirty by thirty. These symbols had been given to Desmond just yesterday by a bizarre species of transparent, fluid-dwelling creatures on the destination world of colony ST5.

"I'll explain later," Armando said when he saw Infinity's frown.

The voice of one of the techs sounded over the intercom system. "I'm resetting the countdown, Mr. Doyle. Is two minutes enough time, or do you need more?"

"We'll be ready in two," Armando replied. "Initiate."

Without hesitating, Desmond continued with his instructions. "The device scans the destination area just before bridging, so don't worry—it won't bridge you into a solid object or anything like that. But you'll arrive a short distance above the surface as a safety measure. You'll drop to the ground, usually only a few inches. Bend your knees slightly and try to stay on your feet."

The building began shaking again, heaving up and down enough that most of the group went to their knees to avoid falling.

"Wait! Please wait a moment." The voice had come from beyond the airlock hatches, which the techs had been in the process of closing. Seconds later, Reece Eagleton entered the chamber, his eyes wide. "Madam President, I'd like to be a part of this group. I beg of you to allow it. Honestly, I don't know if we'll have time for a second group." Tears were forming in Eagleton's eyes.

Millwright turned to Armando. "Can the device accommodate twenty-one?"

Armando shook his head. "It isn't wise to try, especially considering the circumstances."

One of the guardsmen, speaking solemnly, said, "I can wait an hour to join group two."

Infinity recognized the guy as Gideon Stead, who had escorted her and Desmond on a recent trip to Kentucky so that Desmond could see his mother one last time. The trip had gone terribly wrong, and Gideon had proven himself to be skilled and resilient.

Armando shook his head again. "We've already moved three of you. We had good reason for including eight guardsmen in the first group. I won't allow less than five." He hesitated for a moment and then nodded his head slightly as if making a decision. "I'll wait for a later group." He headed for the hatch.

"No!" Infinity cried. "You said you would—"

"I will—later!" Armando said, cutting her off. "This makes sense, and you know it. If we have trouble with the device, I need to be here to troubleshoot. It's my duty to be here."

Infinity couldn't believe this was happening. She stepped toward the hatch to stop him, but then the floor shifted sideways and she went down. Shouts filled the chamber as the room continued jerking from side to side. Infinity managed to get to her knees in time to see Armando closing the airlock hatch from the other side. She heard him shout, "Activate the bridge! Do it now!"

Eagleton scrambled forward, trying to get to his feet but

unable to. He rolled to his side and ended up inches from Infinity.

She could barely hear the tech's voice over the groaning and heaving of the building. "Bridging in five, four, three..."

Infinity grabbed Eagleton by his shirt. "You goddamn son of a—"

The violence, the noise, and the bridging chamber all vanished.

2

MOSS

September *4 - 7:12 AM*

Desmond was weightless for a brief second as he fell several feet to the ground. He landed on a soft surface and managed to stay on his feet. Some of the others lost their balance, though, and collapsed, crying out in confusion. Seconds later, most of them began retching, their stomachs trying to regurgitate the partly-digested food that had existed seconds ago but now had been stripped away by the bridging process.

Desmond stared down at the green surface beneath his feet and realized it was moss. Or some kind of plant that resembled moss.

"This can't be right," Infinity said, her voice full of alarm.

Desmond looked up and then followed her gaze. His gut was already twisted from his attempts to avoid retching, but it tightened even more as he took in his surroundings.

"Unrecognizable terrain," Infinity said. "There's no forest here. Large animals at several hundred yards."

Lush moss in various colors covered the ground as far as Desmond could see in every direction. The sky was astoundingly blue, dotted with cotton-ball clouds. There were no trees. The only structures rising above the flat, mossy plain were the numerous large mounds that dotted the landscape, some of them at least a hundred yards in diameter. These mounds were covered in carpet-like moss.

"Where are we?" Xavier said as he got to his feet.

"Not where we're supposed to be, that's for damn sure," Infinity replied.

Most of the other refugees had now gotten past their nausea and were standing up. Most of them grew quiet as they acclimated to being naked and hairless. As was typical for first-timers, this involved trying to feel their freshly-bald head and cover their genitals at the same time.

The guardsman named Gideon Stead seemed unfazed by the bridging process. He pointed toward the group of animals Infinity had spotted. "No idea what those are, but now they're coming our way."

At least fifty olive-green animals were moving directly toward the group of refugees. Desmond squinted at the creatures. They were large, at least the size of cattle, but they were nothing like cows. They were walking on more than four legs. The legs were hard to count while the creatures were moving, but there were at least six on either side. Their backs were domed and segmented, making them resemble massive pillbugs, the tiny crustaceans Desmond had known as roly polies when he was a kid.

Desmond glanced at Infinity, and their eyes met. He said, "This was supposed to be a world with a divergence of only twenty years," he said.

She frowned, her face lined with concern.

"Where are the trees?" Eagleton asked, his voice weak, either from retching or from fear. "This is supposed to be Missouri, right?"

"It *is* Missouri," Infinity said, not hiding her annoyance.

Eagleton persisted. "It doesn't look anything like Missouri. Someone screwed up. We have to go back!"

Infinity opened her mouth as if to respond, but then she stopped and just shook her head.

Gideon pointed. "That hill. We might be able to take shelter there."

Apparently, Gideon was the only one actually thinking straight. Desmond shook his head to clear away the fear that was growing inside him. He reminded himself that he was a bridger —one of the group's leaders. "Everyone okay?" he asked loudly.

Most of the refugees nodded in spite of their shock.

"Good," Infinity said. "Then we're moving to that hill. Stay together in a tight group. Don't wander off, and don't touch anything. We have no idea what's dangerous and what's not."

The refugees began walking, and Desmond followed behind the last of them. The carpet of moss-like plants was soft, at least a few inches thick. He turned to check on the approaching herd of creatures. The animals were still walking toward them, but at a fairly slow pace. The creatures were now about a hundred yards away, and Desmond could see that they were larger than he had originally thought, perhaps twice the size of the largest cow he'd ever seen.

As the refugees approached the hill, Desmond noticed what Gideon must have been referring to. The entire hillside was riddled with holes. In fact, it seemed that the holes made up a majority of the hill's surface.

The group stopped at the hill's base. Most of them kept glancing nervously back at the approaching herd. The solid parts of the hill comprised a framework of intertwined limbs of some kind of hard material. The meshed limbs on the surface of the hill were covered in fine moss, but inside the hill was a maze of bare limbs, becoming darker toward the center. These limbs—or girders—were apparently supporting the entire hill. The numerous structures had grown together into a massive mound a hundred yards wide and forty yards high. Desmond couldn't help but think of a coral reef. Was it possible the moss had actually created these framework hills as a way to elevate them toward the sunlight?

"We have three choices," Infinity announced. "We climb this mound and hope those creatures don't climb up after us, we run and hope they don't chase us, or we crawl inside and hope there's not something worse in there." She nodded toward the nearest hole.

Desmond glanced back at the approaching herd. The creatures in the lead were now moving faster, walking with an awkward gait due to having so many legs. The closer the things got, the more Desmond thought they resembled hippo-sized pillbugs.

"I'm climbing," said the history professor Chloe. The woman was in her late forties and appeared lithe and fit. She began scaling the mound, clambering up the ladder-like slope on her hands and knees. Several of the others started up after her.

"Be careful," Infinity said, waving for the rest of them to start climbing. "Don't put your weight on the thinner—"

An explosion of flying creatures cut her off, emerging from within the hill. Thousands of the winged insect-like animals the size of cicadas flooded out through several nearby openings, forming a dense, swirling cloud in the air above.

This apparently stirred up another swarm of winged creatures higher up the hill. These were smaller but just as numerous. Then another swarm emerged to the right, and then one to the left. Like a wave working its way around the hill, massive groups of bugs continued flying out of the framework, each group apparently consisting of a different species. Some of the swarms buzzed like angry wasps while others whined like tiny mosquitoes. One group with creatures the size of starlings fluttered with chittering wings as large as human hands. The spinning swarms scattered into the distance as they emerged, disappearing into the nooks and crannies of other nearby hills.

Desmond stood watching the creatures, mesmerized. But then the sounds of the approaching herd broke the spell, and he realized the monstrous creatures were now thirty yards away and closing.

"Get your asses up there!" Infinity shouted.

Desmond and Infinity waited until the other refugees had started up and then began climbing when the herd was only a few yards away. At about fifteen feet up the hill, Desmond paused to look down. The massive creatures had stopped at the base of the hill and were shuffling around with their heads near the ground, perhaps smelling the humans' scent. One of the beasts turned, giving Desmond a better look at its head. Two segmented antennae, each as long as a man's arm, probed the soft moss, touching the plants delicately as if gathering scent molecules. Its leathery head was dominated by two multifaceted eyes, each the size of a soccer ball. The creatures seemed to have no intention of climbing the hill in pursuit.

Desmond let out a sigh and turned to Infinity. He considered saying something but didn't know where to begin. The bridging device had malfunctioned, and he had no idea what kind of world they were on. This was a one-way trip, and they were all going to live the rest of their lives here. From the looks of things, that might be only a few hours, or maybe days. The creatures below were vastly different from anything back home. He could only conclude that this world had diverged from his own far earlier than any of the three alternate worlds he'd bridged to before—including the first one, which had diverged eighty million years ago.

The air was breathable, although he was starting to suspect a higher oxygen content, since he was taking fewer breaths than he normally would, especially considering the stressful circumstances. What effect would elevated oxygen have on their bodies after several hours or days? Were other more toxic gases present? What about predators, or infectious microbes, or parasites? What would the refugees even eat? The largest plants he'd seen so far were only a few inches tall and were without flowers or fruits.

"You okay, partner?"

Desmond started and realized Infinity had been watching him. He nodded. "Just trying to process everything."

"You remember Razor?"

"Yeah." Razor had been Infinity's previous partner. He'd been a fierce fighter, but that hadn't saved him from being killed and eaten by a ten-foot-tall wingless bird. Desmond had watched it happen, and he still had nightmares about it.

"Before Razor's last excursion, he said to me, 'Every world is paradise to some creatures and hell to others. You just have to be the right creature.'"

Desmond considered pointing out the irony of this, considering Razor's fate, but he decided against it.

"Humans aren't powerful or indestructible," she said. "But we are adaptable. That's our strength."

He shook his head. At this moment he was unable to acknowledge that there was any hope.

"Wipe that goddamn frown off your face," she said. "Those

people up there?" She nodded toward the eighteen refugees climbing ahead of them. "They need bridgers, not pussies."

He couldn't help but smile at this. "You do have a way with words," he said as he started climbing again.

The hill consisted entirely of interlaced girders of a brown, amber-like material. Fine green moss covered most of the outer surfaces, sometimes making the footing slippery, but the girders below the surface were bare.

As the hill's slope flattened out near the crest, Desmond heard one of the guardsmen ahead curse and then call out a warning to the others, something about being careful. Seconds later, he realized why when one of the horizontal girders broke beneath his knee, and he narrowly avoided a nasty cut from its jagged edge. He looked around and saw that many of the girders here near the top of the hill were thinner than those at the base.

The group stopped and gathered at the crest, where they could see out for miles in every direction. Desmond gazed out to his left and then to his right, taking it all in. The landscape was utterly alien, but it was also stunningly beautiful. The morning sun was still low in the sky, throwing brilliant light on an endless expanse of honeycombed hills that dotted the landscape. To the west, opposite the sun, larger hills—real hills, with rocky outcrops—rose above the plain. Behind those, faint in the hazy distance, rose even taller hills. Everything was carpeted with tiny moss-like plants, with huge swaths of yellows, oranges, and reds mottling the otherwise green landscape. Apparently some of these plants made use of other light-absorbing pigments besides chlorophyll.

Desmond spotted more herds of large animals grazing or moving about on the flat meadows between the framework hills. He saw more of the giant, olive-green pillbugs but also noticed other species of various shapes and colors, most of them too distant to discern details. If his mind hadn't been stunned by the crushing realization that the bridging device had malfunctioned, the biological fascination within him would now be shifting into overdrive.

He found a secure spot on the hill to sit with his feet dangling into the open cavities below and turned to look at the other refugees. Four of them were doctors. Two were historians selected as arbitrators. Five were national guardsmen. And lastly there was Reece Eagleton, Celia, Lenny, Xavier, and President Millwright's family. Altogether the group consisted of nine women and eleven men. Now naked and hairless, every one of them looked dazed and unnerved, clinging to the hill's strange framework and staring out at their incomprehensible surroundings.

President Millwright turned her head, and her eyes met Desmond's. Without her wavy blonde hair, she was less recognizable, but her strikingly intense eyes were still unmistakable. For a brief moment, her expression seemed to plead with Desmond, perhaps wishing that he might suddenly say something to give her hope. He shook his head slightly, having nothing to offer, and her expression faded.

"What are we supposed to do now?" It was Millwright's daughter. Desmond remembered her name was Isabelle. Her eyes were just as intense as her mother's.

"That's what *I* want to know!" Eagleton said. "What the hell are we supposed to do?" He was awkwardly straddling several girders of the framework, and Desmond noticed he was bleeding in at least two places from the climb.

"We survive," Infinity replied. She eyed Eagleton for a moment. "We work together. We systematically seek out ways to meet each of our basic needs, beginning with protection from potential threats, and then shelter, water, and food. I know you're all scared, but take a moment to look at each of the other people in this group." She waited a few seconds for them to comply. "Every person here is capable and has a set of skills. Everyone here is badass in one way or another. There are twenty of us, and if the bridging device back home is still functional, there will be twenty more in less than an hour. And twenty more an hour after that."

"The bridge-in site is right down there," Desmond said, pointing to where ten or more huge pillbugs were tapping the ground with their antennae. "We'll stay in this area until all groups have arrived, and we'll make the best of an unexpected situation."

He exchanged a glance with Infinity. Her expression told him she had little hope that the bridging device was still working. Desmond was having a hard time being optimistic himself. The device had already malfunctioned, sending them to the wrong alternate world. Even if SafeTrek was still standing and the machinery was still operating, would the device send group two to this same destination world? Or would it fix its mistake and send subsequent groups to the correct world?

The refugees fell silent again. Desmond's eyes were drawn to Celia, her back covered in fresh tattoos, the symbols constituting the "key" to bridging technology. The tattoos had lost some of their ink through the bridging process, but the symbols were still legible. Celia had always kept her hair cropped short, her way of showing solidarity with the bridgers, so her appearance now wasn't strikingly different compared to most of the others. But her eyes were red, perhaps from crying or from lack of sleep.

"Celia, did you and Armando stay up all night getting those symbols inked onto your backs?" Desmond wasn't sure why he had asked this—he already knew the answer. It had only been eighteen hours since he'd bridged back with the symbols in his mind and then quickly scribbled them onto paper.

Celia nodded. "Armando asked me to do it." She shifted her weight to face Desmond. "We thought it best to have two copies, so I—"

The girders under Celia cracked loudly, and she fell through the framework. She grabbed for support but only got a handful of loose moss before disappearing into the hill. Desmond heard several more cracks, followed by a muffled scream.

"Ow! Shit, I can't move!" Celia's voice came from far below.

Desmond and Infinity scrambled to where she had fallen through. The first ten-foot stretch of honeycombed space was reasonably well lit, but things got darker below that. Celia was at least fifteen feet down, her body barely visible.

Infinity immediately began lowering herself through the enlarged opening. "Hold on to something, Celia, so you don't fall deeper!"

"I'm wedged in tight! I think I'm going to need help."

Desmond headed for another opening a few feet to the side and started making his way down. Once he was below the surface, he had to sit on a cross support and maneuver to his left to keep moving toward Celia. Then he had to move back to his right to squeeze through another opening. He rested his feet on a nearly horizontal girder, but it snapped with a loud crack. He caught himself with his arms and cursed, resolving to avoid the thinner beams.

He and Infinity were about ten feet down when Celia cried out, "Oh, shit! Shit, shit, shit! You guys, there's something moving around down there. I think it's coming closer." She began grunting and whimpering, struggling to free herself.

"Don't panic," Infinity instructed calmly. "We'll pull you up in a second."

Desmond doubled his efforts, maneuvering his way through the maze of pillars and angled girders. Finally, he was just above Celia. He followed Infinity's lead, hooking his knees over two beams and extending a hand down to Celia.

But Celia was looking down. "I think there's more than one. They're getting closer!"

"Look up, Celia," Infinity said. "Grab our hands."

Celia was still looking down. "Oh God, what are those things. Shit!"

"Celia!" Infinity demanded.

Celia finally looked up, her eyes wide with panic. She released her hold on the framework and took both of their hands. "Hurry, pull me up!"

Desmond and Infinity pulled, easily extracting Celia's petite body from where it had been wedged into the framework until she found purchase with her feet.

"Can you climb?" Infinity asked.

Celia nodded. But then she gasped and snapped her head downward. "It's on my foot! Ow, shit!" She kicked wildly and a lobster-sized creature flew off, clattered against the framework, and fell out of sight.

And then Desmond saw movement below. Hundreds of the creatures—no, thousands—were scuttling up the framework from the darkness, their scrabbling claws resonating like an approaching hailstorm.

3

SAFE ZONE

SEPTEMBER 4 - 7:39 AM

INFINITY TOOK one look at the advancing legion of skittering creatures and yanked on Celia's arm, pulling her another foot higher. "Climb!" Infinity commanded.

Celia didn't have to be told twice. She climbed past Infinity and Desmond while they were still scrambling to disentangle their legs from the framework. Infinity finally pulled herself loose, but it was too late. The swarm was upon her. One of the creatures, tinted green with foot-long jointed legs, latched onto her calf, digging its claws into her flesh. She kicked it off, but two more quickly grabbed her other leg. She heard Desmond cursing, obviously in the same predicament. She shook the two creatures off, but dozens more were closing in on her. She'd be completely covered within seconds.

"We have to get out!" Desmond yelled.

Infinity glanced one more time at the swarm below and then started climbing, shaking off several of the creatures each time she lifted a leg. "Get off the hill!" she shouted to the refugees above.

Seconds later, she and Desmond pulled themselves onto the surface, several creatures clinging to their legs. They pulled the animals off, tearing their own skin, and tossed them aside.

The other refugees were well on their way down the mound, clambering dangerously fast. Suddenly the creatures spewed forth from below in masses, flowing out through the openings almost like fluid. They swarmed over Infinity, Desmond, and the other humans, resulting in screams of panic and pain. Some of the refugees began tumbling down the slope, knocking creatures from their bodies in the process.

Infinity was in no position to help them. She was busy batting creatures off with one hand and negotiating the descent down the hill with the other. Out of the corner of her eye, she saw Desmond lie down and start rolling down the slope. This seemed to be knocking the creatures from his body, so she did the same. But each attacking creature crushed or dislodged was replaced by more that had scrabbled up through the framework below. Soon the slope became too steep to continue rolling safely, so she angled her body and slid feet first, guiding herself with her hands. Fortunately, the layer of moss covering the framework's outer surfaces saved her skin from serious abrasion.

She hit the ground seconds before Desmond, yanked several of the creatures from her skin, and then rushed to his side and swatted more from his body. His arms and legs were smeared with blood from puncture wounds.

"Des, Infinity, this way!" Lenny's voice shouted.

Infinity was kicking her feet, trying unsuccessfully to keep the endless onslaught of creatures from climbing up her legs, but she diverted some of her attention to look for Lenny. He and the others were fifty yards away, standing beside several of the monstrous bug creatures. Astoundingly, the smaller creatures were not attacking them. Instead, they had stopped a short distance from the refugees, as if there were an invisible barrier holding them at bay.

"Get off me!" Desmond cried, struggling to pull more of the things from his legs.

Infinity grabbed his arm. "Come on!" She started running, dragging him with her. So many of the creatures were covering the ground that Infinity kicked several aside with every step.

A few yards ahead, Gideon and another guardsman were helping President Millwright's husband, who appeared to have broken a leg. Infinity and Desmond caught up to them and helped swat away the creatures that were clinging to the three men and themselves until they all crossed the line where the swarm had mysteriously stopped.

A few of the smaller creatures were still clinging to Infinity, but even these dropped off voluntarily and skittered back to the rest of their kind as she got closer to the nearest of the larger bug beasts. The guardsmen lowered Mr. Millwright to the ground, prompting him to grunt in pain. President Millwright and her daughter rushed over and kneeled beside him.

Four of the bug beasts had turned around and were slowly approaching the humans, sweeping the ground with their antennae as if curious about the strange smell. As the beasts drew closer, most of the refugees backed away, but no one was willing to stray too far, as that would require re-entering the mass of attacking creatures. Hundreds of the smaller creatures now covered the ground just beyond the invisible barrier.

The hippo-sized creatures continued lumbering toward the President's family. Millwright and her daughter stood up, and Infinity and Gideon stepped over and grabbed Mr. Millwright's arms, ready to pull him back from the nearest bug beast.

"No, don't move me again!" Mr. Millwright grunted. "It hurts like hell."

Infinity exchanged a glance with Gideon, and they both waited as the beast continued inching closer. One of its antennae found Mr. Millwright's legs. The jointed feeler tapped his skin lightly.

Isabelle said, "Dad, he'll bite you!"

Infinity shot a look at Desmond. "Do you think it's dangerous?"

"It looks like a huge pillbug to me," Desmond replied. "And its mouthparts are definitely for chewing, not killing."

"I concur," Xavier added. "It's not a predator."

The beast's entire head was now over Mr. Millwright's legs, and everyone became silent. It lowered its head and gently mouthed each of his legs. The man sucked in an anxious breath as the creature put its mouth on his injured knee.

The giant pillbug then backed up, leaving a bubbly layer of clear drool on Mr. Millwright's legs. The beast went back to tapping the ground with its antennae, gradually moving away on at least fourteen legs.

"Holy crap on a cracker," Lenny said. "This day just keeps getting weirder."

Infinity turned and scanned the others. "Is everyone here?"

For a moment, everyone just stared back at her. Then they looked around as if checking.

"Where's William?" asked the historian, Chloe Hunt. She was referring to William Dixon, the historian she'd been paired up with. "He was next to me on the hill. I don't see him." She shouted toward the framework mound, "William!"

Several others called out the name. There was no answer, and there was no one in sight beyond the immediate group. The small, greenish creatures were beginning to fall back from the perimeter around the humans and beasts, moving back toward the hill and disappearing into its depths. But their presence was still too dense for anyone to attempt leaving the area, which was apparently a safe zone.

"William!" Chloe called again. After calling his name a few more times, she turned to the others, her face ashen. "What could have happened to him?"

Infinity thought it was obvious what had happened to him. He had probably fallen into the hill's interior, and it didn't take much imagination to figure out what had happened then. But she knew better than to say this aloud. "When it's safe, we'll return to the hill and search for him. Maybe he ran the other direction and found a safe spot on the other side of the hill."

Chloe just nodded slightly and turned back to stare at the hill.

"Check this out," Lenny said. He was standing just beyond the edge of the safe zone, at a spot where only a few of the green creatures lingered. He picked up one that had apparently been stepped on. He carried it back to the group, dangling it by a single leg. The creature was still twitching. "This ugly mofo is a freakin' arthropod."

Some of the refugees backed away, but Desmond and Xavier gathered around him, obviously curious. Infinity decided to take a closer look too. Big enough to weigh two or three pounds, the creature's body was bottle shaped, with the head at the wider end. Shiny green plates covered its back and underside, with a row of one-inch gray spikes running down its back from its head to the tip of its tail.

"But it's got only four legs," Xavier said.

The legs were jointed, about twelve inches long, and tipped with three-pronged claws. The creature appeared to be built for climbing.

Desmond pointed to a pair of shorter, needle-sharp appendages positioned on either side of the creature's mouth. "Those could be legs too, modified for holding prey or feeding. So there might actually be six."

"This is larger than any insect," Xavier said. "And those monstrosities," he nodded toward one of the giant beasts a few yards away, "they look like invertebrates, but we all know they can't be."

Infinity shook her head. "And how do we know that?"

Desmond, Xavier, and Lenny looked at her like they were surprised by the question.

"Because they're far too large," Desmond replied. "It's an issue of the surface area to volume ratio. If a terrestrial insect, crustacean, or any other arthropod gets much bigger than the largest that exist back on our own world, then the volume of the creature's body increases much faster than its surface area. In other words, beyond a certain size, an arthropod's weight increases too much for its exoskeleton to support it. Arthropods' exoskeletons are made of chiton, which simply isn't strong enough to support a body much larger than your fist. Unless the creature lives in water, of course. Water provides additional support."

Xavier pointed to the twitching creature dangling from Lenny's grip. "Even that thing is too large. Or should be, theoretically."

"Maybe the creatures on this world have exoskeletons made of something stronger than chiton," Infinity said.

Lenny nodded. "Either that, or..." Taking a step forward, he swung the creature over his head and smashed it onto the ground. He then kneeled and pried the largest spiked plate from the creature's back. The plate had cracked, and it now separated from the body with a wet, squishing sound. Lenny poked around in the creature's insides with his fingers. "Well, damnation. Ain't that wicked crisp."

Infinity leaned in closer to see. "What?"

Lenny pointed, his hand covered in blood and goo. "Here, squeeze this muscle." His eyes sparkled with fascination.

She frowned at him and then thrust her hand into the carcass and squeezed. Underneath the soft tissue was a solid object. "It has an internal skeleton," she said.

Desmond kneeled beside them. "Let me see that." He grabbed one of the creature's legs and wrenched the limb free from the body. He then pulled away the green exoskeleton from the top end of the leg like he was peeling a banana. Next he tore away the pink, glistening muscle, revealing a brown, translucent bone beneath.

Lenny whistled. "Toto, we're not in Kansas anymore. These things have internal *and* external skeletons."

President Millwright approached and interrupted them. "We've got a man missing, my husband obviously has a fractured leg, and we have no idea where we are. Is it really necessary to dissect the local wildlife right now?"

Infinity turned to Millwright. "As Lenny was just saying, ma'am, the life here is very different from our own world. That means that this world must have diverged from ours in the very distant past. Which is relevant to our survival."

Desmond cleared his throat. "Um, by very distant past, we're talking about possibly during or before the Cambrian Period."

Millwright shook her head and raised her eyebrows.

"About five hundred million years ago," Desmond clarified.

"Or even before that," Xavier added. "The Cambrian Period was when many of the larger, more complex forms of life evolved. If this world is dominated primarily by arthropods—which it appears to be—then the divergence likely took place before most terrestrial vertebrates—like reptiles, birds, and mammals—even existed."

Lenny wiped his gooey hands on his thigh. "We're up defecation creek with minimal equipment for locomotion, ma'am."

Xavier shook his head. "He's trying to say we're up—"

Millwright held up a hand. "I know what he's trying to say. But maybe we should focus on the positive aspects of this, not the negative."

Eagleton, who had been lurking nearby, spoke up. "The positive? There is no positive, Madam President! It's obvious the bridging device screwed up. It sent us to this God-forsaken world, and then the SafeTrek facility probably collapsed. It's been an hour, and group two hasn't arrived. So we're alone here, and nobody's coming to help. I don't see how we're going to survive even one night!"

Millwright opened her mouth to speak, but Infinity put a hand on her shoulder and said, "Allow me, ma'am." She stepped over to Eagleton and punched him in the throat. Not hard enough to crush his windpipe, but certainly with enough force to shut him up.

He dropped to his knees, clutching his neck and coughing. Infinity grabbed one of his ankles and started dragging him toward the perimeter of the safe zone.

President Millwright stepped toward her. "Infinity, this is not what I had in mind!"

Gideon put out a hand to stop the president. "Please give her a moment, ma'am. Perhaps we could see where this is going?"

Most of the swarm of smaller creatures had retreated back to the interior of the hill, but a few dozen were pacing back and forth at the invisible barrier apparently created by the presence of the larger beasts. Still coughing, Eagleton realized what Infinity was doing and began kicking. She easily deflected his legs, hauled him into the midst of the creatures, and released his ankle. The things began latching their claws onto Eagleton's skin immediately. He frantically swiped at them. She kicked a few of the creatures aside and then kneeled on the man's chest.

"Listen to me!" she snarled. "Armando Doyle was a good friend of mine. In fact, I owed him my life." She shook off a creature that was trying to crawl up her arm. "But now you're here in his place. I'm not happy about that—do you understand me?"

He looked up at her, his eyes wide with panic. "They're biting me!" he croaked.

Infinity snatched the leg of a creature that was going straight for Eagleton's eyes and smashed the thing into the ground the way Lenny had done, cracking its exoskeleton. She dropped the creature and it began kicking, flipping itself over and over in nightmarish spasms.

She grabbed Eagleton's chin and forced him to look up at her. "If you want to be part of this colony, you're going to make yourself as useful as Armando would have been. And you're going to shut the hell up unless you have something helpful to say. Otherwise, you're on your own. And I really don't think you want that. Do you understand?"

He nodded. "Yes! Let me up!"

She rose to her feet. Several creatures were digging into Eagleton's legs, and she helped him pull them off and then dragged him back into the safe zone. She released him.

"Look at me," Eagleton whined, rubbing his legs and then staring at his hands. "I'm bleeding."

"We're all bleeding," Infinity said. "Are you complaining?"

Eagleton looked around at the others, all of whom were bleeding from numerous puncture wounds, and all of whom were staring at him. "No, I'm not complaining."

Infinity glared at him for a few more seconds and then

moved to Alexander Millwright's side to examine his broken leg. Poppy and another med tech named Àurea Gonzalez were already wiping away the bug beast's saliva and gently probing the man's right knee. The knee was red and misshapen, obviously broken or dislocated.

Alexander Millwright was pale and sweating profusely, but he gazed steadily at Infinity. "I take it bridgers aren't selected for their diplomacy skills," he said.

She shrugged. "I'll leave the diplomacy to you and President Millwright."

"For the record, we're glad to have you here with us," the president said.

Infinity nodded. Then she glanced at the bug beasts, which were still moving away slowly. She stood up and spoke to the guardsman with whom she was most familiar. "Gideon, I don't know if it's even possible, but I need you and the others to try to herd those animals back this way. Having them near us seems to be pretty damn important, and we can't keep moving Mr. Millwright."

"We'll do our best, Infinity." He nodded to the four other guardsmen, and they all headed for the creatures. They fanned out, circled about fifteen of them, and tried shooing them back toward the refugees. This didn't have much effect. But then Emily Sanchez, the only woman among the guardsmen, began pushing against the side of one of the beasts, gradually turning it around. The other guardsmen saw this and started doing the same.

Desmond stepped up beside Infinity. "Not exactly what they signed up for, I imagine."

Infinity watched the naked guardsmen grunting and leaning into the two-ton bugs to guide them back. She sighed and turned to Desmond, noting the blood from his puncture wounds. She gingerly touched one of his wounds, inspecting it. It wasn't terribly deep, but it was certainly deep enough to get infected. "I don't even want to think about how these wounds are going to look by tomorrow," she said.

He put a hand on hers, and then his unspoken words filled her mind. "How about we take this one step at a time? This world may not even have bacteria, let alone bacteria that can infect human tissue. We may be safe from infection simply because we're unlike anything else here. For all we know at this point, this world could be a *neverland.*"

She hated it when he used his thought-projection ability on her without warning or permission, but she still couldn't help but smile at him. *Neverland* was a word bridgers used to describe an alternate world that was safe and beautiful, with a pleasant climate—a paradise. The problem was that neither Infinity nor any of the other bridgers she'd known had ever found such a place. Hence the name, *neverland.*

"Holy crap!" Lenny cried, shattering this almost pleasant moment. "Des, Infinity, you have to see this."

Lenny and Xavier were pointing to the west. About seventy yards out, making its way through a cluster of moss-covered pillars, was a long, multi-legged creature. It was broader than it was tall, but still the glossy-black peak of its back was at least knee high. And it was as long as a limousine. It stopped for a moment to inspect the base of one of the moss-covered structures and then kept moving. Below the segments of its outer shell were countless legs, moving in waves from front to back as it walked.

"That's the mother of all millipedes," Desmond muttered.

Infinity had to admit it was an impressive creature. "It must weigh at least a ton," she said. "At least we know there's no shortage of meat here. We won't starve."

Desmond gave her a dubious look. "Yeah, I guess."

She pulled her eyes from the creature. "Enough gawking at the wildlife. How much time do you think has passed?"

"It's been well over an hour, if that's what you're asking," Desmond said.

"Yeah, I thought so too." She glanced over at the bridge-in site. Nothing. "I think we need to proceed as though no one else is coming. Which means every human life in this colony is immeasurably precious."

Desmond nodded toward Eagleton, who was sitting on the ground inspecting his wounds. "Even his?"

"Yeah, even his."

4

___

MANDIBLES

SEPTEMBER 4 - 8:41 AM

SITTING WITHIN THE PILLBUGS' safe zone, Desmond watched the last of the smaller creatures disappear back into the darkened interior of the hill as he considered how to avoid triggering them to come pouring out again.

Most of the original herd of giant pillbugs had wandered off, but the guardsmen were continuously coaxing fifteen or so to stay near the humans. Hopefully this would be enough to maintain the safe zone, which was most likely the result of some kind of defensive pheromone emitted by the creatures.

"William!" Chloe shouted again, despite none of her previous calls having elicited a response. She turned to Desmond. "We have to search for him."

Desmond glanced at Infinity, and she nodded in agreement.

"I'll go look for him," Desmond said to Chloe.

She nodded. "I'd like to go with you."

He considered this. "Well, all we can do is look into the hill's openings and circle around to the back side. I suppose we might get it done faster if there are two of us."

"I'm coming, too," Infinity said.

In spite of Desmond's reservations about having both bridgers leave the refugees, Infinity's look indicated there was no use arguing. So he sighed and shrugged.

Gideon was sitting nearby and said, "If those things start coming out again, get your asses back here, pronto."

Desmond, Infinity, and Chloe quickly covered the seventy yards to the hill. As they were cautiously approaching the slope, Gideon called out, "Bridgers, we may have another problem."

They turned. Gideon was pointing to the west, to the still-visible millipede. The millipede was no longer alone. Beside it were two new creatures. Other than being black, these creatures were not at all similar to the millipede. They stood on four legs and were considerably taller. And everything about them, from their quick movements to their streamlined, powerful build, suggested they were predators. The sun glinted off their glossy-black bodies, indicating that they, too, were likely arthropods with armor-like exoskeletons. One of them suddenly darted in and attacked the millipede, battering it repeatedly with two long, wicked-looking protuberances extending from the predator's face. The millipede rolled onto its side and curled into a tight coil, presumably protecting its more vulnerable underparts.

Even from over a hundred yards, Desmond could hear scuffling and pounding as the two predators attempted to break through the millipede's outer shell. But their attempts were fruitless, and soon they gave up and turned away from their would-be prey.

"Hold still!" Desmond muttered, hoping the refugees would follow this advice even though he had not been willing to shout it loudly enough for them to hear. Then he spoke softly to

Infinity and Chloe. "Most arthropods have compound eyes adapted for seeing motion, and those that don't fly can usually only see a short distance."

Desmond was relieved to hear Gideon command the main group to keep still.

The two predators started making their way to the southeast, apparently having not seen the humans. But then one of them stopped and turned toward the refugees and pillbugs. It swung its head from side to side and clacked its two mandible-like protuberances together, drawing the attention of its companion. Together they started moving straight for the refugees.

So much for the poor-eyesight theory.

"Get next to the pillbugs!" Desmond shouted, although there was no reason to expect that the safe zone would deter these new creatures.

"Goddammit, we need some weapons," Infinity muttered. She turned her back on the refugees and kicked one of the girders at the base of the hill's framework. It didn't break. Most of the girders this low were thicker than the ones they'd seen near the summit, and would be nearly impossible for one person to detach.

But Infinity had the right idea, so Desmond joined her. They kicked the girder at the same time, but it still didn't break.

"Let's go for that thinner one up there," she said, pointing to a spot ten yards up the slope.

"Oh my God!" Chloe cried.

Desmond turned. The two predators had begun moving faster, their legs pounding the soft moss in an odd, loping gait. There was not enough time for Desmond and Infinity to make it back to the group, let alone procure weapons first. The refugees, now hunkering beside the massive pillbugs, were on their own.

As the predators approached the safe zone, the creatures'

immense size became more apparent. They were at least waist high, with bulky bodies that could easily have weighed as much as a tiger's, perhaps four hundred pounds.

A crack came from behind Desmond, and he pulled his eyes from the charging creatures and swung around.

"Dammit, it fell through," Infinity cried. She was already up the slope and had apparently broken off one of the beams, which had then fallen beyond her reach. "I need you to kick one of these while I hold it," she shouted at Desmond.

Desmond started scrambling up the slope. He paused when he was halfway to Infinity and glanced back in time to see the two predators stop in their tracks ten yards from the refugees. The creatures swung their heads back and forth, clacking their mandibles together noisily. One of them rushed forward a few yards to attack but then abruptly backed off. Whatever was creating the safe zone seemed to be working.

"Desmond!" Infinity growled.

He turned back up the hill and finished making his way to her side.

"Kick this one," she said, gripping a relatively thin girder.

He positioned himself over the girder and kicked it with one foot. It broke with a cracking sound. Infinity examined it and handed it to him. Both ends were jagged and sharp. It was only two feet long but had reasonable heft—lighter than stone but at least as heavy as amber, which was what it looked like.

"Des, Infinity, look out!" It was Lenny, shouting from the group of refugees.

"They're coming for *us* now," Chloe cried. She started climbing the framework hill.

"Get your asses over here!" Gideon called out.

But it was too late for that. The predators had spotted them and were steadily approaching at a gallop. If Desmond, Infinity, and Chloe were to try running back to the safe zone, the creatures would be able to head them off easily.

"This one's longer," Infinity said, gripping a girder. "Get over here and break it off."

Desmond scrambled to her side and kicked with his right foot. Nothing. He braced himself and kicked with both feet. This time it broke free at one end. Infinity wrenched it upward until the other end snapped off too. The resulting piece was three feet long and nearly three inches thick—this would make a more substantial weapon. She offered it to Desmond, but he shook his head. Infinity could no doubt wield it more effectively than he could.

The predators reached the bottom of the slope and paused. They rested their front claws on the angled framework and stared up at the humans. At this proximity, the things were terrifying, like creatures from a nightmare. Their two hind legs, covered in glossy exoskeleton segments, were each the size of Desmond's legs, while their two front legs were slightly smaller. The body part to which the legs were attached was covered by one solid plate, also glossy black. Extending backward from that was a multi-segmented tail or abdomen, each segment sweeping out to curved points on either side. But most disturbing was the head. Below two black, fist-sized eyes on the face were six smaller eyes arranged in a horizontal row. The two at either end of the row were angled to the side, perhaps to enhance peripheral vision. Below the eyes was a gaping, meat-grinder mouth, with a pair of ten-inch, sawtooth jaws for chewing, moist with spittle. Just below the mouth were two jointed, arm-like appendages tipped with pincer claws, no doubt for tearing off bite-sized chunks of flesh.

As if these features weren't terrifying enough, each creature had a pair of spiked, antler-like mandibles positioned above the pincer claws. These maroon-colored mandibles, the only parts of the creatures that weren't black, were at least two feet long, and the creatures were gnashing them together repeatedly as they stared up at the humans. These wicked weapons were like monstrous versions of the mandibles of male stag beetles, except whereas stag beetles used theirs simply to exert dominance over other males of their species, these creatures appeared to use theirs for more serious business.

Chloe scrambled up the last few yards to Desmond and Infinity and turned to look down at the predators. "They're not climbing. Maybe they can't climb?"

As if cued by Chloe's question, the creatures began climbing, moving tentatively at first but then gaining confidence.

Infinity pointed to her right and spoke to Chloe. "Go that way! We'll keep them busy. Get to the ground and back to the safe zone."

Without a word, Chloe complied. One of the predators started angling in that direction to cut her off.

Desmond waved his arms and shouted, drawing the creature's attention until it had turned itself back toward them. As the two creatures climbed closer, he and Infinity were forced to start moving up the slope, awkwardly carrying their weapons in one hand and climbing with the other.

"I don't see how we can fight these things, even with these weapons," Desmond said.

Infinity was just ahead of him. "Then we move inside the hill. They're too big to fit through the gaps."

"Are you kidding? Those little green things will eat us alive."

She snorted. "You still think this world might be a neverland?"

He glanced over at her and frowned but then missed grabbing one of the girders and almost fell through.

She paused to look back. "Shit, they're gaining on us. Split up. Maybe they'll follow one of us and the other can make it back to the safe zone. Better one than none."

"No!" he said, puffing from the effort of climbing. "If we do that, you'll just figure out how to make them follow *you*." Again he nearly fell into a gap before catching himself. "And if we figure out how to survive, I want both of us to live here together, happily every after."

"Aren't you romantic." She looked back again. "They're still gaining. Move it!"

They stopped talking and climbed furiously. The slope was now leveling out as they approached the summit. A loud crack came from behind and Desmond turned to look. One of the creatures had broken a girder and was floundering to regain footing. The thinner framework here near the top would hopefully slow down the much-heavier predators. But Desmond noticed the second predator was now moving even faster as the slope leveled out. It, too, broke one of the girders but quickly regained its balance.

At the summit, Desmond realized they weren't going to escape. The creatures, scrabbling and cracking their way over the framework, would be on them in seconds.

Infinity must have known it too. "Inside!" she commanded before dropping through one of the openings.

Desmond lowered his feet into a gap and sat on its edge. A sword-like mandible narrowly missed his face as he slid into the opening. His hip hit a girder, knocking him to the side, and then he came to an abrupt and painful stop straddling another. Something sharp cut into the side of his scalp. He ducked and looked up. The creature's mandibles were inches away, slamming back and forth, gnashing wildly. Dislodged patches of moss and broken pieces of framework showered down on his head and shoulders. The monster was digging its way into the hole to get at him. Through a mesh of criss-crossing girders, he saw that the other predator was doing the same thing above Infinity.

With his groin firmly wedged over one of the beams and the thrashing mandibles inches above, he had no choice but to lift his body and slide to one side. There was no room on his left, so he shoved himself to the right, using all his strength to slam his shoulder into a girder. He slammed it again. It wouldn't break, and there wasn't enough room to get his left leg over the crossbar that had stopped his fall. He was trapped.

Again one of the mandibles gashed his scalp, causing so much pain that he was sure it had cut through to his skull.

Desmond crouched as low as possible as the mandibles clattered back and forth just above his head. "Infinity, I'm stuck!"

"Goddammit!" she grunted. "I'm out of this one's reach, but it's blocking my way back up, and I can't get to you through the framework. Use your weapon. Kill the son of a bitch!"

Desmond realized he was no longer holding his weapon. He spotted it wedged in next to his left knee. He grabbed the weapon and awkwardly maneuvered it back and forth until it was pointed upward. The problem was, with his head held low, it was almost impossible to look up at the creature. He would have to stab blindly and hope the predator's mandibles didn't tear his arm off in the process.

He took a deep breath and then thrust the point of the weapon upward as hard as he could. It hit something solid, and he chanced a brief look upward before ducking back down. The weapon had penetrated the gooey edge of the creature's mouth.

But this had no effect on the monster's efforts.

Desmond repeated the thrust, making contact again. He jabbed a third time. He looked up, but his vision was blurred by fluid running into his eyes, either blood from the creature or from his own scalp. Almost blinded, he thrust the weapon again and again. Still the creature wouldn't give up.

"Desmond!" Infinity shouted.

"I'm still here," he said between thrusts.

"Desmond, look down! The little green fuckers are back."

He paused and looked. In the darkness below he saw the swarm rushing up toward him. It seemed like the framework itself was moving and skittering and clawing over itself to get at him. For a moment complete panic nearly overtook him. He and Infinity were trapped between two hellish deaths, and within seconds they were going to suffer both at the same time. He screamed in fear and frustration and thrust his weapon up with all his strength, again jabbing at the predator's mouth.

Several cracks rang out as the monster above him pushed itself deeper into the hole. Its two mandibles slid past Desmond's face and stopped just in front of his chest and stomach. One of them became wedged tightly between two angled beams. The creature's black eyes were now less than two inches from his face. He could hear its mouthparts grinding open and shut next to his throat, sloppy with saliva and blood. But the creature's jammed mandible kept it from moving its head closer. Desmond heard air rushing in and out as the creature gasped for oxygen, but the sound was coming from somewhere on its abdomen rather than its mouth.

Desmond couldn't move without putting his throat within range of the gnashing jaws. His nostrils were filled with an acrid odor unlike the smell of any animal he'd ever encountered. He stared at the creature's eyes, but they were so close he couldn't even focus on them. The sounds of the approaching swarm's scrabbling claws were quickly growing louder.

Desmond closed his eyes. "I'm sorry, Infinity. I don't think I'm going to make it this time."

"You're not dead yet, bridger! Don't give up."

Desmond felt the first claw sink into his ankle. He winced but fought back the urge to flee toward the larger predator's mouth. Seconds later the smaller creatures had covered his legs, climbing over each other to get to his exposed skin. Then a claw punctured his skin millimeters from his scrotum, and he lost it.

"Get off!" he screamed. He plucked the creature off and began kicking his legs. More creatures closed in from the sides, going for his chest and face. They also began latching onto the monstrous predator.

The predator responded by going berserk. Its feet scrabbled against the framework, and it yanked itself upward, snapping off its own wedged mandible and pulling itself out of the hole.

Desmond wasn't about to pause to see what it did next. He dropped his weapon and began frantically yanking creatures from his body. But each one was quickly replaced by two more.

Something slapped his head twice. "They're gone. Give me your hand!"

He grasped Infinity's wrist and she pulled. "Wait!" he cried. He grabbed the predator's mandible with his other hand and used his feet on the girders holding it in place to wrench it free. "Okay, pull me up!"

Once they were both on the surface, he swatted several more creatures from his body and then began swinging the mandible at the rest as they emerged through the openings, cracking their shells and sending them flying. But it was a losing battle—there were too many.

"We have to roll down!" Infinity said, already flopping onto her side.

Desmond threw himself onto the surface and started rolling after her, holding his new weapon above his head to avoid impaling himself.

5

———————

INVENTORY

SEPTEMBER *4* - *about 10 AM*

INFINITY FINISHED COUNTING the puncture wounds on her body—thirty-seven. And that didn't include the ones she couldn't see on her back. Desmond was in even worse shape, with almost fifty, including two mandible gashes on his scalp. Most of the other refugees had at least a dozen each. Some of the wounds were deeper than others, but without antiseptic any of them could become deadly.

For now, they were alive, except perhaps for William Dixon, who still hadn't been found. And the group had only survived this long due to considerable luck. They were lucky the small creatures from the hill weren't venomous. They were lucky the large predators had allowed Chloe to escape and then had retreated when attacked by the green swarm. And they were especially lucky the docile pillbug beasts somehow created a predator-free safe zone around their bodies.

Fifteen of the pillbug beasts were still hanging around, but only because several of the guardsmen had taken on the task of prodding them back whenever they began to wander off.

Infinity looked over at Desmond, who was lying on the moss beside her with his eyes closed. The two-foot, severed mandible lay next to him, gleaming in the sunlight. "I'm a little envious of your new weapon," she said.

He opened one eye and squinted at her. "Sorry, you'll have to get your own. I earned this one."

She snorted a laugh.

Desmond propped himself up on his elbow and looked out to the south. "They're coming back."

She followed his gaze. Gideon, Lenny, and Xavier were returning from a framework mound that was about a quarter of a mile away. Their mission had been fourfold: stay alive, gather what weapons they could, keep an eye out for any signs of William, and look for possible food or water sources. Apparently the group had stayed alive, and their arms appeared to be loaded with girders from the hill, so they had accomplished at least two of these objectives.

They entered the safe zone and dumped their collected weapons in the midst of the larger group. Gideon pointed to the south. "We saw a few large animals moving around beyond the hill, but none of them spotted or approached us."

"We flushed a few swarms of tiny, winged bugs out of that hill," Lenny said. "But either there's no green terror bugs in there, or we simply didn't piss them off enough to push their attack meters into the red."

"Any sign of William?" Chloe asked. She was sitting on the moss nearby with most of the others.

The three shook their heads solemnly.

"We may have found a source of water, though," Xavier said. "From where we were, we could see a minor valley farther to the south. We didn't try to venture that far, but I'm betting we'll find a stream running through it."

Infinity got up and started picking through the pile of broken girders. She chose one that had a nice jagged point at one end and hefted it to check its balance. The material was dense enough to pack a punch but light enough to be wielded with agility. It would do. But she still needed to figure out a way to make long spears for holding predators out of reach. This would be a challenge, considering she had seen no trees of any kind, and the broken girders were no longer than her arm.

Lowering the weapon to her side, Infinity gazed at the group. Nineteen naked refugees, exposed, nearly defenseless, and huddled together waiting for the next threat to come along. It was time to take control of the situation, to do what humans do best—adapt to their environment.

"We need to quit sitting on our asses and go search for a safe shelter," she said to Desmond.

He nodded and then glanced toward the bridge-in site as if he thought another group might have appeared since the last time he looked. "If we do that, we'll either have to split up or leave the bridge-in site."

Infinity sighed. She stepped over to President Millwright, who was sitting with her daughter and her injured husband. Infinity addressed the entire group. "I'd like everyone to gather around. We have decisions to make." She looked at the two guardsmen who had been making the most effort to keep the bug beasts nearby. "Emily and Steven, can you keep those things close and listen at the same time?"

They both nodded. Everyone else moved in closer. Some of them sat on the moss while others chose to stand.

"As you're all aware," Infinity said, "we're alone on this world. Maybe another group will arrive, maybe not. Regardless, we have no way of bridging home or elsewhere." She hesitated. "I know—it sucks. But we're alive. And as far as we know, we may be the *only* living humans from our own Earth. Which makes our tiny colony pretty damn important."

She looked around at the faces in the group. Most of them stared back at her with hollow eyes, looking like they'd already given up hope. Infinity could hardly blame them—long-term survival here wouldn't be easy, if it was even possible. But the one small thing she could do to make up for her part in Earth's destruction was to make sure this colony had a decent chance. As long as she was still breathing, she sure as hell wasn't going to give up.

She continued, trying to sound confident. "We're going to figure out how to make this world our home. But we've got major problems to solve, and we'll have to work together if we're going to solve them. We need to know exactly what resources we have to work with. And by resources I mean all of you. What are you good at? What can you offer this colony?" She paused, wondering if they should even be wasting valuable time with this, time that could be used searching for shelter.

"I'll start," she said. "I'm Infinity Fowler. Since I became a bridger almost five years ago, I haven't told other people this— only other bridgers. But my real name is Passerina Fowler." She glanced at Desmond, whose brows were raised in surprise. "Why am I telling you this?" she asked the group. "Because I'm not a bridger anymore. I'm a colonist now, and all of you are my new family. If I have to, I'll give up my life to protect any one of you." She made a point of making eye contact with Eagleton, who returned her gaze without expression.

She went on. "To be honest, that's about all I have to offer. I'm trained in short-term survival techniques—bridging excursions were only thirty-six hours. I have training and experience in fighting with bare hands and with primitive weapons." She held up her crude spear. "Right now this is about all we have, but in a world of armor-covered creatures, we're going to need more. Anyway, fighting is pretty much all I've ever done, so it's what I've got to offer." That was all she needed to say, so she nodded at Desmond to take his turn.

He got to his feet and cleared his throat. "Desmond. I've bridged only three times before this, so I don't have Infinity's level of experience or training. But I've learned a few techniques and strategies. And, like Infinity, I'm willing to risk my life to protect any one of you. My academic background is in evolutionary ecology. That might help us to understand the bizarre lifeforms in this place. The more we understand, the better we can avoid being at the bottom of the food chain." He hesitated. "Oh, and I have a knack for remembering certain types of information, such as long sequences of names or numbers. For whatever that's worth."

Xavier was next. He got up, self-consciously holding his hands over his groin. "Xavier Cahill. Like Desmond, my background is in biology. To be honest, it's absurd that I'm even here with all of you. It's only because I'm Desmond's friend, and because I happened to survive a previous bridging excursion. It was my family's money that funded that excursion. I've lived most of my life in New York City, and I'm starting to realize that, other than the two-week canoe trips I took every year with my father when I was younger, I have few life experiences that will be helpful to this group. May God forgive me for being here in place of someone more worthy." He lowered his eyes and then sat back down on the moss.

Lenny got to his feet. "Don't let Xavier's nauseatingly self-deprecating words fool you. On the previous excursion he mentioned, I was injured and nearly comatose, and he saved my sorry ass. We were holed up in a cave, and I was unconscious when we were attacked by a flock of birds from hell. Xavier was also injured, but still he fought off those birds until they finally quit attacking, which was pretty much the next morning. He may look and talk like a wussy nerd, but I trust him with my life."

This actually drew a few chuckles from the group.

"Anyway, I'm Lenny Stiles. At the risk of making biologists seem like we're a dime a dozen, I'm also a biology grad student. My superpower? I may not be able to turn water to wine, but I can turn every goddamn bummer into sunshine and rainbows. I'm what you'd call an optimist. And it seems to me that's what we need right now. This place ain't the hellhole you might think it is. It's an opportunity. With Des and Infinity leading us—no offense, Madam President—we'll tame this no-man's land and make a future here. We came here to kick ass and chew bubblegum, and we're all out of bubblegum."

Lenny flashed his idiotic grin at the group. "Oh, and by the way, I've done a fair bit of rock climbing, I've competed in triathlons, and I've been a hunter and fisherman all my life. I'm wicked frosty and ready to do what needs to be done."

Infinity stifled a smile. Desmond had recently told her that Lenny was actually a pacifist and had never been in a fight in his life. But his attitude was a force to be reckoned with. It would be an asset to the group.

Celia stood up, looking around demurely at the others. Physically, she was smaller than anyone else in the group, including President Millwright's petite daughter. "I'm Celia Pickett. I was assistant to Armando Doyle, director of SafeTrek, until we learned that the Earth was imploding. Since then my duties have, well... expanded considerably. I'm afraid I have little to offer under these circumstances." She gestured out toward the alien landscape. "I know quite a bit about the bridging device, but that's of no value here. During the night last night, I had these symbols tattooed on my back." She turned a complete circle, showing the nine hundred freshly-inked symbols. "Supposedly they're some kind of key to unlocking hidden features of the bridging devices. We thought we would be bridging to a world similar to ours, in which case they might have been useful. But obviously they're not now."

She started to sit down but then hesitated. "I've taken self defense classes—I suppose that might be useful. You know, to fight off rapists and such."

"Poppy Safran." The med tech raised her hand without getting up. "I'm an emergency physician. I was an ER doctor before SafeTrek recruited me." She nodded toward the med tech next to her. "Four of us in the group are physicians, and I imagine I don't need to explain why we were selected. But to be perfectly frank, physicians aren't trained to treat patients in a place completely lacking in... basically everything. We have nothing to work with here. But I'll do whatever I can to be a valuable member of the colony."

Poppy had always been Infinity's favorite med tech, and Infinity knew the woman had an unusual hobby. "Anything else you want to tell the group about yourself, Poppy?"

Poppy half-smiled. "Well, I'm a spelunker. Missouri has a lot of caves, and years ago I joined an active spelunking group. Weekend adventures, mostly. I don't know how useful that will be here, though. Also, I've always been interested in plant-based medicines and natural healing. But the plants here are completely different, so...." She trailed off, apparently finished.

"Àurea Gonzalez," said the med tech beside Poppy.

"And Sarah Suzuki," said the med tech beside her. "Àurea and I also worked previously as ER doctors before coming to

SafeTrek, I suppose drawn by the unique and exotic opportunity."

"And by the money," Àurea added. She put a hand on Sarah's. "Sarah and I were in school together and even did our internships together in Saint Louis. We mostly have the same hobbies. Mainly kayaking and hiking, neither of which are likely to be helpful to this group."

"We're doctors, of course," Sarah said, "but I agree with Poppy—with no technology or tools, our abilities are limited."

Àurea moved her hand to Sarah's shoulder. "But we feel lucky to be here, especially to be here together. You can count on us."

Infinity had long suspected Àurea and Sarah were a couple, and it had never mattered, even when they'd been selected as members of a colony of 720 refugees. But now that the colony had apparently been reduced to only nineteen, things might become interesting when and if the group survived long enough to start thinking seriously about increasing the population. Saving the human species, after all, was the purpose of this colony.

Of course, none of this even mattered if they couldn't figure out how to survive here.

The man next to Sarah raised his hand. "Richard Hussain. I'm the only doctor here who didn't already work for SafeTrek. I have no family, so I applied for a spot with one of the colonies. I'm actually an OB-GYN." He paused and eyed the group. "I don't suppose I need to explain why that was considered important. And so, here I am. I agree with these good doctors that emergency trauma treatment is greatly inhibited by the lack of technology and facilities. But I'm happy to say that for most of human evolution we have given birth in primitive conditions. It may be more difficult without technology, but I think I can handle most situations. If the occasion arises, that is."

Some of the refugees shot awkward glances at each other. Others looked down at the carpet of moss.

Chloe got to her feet. "My name is Chloe Hunt. My background is in modern US history, and I—" She stopped talking and stared to the west. "What is that?"

Infinity looked. Several hundred yards away, a massive creature was approaching, much larger even than the huge pillbug beasts. The thing was mostly gray, and it walked on four spider-like legs, each as thick as Infinity's torso. The legs angled up from the body to a joint, where they angled back down, ending in thick, club-like feet. The stocky, squarish body appeared to be mostly head, with no distinct abdomen. Whatever the creature was, it was coming straight for the cluster of humans and pillbug beasts.

The guardsman Emily said, "Move back here! Get behind these pillbugs." She was shoving one of the bug beasts, driving it closer to another. She ran to a third and started pushing it closer as well.

"Do what she says," Infinity commanded, trying to keep her voice low, although it was obvious the creature already knew they were there. She moved to Alexander Millwright's side. "We'll carry you, sir."

He held up a hand. "Just help me up. I'll lean on Hayley."

Together, Infinity and President Millwright got him to his feet, and seconds later everyone was gathered with the bug beasts loosely arranged around them like a defensive circle of covered wagons. The approaching creature continued closing in on them at a steady walk.

"Stop, you bastard," Infinity muttered as the thing got close to what should have been the safe zone's boundary. But there was no reason to expect that every type of animal would avoid the pillbug beasts. When the approaching creature was fifteen yards away, she put Alexander's arm over her shoulder, ready to haul him away if necessary. The creature slowed down, but it didn't stop. She was about to order the refugees to run, but then the monster finally came to a halt. It took several steps to the right and then to the left.

"Yeesh, this is the coolest bug we've seen yet," Lenny muttered.

Cool was the last word Infinity would have used to describe it. In fact, she wasn't sure whether there *were* words to describe it. The thing stood perhaps twelve feet tall at its highest point, which was the rounded top of its head. A long, leaf-like structure protruded from each side of the head. These were black and flattened, with their slightly concave surfaces facing forward like two satellite dishes. At the end of each of these structures, perhaps three feet out from the creature's head, was attached a gray, flexible cord. These cords arched up slightly and then hung down in front of the creature's legs, their ends dangling freely on either side of its face. The most striking feature of these cords was the softball-sized orb at the end of each one. The orbs were translucent pink and seemed almost to glow.

Infinity couldn't find anything that looked like eyes. Perhaps the eyes were simply too small to be seen from this distance— about eight yards. The creature's mouth—like those of the mandible predators—was equipped with several pairs of appendages, apparently for grabbing, tearing, and chewing.

After pacing back and forth at the perimeter several more times, the massive creature angled off toward the nearby framework hill containing the swarm of vicious green creatures. When it reached the hill, it stopped at the base and leaned forward as if looking into or smelling the structure's interior. Abruptly, it lifted its front half and slammed its feet onto the girders about ten feet up the slope. In this propped-up position, it lowered its two translucent orbs through the gaps between the girders.

"Are those things lights?" Desmond asked.

No one attempted to answer. The orb did appear to be glowing within the hill's darkened interior.

The creature began emitting a buzzing sound, like static, interspersed every half second or so with loud clicks.

"You've got to be kidding," Lenny said. "The damn thing is fishing."

Infinity could see movement within the hill—flashes of green. Lenny was right—the monster was attracting the swarm that had attacked the humans. But the small creatures weren't pouring out of the mound as they had done before. Perhaps they were wary of the hulking monstrosity above them. The creature slowly raised its left cord, coaxing one of the green creatures to follow the glowing sphere. When the smaller creature was almost to the outer, moss-covered girders, the monster lunged forward with surprising speed. Infinity couldn't see its mouth, but could hear its crunching, chewing sounds as it enjoyed its catch.

Soon the monster had caught a second creature, and it showed no signs of stopping there. Considering its size, it could probably eat fifty of the little green shits.

Infinity turned back to the other refugees. "Well, I guess we're safe as long as we stay near these pillbug beasts."

"I propose we call these things *isopods*," Xavier said. "You know, for the sake of clarity. And for that matter we need a name for the green bugs that live in that hill. I propose *skitterbugs*."

"Agreed," Desmond said. "But I'm naming the black predators that almost killed me and Infinity. *Tiger beetles*. They're as big as tigers and as mean as the tiger beetles from our world."

Lenny nodded. "Fair enough." He pointed at the creature fishing for skitterbugs. "And that freak of nature—that's a *colossal anglerbeast.*"

Xavier frowned. "*Anglerbeast* is good enough. No reason to go overboard."

Infinity shook her head and looked at Desmond. "And you actually shared an apartment with these two?" She glanced around at the group. Everyone was still huddled close, so she turned to Chloe. "Please continue. I think we should hear from everyone."

Chloe nodded and started again. "Chloe Hunt. My background is in modern US history, and I was to act as an arbitrator between our colony and the human inhabitants of this version of Earth. Needless to say, I now have little or no value to this colony." She glanced toward the framework hill where the creature—the anglerbeast—was still catching and devouring skitterbugs. "William Dixon and I were included in group one so that we could begin conferring with the people of this world immediately upon our arrival. When SafeTrek asked me to select a second historian for the group, I selected William because I knew him well and admired him. We weren't married or even dating, but I think we both assumed we would pair up after starting a new life here. I guess that's not going to happen."

After several seconds of silence, Desmond said, "We're sorry he's gone, Chloe."

She nodded and looked down at the ground. "I'll do what I can to help. I'm not as young as most of you, but I work out a lot, and I compete regularly in jiu jitsu tournaments. I intend to carry my own weight."

"Thank you, Chloe," Infinity said.

Eagleton cleared his throat. "I think you all know who I am.

Reece Eagleton. I'm the Regional FEMA Administrator for Region VII—Kansas City."

Infinity couldn't help herself. "You *were* a FEMA Administrator. Now you're a refugee, like the rest of us."

He frowned but nodded. "Yes. Quite right. However, I have a great deal of project-planning experience. I believe I can be useful as we establish a colony and then eventually transition into a true civilization." He sighed. "Other than that, I'm sorry to say I have no specific skills for this environment. I suddenly find myself wishing I had taken the time for a few hobbies, or for binge watching some of those wilderness survival shows." He pursed his lips and glanced to the man on his right.

"Gideon Stead," the guardsman said, nodding grimly. "I think I'm here simply because I happened to accompany Infinity, Desmond, Xavier, and Lenny on a recent drive to Kentucky. Things went south on that trip, and we were lucky to make it back to SafeTrek." He gazed directly at Infinity. "I don't know if I deserved it, but I'm grateful for being chosen."

Infinity nodded.

"I've had a fair amount of hand-to-hand training, which may or may not be useful here," Gideon said. "I wasn't trained to fight skitterbugs or tiger beetles. But like our bridgers, I'll give my life to protect any member of this group. You can goddamn count on that." He then nodded to one of the guardsman who was still wrangling the isopods.

The guy paused and said, "Steven Irizar. Ditto to most of what Gideon just said. Grateful to be here, considering the alternative. Basic combat training. And willing to do what it takes for this colony. Oh, and I've been told I have a knack for finding trouble. Or maybe trouble finds me. If we come to a place we need to explore, send me in first. If nothing bad happens to me, I guarantee nothing bad will happen to anyone else." He hesitated. "If you think I'm kidding, I'm not." He then went back to nudging one of the creatures toward the group of refugees.

The remaining three guardsmen, Alfie Lewis, Tyrone Hodson, and Emily Sanchez reiterated pretty much the same thoughts: they were glad to be in the colony, and they were willing to contribute whatever was needed of them, including their lives if necessary. Emily added that she had lived around farm animals all her life, which was why she had gotten the idea to try pushing the huge isopods to guide them back to the desired location.

After Emily finished speaking, the area became quiet other than the gentle shuffling of isopods and the crunching of skitterbugs from the side of the hill. All eyes turned to President Millwright and her family.

The president nodded to her daughter. "Go ahead, honey."

The girl looked down at her hands timidly. She was only about six years younger than Infinity—perhaps twenty-three—but in spite of her skitterbug wounds, her otherwise unscarred, youthful skin made Infinity feel like an embattled old woman.

"My name's Isabelle Millwright," she said. "I think you all know why I'm here—I'm the president's daughter. I've recently finished my bachelor's degree in political science, which I guess will be useless here. I don't have any survival skills whatsoever. And now that I know how valuable the rest of you are, I'm thinking that it really doesn't seem fair that I'm here in place of someone else." She lowered her gaze to the ground, apparently finished.

"Perhaps Isabelle is right," President Millwright said. "Perhaps it isn't fair that she, or I, or Alexander are here. But I can tell you how Isabelle is valuable, and not just to me and Alexander. Isabelle has always been a beacon of light. She has this way about her, of seeing the best in everything and everyone. It lifts your mood to simply be around her. And I can tell you that there have been many occasions in which I don't think I could have endured the pressures of my job if she hadn't decided to live with us in the White House. I believe you'll soon understand what I mean. Talk to her, get to know her, and you'll feel the same glow. Because of that, I believe her value to this group will be immeasurable."

Isabelle still didn't look at anyone. She just shook her head slightly, clearly embarrassed.

"Now that's something I can relate to," Lenny said. "I have the same effect on people, if I do say so myself."

At this, Isabelle Millwright finally looked up. She smiled warmly at Lenny, and Infinity noted that her gaze lingered on him for several seconds.

"My wife is right," Alexander said. "Isabelle can lift anyone's spirits just by being nearby. And my guess is that this colony will need as much of that as possible." He shifted his body, grimacing from the pain this caused. "That brings us to the very unpleasant business of my worth to this group. As an immigration lawyer with no useful hobbies to speak of, there is little for me to say. Had I not broken my leg, I would have at least been able to help with securing and preparing food, as I'm a decent cook. But now I'm nothing more than a liability. That's the plain and simple truth."

Several seconds of uncomfortable silence followed.

"Broken legs heal," Infinity said. "And we've got four doctors, which means it's possible you'll regain full use of that leg. Every person here is valuable. And now we at least know a little more about each other, so let's—"

President Millwright cut her off. "I don't get a free pass, Infinity. It's my turn."

Infinity had actually been hoping Millwright would do this, and she nodded, inviting her to go ahead.

Millwright got to her feet and stepped forward, baring her body to the entire group with an undeniably dignified expression. "I'll keep this brief, which may surprise some of you." She paused, but no one even smiled. "I've always made it a point to tell it like I see it. No sugar coating, if you will. And here's the way I see it. Isabelle is a precious thing in any setting, including this one. But Alexander and I, we are of little value to you here. I was the leader of the free world back home, but I have no expectation of being your leader here." She paused while everyone absorbed this information.

"Hell, you may decide you want to dispense with the concept of leaders altogether," she said. "But regardless, this environment would require leaders with entirely different sets of skills than those I possess. I'm out of my depth, or at least I feel that way. So, Alexander and I will simply try to be what you need us to be. Hopefully we'll learn skills that will make us useful in some way. In the meantime, I'll take the liberty of offering what I consider to be an invaluable bit of advice. Alexander and I are obviously the oldest here." She glanced over at Lenny. "Perhaps our super power is our hard-won wisdom. My advice is this: never forget what made our civilization great." She paused again.

"It wasn't military power, or wealth, or technology," she continued. "All of those things were the *results* of a great civilization. Remember what it was that made our civilization great in the first place. It was altruism. The tendency to behave in ways that benefit others, even at our own expense." She shot a look at Desmond. "I'm borrowing this concept from your field, the study of the evolution of populations. Altruism has emerged because it benefits the entire population, although it sometimes costs the life of the altruistic individual. A prairie dog sees an approaching hawk and gives an alarm call to its siblings and offspring. This draws the hawk's attention directly to the altruistic prairie dog, but it gives the prairie dog's family a chance to escape.

"That example is a simple one—the prairie dog increases the likelihood of its genes being passed on to later generations by saving its offspring. But in humans there is a more complex behavior, called psychological altruism. It is a result of *empathy*, the ability to understand when others are in need. And it is the result of *caring*, which is the desire to alleviate that need. Without altruism, civilizations would fall. Or, in our case, a civilization will never rise."

She stopped to gaze around at the group, making eye contact with every refugee before continuing. "I don't deserve to be here, yet here I am. So I owe a debt to the human race. I intend to repay it. To one degree or another, I imagine each of you feels the same way." She turned to Infinity, apparently finished.

Damn, the woman had a presence. No wonder people had voted for her.

6

SOUTHEAST

SEPTEMBER 4 - AFTERNOON

DESMOND WATCHED another twenty-foot millipede as it slowly made its way over the top of a distant framework hill. He wondered if perhaps it was feeding on a specific type of moss that grew there. To the south, he could see a herd of hundreds of unidentified brown creatures grazing in an open moss field. The anglerbeast had wandered off hours ago, but Desmond had seen two more since then.

He glanced at Infinity, who was sitting upright on the ground beside him, meditating. He spoke softly to her. "You know why grazing animals herd together instead of living individually, right?"

She spoke without opening her eyes. "I do, but I'm pretty sure you're going to tell me anyway."

"There are several reasons, but by far the most important is to protect individuals from predators. Large herds are only found where predators capable of killing the grazing animals are common."

She opened her eyes and got to her feet. "We already know this is a predator-rich world. But we still have to go."

"I know we do. I'm just saying."

The group had come to the conclusion that some of them would have to leave the safety of the isopods to do more extensive exploring. They needed to find water and to start experimenting with possible sources of food. They hadn't seen any plants other than a few varieties of moss, each no more than a few inches tall. The moss might be edible, but it could just as easily be toxic. Arthropods, both large and small, were abundant, but without wood to burn, the colonists would probably have to eat their meat raw.

Lenny and Xavier approached, each of them carrying a hill girder as a weapon.

"We're as ready as we're going to be," Xavier said.

Lenny swung his weapon like a baseball bat. "I declare, kids, this is going to be just like old times. Only problem is, on our first excursion I was scared shitless and almost died."

Desmond picked up his mandible weapon. There was no point in waiting any longer. The plan was for the four of them to methodically venture out a mile or so in every direction until they found something—anything—that the colony could use. A dry, unoccupied, defensible cave would be nice. But what were the chances of that?

Infinity went to check on Gideon and the other guardsmen, who were becoming increasingly frustrated with trying to persuade the isopods to stay nearby. Meanwhile, Desmond went to President Millwright's family. Alexander looked miserable, and his leg was covered in dark bruising from mid-thigh to mid-calf. Two of the longer girders lay beside him, intended to be used as a splint, but there was no way to fasten them to his leg.

"We're ready to go," Desmond said. "We'll try to bring back something we can use to finish your splint, Mr. Millwright. Just so you know, though, I'm pretty sure any cord we use will have to be made from animal parts, perhaps by braiding tendons or intestines."

The man nodded. "If it will help prevent pain in this leg, I don't care where it comes from. And thank you."

"Please be careful," President Millwright said.

"We intend to." Desmond lightly slapped his mandible weapon into the palm of his free hand. "We're all armed, and we're only going—"

"Hey, we need help here! They're not responding."

It was Emily Sanchez. She and Alfie Lewis were leaning into one of the isopods, trying to turn it, but the massive beast was done cooperating. It and all the others were walking away as a group, heading southeast.

Desmond and most of the others ran to help. Together they pushed on the creatures, as many as five people per isopod. They stood before the creatures, yelling and waving their arms. Desmond even resorted to jabbing one of them with his mandible. But the creatures wouldn't deviate from their course. They walked past the base of the framework hill and continued southeast, forcing the refugees to move with them. Desmond stopped, realizing his efforts were useless. Something had triggered the isopods to move off as a group. Perhaps this was something they did each afternoon at a specific time. Or perhaps they sensed danger approaching. Whatever it was, they were determined, and they were far too large for the humans to contain them against their will.

Soon the herd had traveled several hundred yards, leaving Alexander, the president, and Isabelle far outside the ten-yard safe zone created by the isopods.

Desmond shouted to Infinity, "We can't leave them behind." He pointed back at the Millwrights.

She frowned, as if she hadn't realized how far the isopods had moved. "Keep trying," she shouted to the others. "We have to get these bastards to stop!"

Desmond and Infinity ran back to the Millwrights.

As they approached, Alexander shook his head. "I don't... I don't think I can do this. You have no idea how much it hurts."

"Yeah, this isn't going to be pleasant," Infinity said, grabbing the man's arm. "But we're not leaving you here."

Desmond took Alexander's other arm, and together they lifted him up.

He screamed.

Desmond and Infinity paused and glanced at President Millwright. She had one hand over her mouth, and tears were forming in her eyes. "I'm sorry, Alex," she said.

They put Alexander's arms over their shoulders and began making their way toward the herd and the colonists, with President Millwright and Isabelle following.

Alexander grunted a few times, obviously trying to stifle cries of pain, but then Desmond stumbled, barely catching himself, and Millwright let out another scream. They kept moving, passing by the framework hill filled with skitterbugs.

"I think we should go faster," Isabelle said, the first time she had spoken since they had returned for her father.

Desmond's eyes met Infinity's. She furrowed her brows. "Why?" she demanded.

"Those things—the skitterbugs—they're coming," Isabelle said. Her tone was oddly calm. "Please go faster."

Desmond glanced back, and his gut clenched tight. The slope's nearest edge was only fifty yards back and masses of skitterbugs were pouring out through the openings.

"Go!" Infinity shouted. "You two run ahead. We'll be right behind."

Desmond and Infinity picked up their pace, eliciting more screams from Alexander.

"We'll help," President Millwright said. "How can we—"

"Just do what she says, Hayley!" Alexander cried. "Get out of here!"

The mother and daughter complied and ran past them, shouting to the other colonists to get their attention.

Desmond glanced back. Some of the skitterbugs were already within ten yards and getting closer. "We need to run," he said.

They picked up the pace again until they were moving as fast as they could with Alexander's weight between them. The poor man had no choice but to endure having his feet dragged. He cursed a few times but then his words became animalistic grunts, and Desmond sensed that the man would soon pass out.

Desmond looked back again. The skitterbugs had not gained any ground. Apparently they were built more for climbing than for running on flat ground.

The other refugees had heard the Millwrights' cries and some were now running to help. By the time they arrived, Desmond and Infinity were well ahead of the pursuing swarm. Gideon and Alfie took over assisting Alexander, and soon the entire group was back among the isopods.

Winded, Desmond rested with his hands on his knees for a moment and then turned back in time to see the skitterbugs come to an abrupt stop ten yards from the nearest isopod. The safe zone was apparently still effective even with the isopods on the move.

"He's unconscious," Gideon reported. "But we're not putting him down until the isopods stop walking."

The beasts were moving steadily at about two miles per hour, each of them walking on seven pairs of legs. Several refugees were still trying to turn them back, but it was now obvious that it was a useless effort. The group had no choice but to keep pace with the isopods.

Eagleton approached Desmond and Infinity. "Don't you think we're getting too far from the bridge-in site? What if another group arrives?"

Infinity sighed. "What exactly do you suggest we do?"

"I don't know, but if the technicians fix the bridging device and send another group, we need to be there."

Infinity looked like she was going to punch the man in the throat again, so Desmond spoke up. "We're kind of playing things by ear right now. Our immediate survival is our first priority. Once we have that under control, we can worry about the bridge-in site." He eyed Eagleton for a moment. "If you have an idea or solution, we'd love to hear it."

Eagleton frowned. He then drifted back over to one of the isopods and started trying to push it in the other direction, which still had no effect.

The skitterbug swarm maintained a line at the border of the safe zone for a while but soon turned back. The isopod herd continued moving southeast, with the human refugees reluctantly following. Eventually, the bridge-in site became obscured by the framework mounds arranged more-or-less regularly over the entire moss-covered plain.

EVENING

ALEXANDER MILLWRIGHT HAD REGAINED consciousness several times, each time begging to be left behind so that he could rest on the ground without constant pain. Desmond felt sorry for the man, almost to the point of agreeing that leaving him behind would be the most humane thing to do. But each colonist's life was now precious beyond measure. Besides, if they left him behind, his wife and daughter would likely want to stay with him. And that would tempt the entire group to stay, without the isopod safe zone to protect them. So they trudged on, carrying and dragging the poor man.

Desmond estimated they had been walking for at least two hours. The sun was getting low on the horizon. And still the group hadn't had a single drop of water to drink or anything to eat. The only break they'd caught was that nearly every square foot of ground was carpeted with soft moss. But even so, Desmond had a few bleeding wounds on his feet from those areas where the moss had given way to wide sheets of bare, inhospitable bedrock.

The conversations had eventually dwindled until the refugees were marching in silence, following the isopods in exhausted solemnity to an unknown destination.

And then the rain began to fall.

Without containers, sheets of plastic, or any other materials to gather the drops, the colonists resorted to walking with cupped hands and trying not to stumble as they held their mouths open to the sky. In this way, Desmond took in the equivalent of several decent swallows of water over the next twenty minutes or so. The Guardsmen actually got onto their knees and sucked water from the saturated moss. Desmond noted that the doctors opted to avoid this approach, and he decided to trust their judgement and remain on his feet. Fortunately, Alexander regained consciousness during the shower, and with some help he was able to hydrate himself.

The rain ended as quickly as it had begun, but it had lifted the group's spirits. Conversations picked up again, and even the isopods seemed to walk with a bit more energy. Desmond noticed that Lenny and Xavier were now walking on either side of Isabelle Millwright. Curious, he dropped back and joined them.

Not surprisingly, Lenny seemed to be doing most of the talking. "So, be honest—is life in the White House like they show it on TV, with a gazillion people all walking in different directions at once while drinking coffee and having pithy conversations?"

Isabelle shrugged slightly. "I'm afraid I never watched much television."

Desmond was about to tell Lenny to leave the poor girl alone, but then Isabelle smiled and said, "But I can tell you this. I've found that I can freak most of those people out by stopping them and saying, 'Do you know where my dad is? I need to tell him about my mom's accident.'"

After a few seconds of silence, Lenny smiled broadly. "That's wicked awesome."

"She's pulling your chain," Xavier said.

"The White House is a stuffy, sober place," Isabelle said. "You'd think it'd be fascinating, right? And it is, but only for the first week or two. Try being there three years. I would imagine living at a bridging facility is much more exciting. I bet you guys have some good stories to tell, right?"

"Sure," Xavier said. "If you like horror stories."

Lenny let out a one-puff laugh. "Getting a hangnail would be a horror story to Xavier. Try to imagine, if you will, a world dominated by large birds instead of mammals. Now try to imagine that some of those birds live in villages and raise crops. They even have pets. You know what they have for pets?"

Isabelle tilted her head. "Uh... birds?"

"You got it. Kind of like Goofy, who is a dog, has Pluto, who is also a dog, as a pet."

Desmond was tempted to interject with the fact that both Lenny and Xavier had spent most of that excursion holed up in a cave high on the side of a cliff, but he decided against it. It was becoming obvious that Lenny was smitten with the president's daughter. And from the way she was looking at him, Desmond got the feeling that the sentiment might be mutual. As usual, Lenny was oblivious to being out of his league. But then again, maybe he wasn't. Everything—quite literally—had changed in the last twelve hours.

Desmond left his friends and moved ahead to catch up with Infinity again. He walked up beside her, but before he could speak she held up a hand.

"Do you hear that?"

He listened. He heard a barely-audible thrumming sound, almost like there was some kind of machinery running below the ground.

"They're stopping!" Emily shouted from the front of the group.

Desmond stood on his toes to see the isopods at the front of the herd. Emily was right. They were coming to a stop at the base of a framework hill. And distributed around the hill's perimeter were more isopods, perhaps the rest of the original herd. The creatures were spaced almost evenly, and although

Desmond couldn't see the other side of the hill, he suspected that they had distributed themselves all the way around. The fifteen isopods the humans had been following were now inserting themselves into the formation, and the others were shifting positions to make room for them.

As Desmond and Infinity followed the last trailing isopods closer to the hill, the thrumming sound became louder. Whatever the noise was, it was coming from the hill's dark interior.

"I don't like this—not one damn bit," Infinity said.

Desmond didn't like it either. The thrumming coming from within the hill sounded like what he imagined he'd hear if he pressed his ear against a beehive.

The last of the isopods joined the others around the hill. And then, as if triggered by the completion of the circle, the isopods toppled onto their sides, drew their legs up tight to their bodies, and curled into armor-plated spheres.

Desmond stared at the creatures—none of them were moving. The refugees shuffled their feet and glanced at each other. Gideon and Alfie lowered Alexander to the ground. President Millwright kneeled beside him and placed a hand on his cheek. He moaned softly, indicating that he was semiconscious.

"Now what are we supposed to do?" Chloe asked.

The sun was now low enough to throw a long shadow to the east of the framework hill.

Desmond turned to Infinity. "This is rather anticlimactic. I was hoping they'd at least lead us to a water source. I think they're going to spend the night here."

"Don't let your guard down yet," she said. "I'm more concerned about what's inside the hill. And why in the hell these things chose this location."

Xavier came up from behind and stood between them.

"Maybe they find the humming sound to be comforting. It might help them sleep."

"I don't find it comforting in the least," Infinity said.

Desmond stared into the hill's dark interior through the openings between moss-covered girders. "Whatever creatures are making the sound, there must be a lot of them. Let's hope they're friendlier than skitterbugs."

Gideon approached the group. "It'll be dark soon. Any thoughts on our next course of action?"

Desmond looked at Infinity and raised his brows. She was far more experienced than anyone when it came to spending the night on alternate versions of Earth.

She pursed her lips and studied the hill for a moment. "I say we stick with the isopods. We're still alive because of them. Once the sun sets, this area could be crawling with far more predators than what we've seen today." She paused to wipe some grit out of one of her eyes. "Goddammit! We really needed a chance to explore."

"Look, we've observed the isopods' behavior for almost an entire day," Desmond said. "They seem to move around and graze on the moss all day, and then they come here to spend the night. They didn't try to go to standing water at any point, so we can assume they get their moisture from the moss they eat, or possibly from the rain."

Xavier continued his reasoning. "So if we continue to follow them, we die of thirst. Or we starve. And then the isopods leave our bodies behind to be picked to the bone by skitterbugs."

Infinity shot him a look. "What did I say to Eagleton about only making helpful comments?"

Xavier frowned. "Sorry, I was just...."

"But you're right of course," Infinity said. "We can't keep

doing what we've been doing and expect different results. We're going to have to leave the isopods, either now or in the morning."

"We've got maybe an hour of daylight," Gideon said. "Taking off on our own now wouldn't be wise."

Infinity looked to Desmond. He considered again the humming sound coming from within the hill. That was an unknown—maybe it was harmless, maybe not. But out here there were tiger beetles, anglerbeasts, and probably countless other vicious creatures they hadn't yet seen. He nodded in agreement.

"Okay, you're right," Infinity said. "This isn't the time to be away from the isopods' safe zone."

"Assuming they even create a safe zone while curled up and sleeping," Xavier added.

Infinity sighed. "Yes, assuming that. If the isopods stay here until morning, and no predators cross into the safe zone, we'll stay here with them. Everyone agree?"

At least half the refugees were now gathered around, listening, and they all nodded.

AFTER SUNSET

"THERE'S ANOTHER ONE," Desmond whispered to Infinity. He could see the creature's outline in the darkness and could hear its feet thumping the mossy ground. Heaving inhalations coming from somewhere on its body grew louder as it drew nearer. But like all the others before it, the creature stopped about ten yards out from the isopods, which were still lying dormant like a string of massive beads around the hill's perimeter. The creature paced back and forth, a featureless black specter that might be either harmless or deadly.

"Infinity!" he hissed. Apparently she was asleep. As far as Desmond could tell, the others were sleeping too, except for the med techs, Àurea and Sarah, who had volunteered to keep watch for the first two-hour shift.

Desmond sighed and allowed his head to drop back down onto the soft moss. He tried to convince himself that this creature, too, would eventually decide to wander off. He stared up at the sky. A few clouds were obscuring some of the stars, but the constellations he could see were familiar to him—the only part of this world that *was* familiar. But instead of comforting him, they made him miss home fiercely.

Was there anything left of his world? Perhaps today had been the predicted, much-feared implosion tipping point. Weeks ago, geologists had used digital models to predict that the frequent minor earthquakes occurring were actually leading up to a series of major geologic events. The very first of these events was certain to wipe away most forms of life and all signs of civilization. The events would get worse after that, but no one would be around to see them. Had the first event occurred today? Perhaps the event had been in its beginning stages as this first group of ST6 was departing. Perhaps if they'd waited one more minute they would have died along with everyone else. Desmond would never know.

He thought of his mom. Had she died a brutal death? And Infinity—she had run away from home at fourteen. Was she having regrets that she had never once tried to contact her parents?

He closed his eyes. The droning from within the hill was still audible in the background, although its volume seemed to ebb and flow every few minutes. The sound kept penetrating his thoughts every time he was on the edge of sleep. The thrumming wasn't particularly unpleasant. But there was something about it, the way it pushed its way into his mind, almost like it was trying to speak to him.

Finally, he felt his body getting light as his thoughts gave way to exhaustion. Thrumming, buzzing waves of sound rose and fell, eventually carrying him to sleep.

7

───────

SMOKE

September 5 - Morning

INFINITY SENSED something large moving near her. She opened her eyes. Not three feet away, a two-ton isopod was waking up, unrolling itself, and rocking toward her to get to its feet.

Desmond was sleeping beside her, and his legs were dangerously close to being crushed by the lumbering creature's attempts. She grabbed his arm and pulled him toward her.

"What... what are you doing?" He stammered.

Infinity got to her feet. In the morning light, she could see that the other isopods were opening up as well, some of them rolling much too close to sleeping colonists.

"Hey, wake up!" she shouted. "Move out of the way."

Several refugees immediately became alert, and they started shaking the others awake. Seconds later, everyone was safely out of the way as the isopods finished pushing themselves upright. The massive beasts shuffled back and forth, some of them rubbing against the base of the framework hill as if scratching their sides.

"I'm sorry, Infinity," said the guardsman, Tyrone. "I was on watch, and I thought I was wide awake. Next thing I knew, you were waking everyone up."

"Don't sweat it," she replied. "The isopods obviously kept the predators away." Now that she thought about it, she too had slept far more soundly than she had expected to. She hadn't stirred at all during the night, and now she felt surprisingly alert.

Desmond got to his feet and rubbed his eyes. "Man, I was out cold."

"It might be the elevated oxygen level," Poppy said. "I noticed yesterday that breathing is easier here than back home. That can only mean that the oxygen level is higher, which could explain why we slept like babies."

"It could also partially explain how these arthropods grow to such immense sizes," Desmond said.

Xavier had been focused on inspecting his skitterbug wounds, but now he spoke up. "Um, I agree that this air has more oxygen. But I think we're ignoring the elephant in the room. This humming sound—it gets into your head. I'm pretty sure it had a lot to do with why I fell asleep so fast. Normally, a sound like that would drive me insane. Doesn't anyone else think it's a little weird?"

"He's right," Gideon said. "The last thing I remember before falling asleep was focusing on the sound. It definitely pushes its way into your brain, but in a good way. If that makes any sense."

Everyone contemplated this silently. Infinity had to agree. The sound was strangely mesmerizing. Which was probably a good reason to get away from it as soon as possible.

"Good God almighty," Richard Hussain said. "Would you look at that sunrise."

They all turned. The sun was just coming up over some rocky hills in the distance, illuminating the surrounding expanse of smaller, domed framework hills. Infinity realized for the first time that the ground in this area gradually sloped downward to the north, allowing them to see miles of broad plain dotted with hundreds of framework mounds. The bright green moss contrasted with the orange and blue sky, creating a breathtaking image. Herds of grazing animals, some numbering in the thousands, created an additional layer of patchwork colors.

A movement in the distance caught Infinity's eye. She squinted, and then her chest tightened. A column of smoke was rising from one of the mounds, spiraling upward in dark plumes. "Do you see that?" she said, pointing.

"Yes, and there," Desmond said, pointing to another column of smoke farther to the east.

Infinity scanned the entire plain and spotted smoke rising from the tops of five framework hills.

"There's something here intelligent enough to make fires?" Xavier said.

Lenny stepped up between Infinity and Xavier. "Not possible, Kemosabe. This is a world of arthropods, remember? Besides, look closer at that smoke. Have you ever seen smoke move downward?"

Infinity stared at one of the columns. Lenny was right. A swirling plume near the top of the column abruptly reversed direction, moving back down toward the hill's peak hundreds of feet below.

"Those are living creatures," Desmond muttered. "A swarm of bugs."

Celia's voice came from the back of the crowd of staring refugees. "Something's happening!"

Infinity turned and saw that the isopods were becoming restless, shuffling back and forth and rubbing more aggressively against the side of the mound. But then Infinity noticed what Celia had been referring to—something inside the hill. The thrumming sound was intensifying. Infinity instinctively stepped back from the mound. All the other humans did the same except for President Millwright and Isabelle, who were huddled beside Alexander a few yards from the isopods. The humming continued to grow until several refugees covered their ears from the noise.

A dark cloud erupted suddenly from the hill, spiraling upward. The cloud continued pouring out, rising amidst an almost deafening surge of sound, until the column was well over a hundred yards tall.

Infinity squinted at the smoke, trying unsuccessfully to discern individual winged creatures. Either they were too small, or this really was smoke. Loud, buzzing smoke, which was impossible.

It had to be tiny, living creatures, she decided. The question was, were they dangerous? The isopods were staying put beside the hill, so retreating from the column of smoke would mean leaving the safe zone—another dilemma. And again, the group would have to act reactively instead of proactively. Infinity was getting damn tired of this environment being so unpredictable.

She turned to the refugees. Several of them were watching her with wide eyes, waiting for a directive. "Stay here, stay together," she shouted. That was it. That was the best advice she had to offer. At least until the smoke creatures became a threat.

The humans stared up at the shifting, swirling column. The way the plumes were moving made Infinity doubly certain that she was looking at a mass of living creatures. She had seen vast flocks of birds surge in one direction and then the other, dropping and then rising in fluid waves of motion. Although she couldn't make out the individuals in this cloud, the swarming movements were unmistakable.

Desmond nudged her shoulder. "This just keeps getting more surreal," he said, pointing to one of the isopods.

The beasts were now frantically scuffing the side of the mound with their bodies. Not only that, but they were also changing in appearance. Their olive green exoskeletons were turning brown. But not uniformly. The brown color was appearing in splotches, with each splotch gradually spreading. Infinity realized the splotches were actually a substance being excreted from specific spots between the creatures' broad armor plates. The substance was oozing out, some of it even running down the isopods' sides and dripping to the ground.

"I think the scraping is what's stimulating that stuff to come out," Desmond said. "Absolutely fascinating!"

Infinity shot him a sideways glance. What she found fascinating was Desmond's mind. Faced with unpredictable and possibly deadly creatures, all he could think of was how biologically interesting they were. Maybe she needed his fascination to balance her hardcore nature, but it was a mystery how he had survived to adulthood. Once again, it was obvious he had lived a life nothing like hers.

The smoke column swirled high above them for another minute or so and then began to retract. Soon it had been reduced to a dense, oval-shaped cloud just above the hill. The buzzing sound started to become softer, less frenzied, as the oval began flattening, its sides pouring down the hill's slope like liquid and spreading outward. Infinity's chest tightened again as she watched the stuff flow nearer to the colonists.

The swarm quickly enveloped the isopods, swirling around the beasts and then alighting upon their bodies, covering them completely. The isopods held completely still throughout this process. Infinity shuddered at the thought of her entire body being covered by the tiny creatures like that. If in fact they were even creatures at all—she still couldn't make out individual specks within the swarm.

The buzzing sound continued to dwindle until it was almost silent, the quietest it had been since the colonists had arrived the previous evening.

"Millwrights," Infinity hissed. "Just stay as still as you can," The family was only a few feet from the nearest isopod, and she worried any movement might draw the creatures to them.

"They're feeding on the stuff the isopods secreted," Desmond whispered. "They must have some kind of mutualistic relationship."

Again Infinity shot him a glance. "Or maybe they're eating the isopods."

He shook his head. "No, the isopods wouldn't hold still if that were the case. Mutualism makes sense—the isopods feed the swarm of creatures and protect them at night by sleeping around their mound."

"Then what exactly does the swarm provide for the isopods?"

He shook his head again. "I don't know that yet."

She sighed and stared at the nearest isopod. The creature's surface flowed with movement. Ridges and depressions constantly shifted, faded, and then reemerged.

"I think it's okay," a muttering voice said.

Infinity turned to see Eagleton stepping cautiously toward the Millwrights and swarm-covered isopods.

"Stop moving!" Infinity ordered.

"What the hell is he doing?" Gideon whispered behind Infinity.

"It's okay," Eagleton repeated. "There's something about it. I can hear it... they aren't going to hurt us." He was now only a few feet from the nearest isopod. "I can see them now. They're extremely small. And they're harmless, I *know* they are."

"Eagleton, back off!" Infinity said.

But he kept ignoring her. "Listen," he said. "Can't you hear it?" He extended a hand, almost touching the isopod's roiling surface.

"Everyone be ready to run," Infinity said. "Mr. Millwright, if something happens, Desmond and I will come to you and haul you away from the hill. Be ready."

The guardsman Alfie Lewis spoke up. "Eagleton's right. I can hear them. It's like they're talking inside my head." The guardsman stepped forward, leaving the cluster of refugees. "I don't think they can hurt us. Their sound is, you know, kind of pretty."

Now Infinity was hearing something too, as if the swarm's buzzing had coalesced into some kind of soft, pleasant music. Or maybe it was simply a thrumming frequency that meshed perfectly with her brainwaves. Whatever it was, it was calming. Which made her even more skeptical and alert. She'd spent a lifetime learning not to trust anyone or anything that initially seemed agreeable.

"They're right," Desmond said, his posture suddenly relaxed. "These things are incapable of hurting us. I'm sure of it."

Infinity grabbed his arm. "Stay where you are, or I'm going to knock you out and drag you away from those things!"

The situation was deteriorating beyond her control. Several others stepped forward, making comments about how the creatures couldn't hurt them.

"Stop, goddammit!" Infinity commanded. "We don't know—"

The group had stopped. They were wide-eyed, but they weren't looking at her. She turned. The cloud was lifting from the isopod in front of Eagleton. Swirling in the air, the swarm drifted closer to him. The edge of the swarm came within inches of his face, and he held up his hand to block them from coming closer. The swarm stopped advancing and hovered before him. At this distance, Infinity could make out individual creatures—tiny dots, like impossibly small flies.

The cloud before Eagleton began changing shape. The flies moved closer together, forming a swarm so dense that no light shone through from the other side. And still the mass condensed, until it was almost black. Its shape continued to change.

Infinity felt her hand grasping for Desmond's. She found it, and she clenched him as tightly as she could, afraid that he might try to step away from her and approach the impossible thing she was seeing.

The swarm had taken the shape of a human. There was no mistaking it. The densely-packed flies were hovering in the shape of a man with two arms, two legs, and even a penis. The figure's surface, if it could be called a surface, was uniformly black, but the contours of the eyes, nose, and mouth were plainly visible. The figure was facing Eagleton, not two feet in front of him. It raised one hand and held it before its face, in the same way Eagleton had done seconds earlier.

Eagleton turned back toward the other refugees, a stunned look on his face, quickly replaced by a broad smile. "I told you, they won't hurt us. They're trying to communicate!"

"That's impossible," Desmond said, barely above a whisper.

"Well, it's happening," Infinity replied. "And don't even think about calling it fascinating."

Eagleton held his palm up and waved it back and forth before his face. The swarm figure repeated the gesture.

The other refugees remained quiet, apparently too stunned to speak.

"Reece Eagleton," Infinity said loudly. "I want you to back away slowly. We need to get out of here. Now."

Eagleton turned to her, as did the figure beside him. "It's intelligent. I'm betting it can help us. This is exactly what we needed."

Infinity gritted her teeth. "We don't know that!"

Eagleton turned back to the figure. "I know it. I'm sure of it." He then extended a hand. The figure did the same, and the two hands touched, one made of flesh and the other composed of thousands of winged creatures. "See? It's intelligent!"

The figure began transforming rapidly. Within the time it took Infinity to open her mouth to shout another order, the swarm dissolved and congregated into a dense sphere around the point of contact with Eagleton's hand. It then rushed up the man's arm. Within a few seconds it had covered his entire body. Eagleton sputtered and let out an inhuman gargling sound.

Several refugees cried out, and the entire group stepped back in shock. Infinity kept her eyes on Eagleton, but in her peripheral vision she saw President Millwright and Isabelle trying to drag Alexander away from the horror.

Eagleton dropped to his knees and began swiping at his face, all the while coughing and sputtering. Although he was no longer visible through the swarm, the creatures were clearly entering his mouth and nose.

Infinity shook away her shock and glanced around. Some of the flies had quit feeding on the isopods and were forming a substantial cloud in the air above Eagleton as he struggled. She had to do something.

"Everyone move back to a safe distance," she ordered. Without waiting for them to comply, she ran to Eagleton's side.

Regardless of how much she despised the man, he was part of her family now. Aware that it would only take the swarm a few seconds to engulf her, she moved in and started frantically swiping the creatures from his body.

A hand grabbed her elbow. "Infinity, don't touch them!" It was Desmond.

She shook him off. "I'm not letting him die like this."

"The same thing will happen to—"

Infinity suddenly realized why Desmond had stopped talking—Eagleton had quit struggling. His body was still covered in flies, but his face was now exposed and he was gazing up at them without expression.

"Reece, are you okay?" Desmond asked.

Eagleton opened his mouth, and a wisp of hundreds of flies spiraled out. "What are you?" he said, his words stilted and strained.

"Reece?" Desmond said.

Eagleton's eyes blinked a few times. "You are different. What are you?"

"What the hell do you mean?" Infinity demanded. Eagleton's behavior was pushing her wariness to a whole new level.

Eagleton's face remained expressionless. "Reece Eagleton allows us to talk to you. We have not encountered you before. What are you?"

Infinity exchanged a glance with Desmond. He shook his head slightly, like he couldn't believe what he was seeing and hearing. She then glanced at the other refugees. They were too far away to be able to hear what was happening, except for the Millwrights, who had ceased their efforts to drag Alexander away and were now crouched with him, watching the conversation closely.

"How are you doing this?" Desmond asked the figure on its knees.

"Please tell us. What are you?"

"We're humans," Infinity said. "We came here from an alternate version of this world. That's why we're different. That's why you haven't encountered us before."

Eagleton stared, shifting his eyes from Infinity to Desmond and back. "We do not understand. But Reece Eagleton has eyes that allow us to see in a new way. We have seen with many eyes, but we have not seen with eyes like these. We like these eyes."

Infinity had no idea how to respond to this.

"You're intelligent," Desmond said. "So where are you? Where is your body? Your mind?"

"We are here. Above you. On Reece Eagleton's body. Feeding on the nectar of the ones you call the isopods. We like these eyes. We will keep these eyes. Please come into our hive with us."

Desmond pointed to the framework hill beside them. "You want us to go in there?"

"Yes. Please come. We will keep you and your eyes."

"Like hell you will," Infinity said. "Give us Reece Eagleton back, and we'll go away and leave you alone. Otherwise we're going to kill all of you."

Eagleton stared at Infinity for a few seconds. "We do not believe you are able to kill all of us."

Infinity's mind raced. Eagleton's life—perhaps all the colonists' lives—might depend on what she chose to say next. "Don't underestimate what we are able to do. We *will* kill you. Release Reece Eagleton."

"We like the way you speak," Eagleton said. "We have not spoken in such a way before. We will keep you. We will speak to you often. You will come into our hive."

"To hell with this," Infinity said. She punched Eagleton on the side of his head, nearly knocking him onto his side. She followed up with a kick that sent him to the ground and then straddled his body, slapping his skin and grinding handfuls of bugs into mush. Within seconds she had smeared dead creatures over the man's entire chest. She then began slapping his shoulders and head.

She felt Desmond's hands slapping at her own head and back, and the creatures blanketed her face, blocking her vision. She swiped at her eyes and mouth, but the things were already filling her nostrils.

"Infinity!" Desmond shouted, but the flies were filling her ears, making his voice sound muffled.

"Grab her legs!" she heard another voice saying. "Go, go, go!"

Infinity kept hitting and clawing at her face as she felt herself being roughly dragged and carried away. Abruptly, she fell to the ground, and then she felt hands all over her, swiping and grinding, until every inch of her body felt sticky with crushed bugs. She wiped more of them from her eyes and then tried to blow them from her nose. But she'd been holding her breath and didn't have enough air left. She opened her mouth and gasped, sucking in countless flies. She started coughing and spitting until finally she felt like she could breathe again.

She heard screams and angry shouts.

"They need help!" Chloe said.

"Then go," Desmond's said. "I'll stay with Infinity."

Infinity rubbed her eyes furiously to clear them. Finally she forced them open. Desmond was kneeling above her but staring back toward the isopods. She sat up and looked. Some of the refugees were dragging President Millwright and Isabelle away from the mound, both of them kicking and screaming. Near the isopods, Alexander—at least Infinity thought that's who it was—was writhing on the ground, completely covered in flies.

"Let me go!" President Millwright screamed as she and Isabelle were dragged away from the mound. "Alex, oh my God, we have to help him!

Tyrone tried calming her. "Please, ma'am. There's nothing we can do."

The president and her daughter continued to struggle and had to be restrained from running back to Alexander.

Infinity coughed and spat one more time. She shrugged Desmond's hand from her shoulder. "I'm okay." She got to her feet.

She and the rest of the refugees were fifty yards from Eagleton and Alexander. Mr. Millwright had stopped struggling. He was still covered with flies, except for his face. A couple yards to his right, Eagleton was now on his feet. The flies had left him—all but those Infinity had smashed into his skin. Above the two men, a growing swarm was hovering like a black storm cloud.

Infinity was struggling to process all that had happened in the last few minutes. She shook her head and decided there simply wasn't time to think about it. With only fifty yards between the swarm and the other refugees, the tiny flies could probably expand outward and overtake them at any time. In fact, why hadn't the creatures done so already? Were they unable to see this far? Were they afraid to move away from their hive?

"Alex, are you okay?" President Millwright shouted.

Alexander was now sitting up, and the flies were vacating his body, like a tendril of smoke rising to join the hovering cloud above. He was looking out at the refugees. "Hayley! I'm okay. You can come back now."

The president started to get up, but Tyrone put a hand on

her shoulder. "Hold on, ma'am, it may not be safe." He looked at Infinity and she nodded in agreement. She was still uneasy about the situation.

"Come on, Hayley, it's safe," Alexander said. "They won't hurt you or anyone else. They're curious about us. Please, I need help."

"I'm going to my husband," President Millwright said. "Stay back here if you want, but I'm going to help him get away from those things."

Tyrone glanced at Infinity again. "What do you think?"

Eagleton called out, "You can all come back. There's nothing to be afraid of."

Infinity shouted, "Reece, help Mr. Millwright up and get him over here. We're leaving."

Eagleton moved to Alexander's side. "No, we'll be staying here, where it's safe."

President Millwright got to her feet. "Let go of me!" She broke away from Tyrone and took off toward her husband.

"Dammit!" Infinity said, taking off after her.

But Steven Irizar intercepted her. "Remember what I said about me finding trouble? Let me go. If nothing happens to me, we'll know it's safe for everyone." Without waiting for a reply, he ran after the president.

Tyrone took off behind him. "We'll carry all three back if we have to, Infinity," he said over his shoulder.

The two guardsmen caught up to President Millwright just as she was kneeling down beside her husband. Infinity couldn't hear what they were saying, but they appeared to be arguing with Eagleton.

Desmond, Lenny, and Xavier stepped up to her side. Desmond said, "Either Eagleton lost his mind when those flies covered him, or—and I can't believe I'm saying this—there's something intelligent in that hill that really did speak to us through his body."

"I favor the insane Eagleton idea," Xavier said. "It's a lot more feasible."

"Spare the fake skepticism, brothers," Lenny said. "You believe, as well as I do, that it's the flies themselves. It's a hive mind. A collective intelligence."

Infinity narrowed her eyes at him and shook her head.

"Not possible," Desmond muttered.

Lenny huffed. "Yeah, and neither is a hippo-sized arthropod. Oh, except for the isopods. And the colossal anglerbeast."

"It's just *anglerbeast*," Xavier reminded him.

Infinity sighed and turned back toward the hill. The two guardsmen's stiff posture suggested their argument with Eagleton was becoming heated. Steven and Tyrone kneeled down to pull Mr. Millwright to his feet. The cloud of flies suddenly descended on the two guardsmen and engulfed their bodies. A split second later, the cloud also covered President Millwright. The three dropped to the ground, fighting to brush the creatures from their skin.

Infinity made a quick decision, one she should have made before they'd lost the president and two guardsmen. "We're getting the hell out of here," she said. She spun around and scanned the surrounding area—nothing but the moss-covered plain, dotted with framework hills for at least a mile in every direction. She pointed to the nearest rocky hillside, which lay about a mile to the west. "That's where we're going."

"We can't just leave my mom and dad here!" Isabelle cried.

Poppy Safran spoke calmly. "Isabelle is right. We can't leave five of our people behind to die."

Infinity gritted her teeth. The survival of the entire group was at risk. Her gut instinct was screaming at her to get everyone out of there and keep the remaining fourteen alive. Five dead was better than total extinction.

Chloe pointed. "Look, I think they're going to be okay."

Infinity turned. The flies were streaming upward from the bodies of the president and two guardsmen to rejoin the cloud above. Seconds later, the three of them sat up. They got to their feet. Along with Eagleton, they stood over Alexander, who appeared to be struggling to get up. But Eagleton, the guardsmen, and the president ignored him, their gaze instead directed out at the rest of the refugees.

And then Alexander did get up.

"Daddy?" Isabelle said, too softly for her father to hear at this distance.

Eagleton began walking away from the hill, and the others followed, including Mr. Millwright, his broken leg skewed unnaturally out to the side as he limped along behind the others. The cloud of flies hung back, still hovering over the isopods at the base of the hill.

"They're not going to hurt us," Eagleton said when he was halfway to the group.

"Reece is right," President Millwright added. "They're curious about us."

"They don't know what we are," said Tyrone. "They're curious."

"Daddy?" Isabelle said, this time louder.

"I'm fine, Izzy," her dad replied. The man was smiling, but Infinity could now hear his knee cracking each time he put his weight on it.

"I really, *really* don't like this," Infinity muttered. But what could she do? The others weren't willing to leave anyone behind.

Isabelle broke away from the group abruptly. "Daddy, I'll help you! We need to help him, Mom!"

As Isabelle rushed to get to her dad, Tyrone stepped out and hit the girl in the face. Isabelle crumpled to the ground, groaning and holding her nose with her hands. Blood poured out between her fingers.

"I've got this one," Alexander said. He grabbed his daughter by one of her ankles and started dragging her back toward the waiting swarm, his knee crunching and twisting at odd angles.

Infinity rushed out to meet the incoming refugees. "What the hell are you doing?" Her first inclination was to attack them, but Millwright was the president, a fact that gave Infinity pause.

"We're trying to tell you, they won't hurt us," Millwright said, smiling.

"Take 'em down!" Gideon cried. He and Desmond rushed past Infinity and tackled Tyrone. But then Eagleton and Steven closed in and began pummeling Desmond and Gideon with vicious blows.

Everything was going to hell.

"We need you to come with us," Millwright said as she closed the distance between herself and Infinity. The woman was still smiling, her eyes sparkling the way they always had on television.

Infinity shook off her hesitation. She thrust her right foot into Millwright's gut. Infinity threw her knee up as the woman doubled over, crushing the face of the former President of the United States.

8

———

ESCAPE

September 5 - Morning

Brutal blows landed on Desmond's shoulders and back, and he soon lost his grip on Tyrone, leaving Gideon to handle the guardsman on his own. Desmond managed to get to his knees and realized his attacker was Eagleton. He'd had no idea the man could hit so hard. "Stop, Reece!" he cried. "What are you doing?"

Eagleton gazed at him with narrowed eyes. "I asked politely and you refused. You're not being cooperative."

Gideon was still wrestling with Tyrone nearby, with Steven attacking him from above. Desmond glanced back at Infinity. She was struggling with President Millwright, whose face, chest, and abdomen were now covered in blood.

While Desmond was momentarily distracted, Eagleton lunged forward and grabbed his wrist.

"We need your cooperation," Eagleton said, dragging Desmond toward the hill.

Desmond tried to yank his arm free, but Eagleton's grip was surprisingly strong. Desmond managed to get to his feet, throw his free arm around Eagleton's neck, and take him to the ground.

"Stop fighting," Eagleton grunted. "You're coming with me."

At that moment, several refugees piled on top of them. In a frenzy of flailing arms and legs, they helped Desmond pin Eagleton to the moss-covered ground.

Eagleton stopped struggling. "You're making a mistake. If you just come with me, you'll understand."

Desmond pushed himself up and put one knee on the man's chest. "That's not going to happen. Why should we trust you?"

Eagleton's face was oddly relaxed. "I told you, they won't hurt us. They want to know what we are."

Desmond glanced around quickly to assess the situation. Six refugees were now fighting to restrain Tyrone and Steven. Infinity had taken President Millwright to the ground and seemed to have her immobilized, although Millwright was still struggling.

Movement to Desmond's right caught his eye. It was Isabelle. She had broken away from her father and was now running. Alexander was pursuing her, walking awkwardly on his broken leg. And now he was carrying the mandible weapon Desmond had abandoned.

"Hold Eagleton down!" Desmond ordered the refugees beside him as he got up off the man's chest.

Isabelle had stopped next to her mother and Infinity, and was staring down at them, perhaps struggling to comprehend what was happening. Alexander came up behind her with the mandible raised, as if he intended to kill his own daughter.

"Look out!" Desmond cried.

Isabelle turned and saw her father. "Daddy?" she whimpered as she stumbled backward.

Desmond rushed toward them as Alexander lifted the weapon higher to swing it. "No!" he screamed, hurtling into Alexander just as he started swinging the mandible downward. Desmond's head rammed into the man's chest so hard that everything went dark, and he felt himself tumbling to the ground amid a jumble of grunts and scuffling hands and feet.

He came to a stop flat on his back. He blinked at the sky, trying to bring the gentle-looking clouds into focus.

"Get up, Desmond. Now!"

Infinity's voice galvanized him into action. He sat up, still blinking.

"Grab your weapon! It's to your right."

He turned and saw the weapon. Alexander had gotten to his feet and was staggering toward it. Desmond snatched the weapon before Alexander could reach it and stood up, facing the man.

"Let me go!" Mrs. Millwright sputtered.

Infinity had the president in a chokehold, and she eyed Desmond intently. "Try not to kill him, but do what you have to," she said.

Desmond turned back to Mr. Millwright.

"You're making a mistake," Alexander said. "Put that down and come with us." The man took a wobbly, bone-crunching step closer.

Desmond lunged in, swinging the mandible at Millwright's broken knee. The leg folded at a sickening angle and the man collapsed. Alexander struggled to get up, and Desmond stood over him, ready to strike again if necessary. But now the man's broken leg would support no weight at all. As he floundered, his face showed no signs of the pain he should have been feeling.

"You are not... cooperating," Alexander said, his words punctuated by his efforts.

"Sorry to disappoint you," Desmond replied, turning his attention back to Infinity and the president.

Infinity had gotten up and was standing over President Millwright, who was lying still on the ground. Isabelle stood beside them, staring down wide-eyed at her mother.

"Is she dead?" Isabelle asked.

"No, I just choked her out. But she won't be unconscious long. We're taking her and we're getting the hell away from that swarm."

"What about my dad?"

Infinity sighed and turned to Desmond.

He looked at the other refugees. Together they had successfully pinned Eagleton and the two guardsmen to the ground. But how could fourteen people manage to carry or drag five others who had apparently been possessed? And would moving them away from the swarm even make a difference? Maybe not. But losing five members of the group was unthinkable. "We need to haul them—all of them, including Mr. Millwright—as far from this hill as we can," Desmond finally said.

Infinity nodded once. "It won't be easy, but I agree." She spoke to the entire group. "We need two more of you over here. We're going to carry all five of them toward those hills." She pointed to the west.

Xavier said, "We can barely hold them down as it is!" He was sitting on one of Tyrone's legs.

"They want us to come back," Eagleton said.

Tyrone lifted his head. "Yes, we have to go back." He grunted fiercely and kicked Xavier and Lenny from his legs. He shoved the others off and jumped to his feet in an instant. He then kicked the med tech, Sarah, in the head, knocking her off Eagleton. In a flurry of violence, Eagleton freed himself and joined Tyrone in shoving the others off of Steven. The three possessed men threw a few more blows at the refugees, who were trying to take them back down, and then they sprinted back toward the swarm.

"Let them go!" Infinity ordered. "Get over here and help us with the Millwrights."

As the refugees made their way over, Desmond turned back to Alexander. The man had somehow managed to get to his feet.

Alexander took a tentative step toward the swarm, but his leg folded to the side, so he resorted to hopping on his good leg. Desmond and several others grabbed his arms and stopped him.

"I have to go back," Alexander said.

Desmond grabbed him around the waist and shouted, "Get him on my shoulders!" Alexander struggled as the others lifted him up until Desmond had shouldered him in a fireman's carry. The man still refused to cooperate, so several refugees had to stay beside Desmond to restrain Alexander's good leg and his arms.

President Millwright began regaining consciousness as the others were lifting her onto Infinity's shoulder. She began struggling and Infinity ordered four people to surround her and help restrain the woman's arms and legs.

"All of you need to come with me!" Eagleton called out. "They aren't going to hurt us."

Desmond craned his head around and saw that Eagleton, Steven, and Tyrone were standing beside the framework hill, watching the group intently. The cloud of flies was gone, although Desmond could still hear the constant thrumming. The swarm had apparently returned to the hill's interior. The isopods were now lumbering off as a herd, probably heading out for another day of moss-grazing.

Desmond called out to Infinity. "The isopods are leaving. Should we follow them—stay in their safe zone?"

"All I care about right now is getting away from that damn swarm," she said. "What do the rest of you think?"

Gideon spoke up as he restrained one of Alexander's arms. "We decided last night we needed to split from the isopods. We need water, food, and shelter. We may find one or more of those near the hills to the west."

Everyone seemed to agree with this, and so they began trudging toward the nearest rocky hillside.

ALEXANDER WASN'T GIVING UP. Slung over Desmond's shoulders, he struggled and pleaded, and they had to assign another refugee to hold his head and prevent him from biting Desmond's arm. Surprisingly, Alexander still hadn't complained about the pain in his leg. It was as if the man could no longer feel pain.

After Desmond had walked perhaps a quarter mile, he began staggering, and he saw that Infinity was doing the same under President Millwright's weight. He was almost relieved when someone spotted a distant anglerbeast to the north and the group quickly decided to stop and get down low to avoid being spotted.

He and Infinity waited while the others lowered the Millwrights to the moss, and then they all flattened themselves to the ground, forcing their two captives to lay prone.

Alexander suddenly shouted, "Hey, over here. We need help!"

Desmond punched him in the side of the head. "You're going to get us all killed!"

Alexander was apparently dazed by the blow, but then his wife started shouting. "We're here! Come this way!"

The huge creature had been lumbering toward the east, but it abruptly changed direction and began heading straight toward them.

The group had left all of the broken girders behind in the confusion, so the only weapon they had was Desmond's mandible, which Lenny was now carrying. It would be useless against a creature as large as the approaching anglerbeast. It was possible the creature was a specialized predator, feeding only on the skitterbugs it lured out of framework hills, but Desmond wasn't willing to bet on this.

He scanned the area. The nearest framework hill was a couple hundred yards away. He glanced at Infinity.

Apparently she had already guessed what he was thinking. "We don't have any other choice," she said. "It's the closest shelter."

He nodded and they both jumped up.

"Hurry, pick them up." Infinity gestured at Mr. and Mrs. Millwright. The refugees gathered around the two prisoners, hoisted them off the ground by their arms and legs, and started running for the framework hill.

Mr. and Mrs. Millwright both began shouting, apparently hoping to draw the creature's ire and encourage it to speed up. Desmond could only guess why they thought this would help their situation. He turned to check on the anglerbeast. It was definitely pursuing them, but its sheer size and mass made it a slow runner. It was loping along only slightly faster than the refugees could run while carrying the two struggling captives.

They arrived at the framework hill a hundred yards ahead of the anglerbeast. The base of the structure had plenty of openings, but the interior near the ground was cluttered with clumps of old, dead moss and loose girders that had broken and fallen down through the framework.

Desmond didn't have to tell the refugees to start climbing—they already had, and they were working cooperatively to haul the president and Alexander with them.

They all stopped about ten yards up the slope, high enough to be out of the creature's reach. As the anglerbeast approached, it slowed to a walk and then stopped at the hill's base. The flattened, leaf-like appendages on either side of its head shifted and turned like data receivers carefully pinpointing the humans' direction. Below the flattened appendages dangled the creature's two translucent pink orbs. Like the first anglerbeast Desmond had seen up close, this one had no eyes, at least none that were obvious.

"We're up here," Alexander said, apparently speaking to the creature. "We need your help."

"Yes, we're here," President Millwright said.

"Shut the hell up!" Infinity growled.

But short of knocking them both out, Desmond doubted there would be a way to shut them up.

The creature hefted its massive bulk and slammed its front two feet onto the framework.

"Yes, climb up," Alexander said.

Then the creature did something Desmond had thought was impossible. It raised one of its hind legs and planted it on a low girder. It pulled itself up until its other hind foot found purchase on the slope.

"Great, it's climbing," Xavier said.

The anglerbeast took another tentative step. A twittering swarm of locust-sized, winged creatures erupted from the hill to the side of the anglerbeast.

The refugees had no choice but to move up, hauling their prisoners with them.

The creature kept coming, climbing faster now.

"I can't believe I'm suggesting this," Desmond said, "but I think we're going to have to get inside the hill." The thought of being trapped again made him sick to his stomach, but this creature was only going to move faster as the slope leveled out at the top. It was certain to overtake them.

"He's right," Infinity said. "Get yourselves in deep enough to be out of its reach."

"I don't wish to go inside this hive," President Millwright said. "I want to go back to my own hive."

"Yes, back to our own hive!" her husband echoed.

"Get your ass in here," Gideon said. He had already lowered himself into an opening between the girders, and he grasped Alexander's wrist and pulled him in face first. Several others shoved the man's legs into the hole, and then Emily climbed down on top of him, kicking him and forcing him lower.

The remaining refugees did the same with Mrs. Millwright, climbing in after her until the entire group was deep within the framework. The creature finished making its way up the hill and stopped directly above them. Pieces of moss and dirt showered down, bouncing from one girder to the next on their way to the darker depths below.

"If that thing's too heavy and comes crashing through, we're all royally toasted," Lenny said.

Desmond hadn't thought of this. He'd been too busy trying to get his mind off the possibility that this hill might contain another colony of skitterbugs.

The anglerbeast's flat sensors swiveled back and forth again, apparently searching for them. It then lowered the front of its body and dangled both its pink orbs into the hill. The orbs began glowing with strikingly bright bioluminescence as they continued moving downward, and the cords they were attached to gradually stretched to twice their original length. One of the orbs stopped just above Desmond's head. The creature began emitting a buzzing, clicking sound, the same sound the previous anglerbeast had used to lure skitterbugs out from the center of the hill.

"Well, crap," Desmond muttered.

The orbs bobbed up and down as the creature contracted and relaxed the cords. This went on for several minutes as the humans clung to the maze of girders. Desmond peered into the darkness below, watching and listening for approaching skitterbugs. Or perhaps something even worse.

But nothing came. Finally, the anglerbeast retracted its orbs and made its way down the slope, loudly cracking several girders in the process. In spite of the Millwrights' annoying calls to the creature, it wandered off. The Millwrights fell silent.

After a minute or so, the med tech, Sarah Suzuki, spoke up. "Maybe a hill like this one would make a good shelter. You know, one without a swarm of killer bugs in it."

"It would at least protect us from the larger predators," Àurea added. "And we might be able to break away some of the girders to create an open space."

Sarah said, "We just need to find a source of water and then choose a suitable hill nearby."

Desmond stared into the hill's interior. Since this hill wasn't home to a colony of skitterbugs, it was likely other hills would be empty as well. And since there were no trees from which to fashion logs for building houses, the only other option he'd come up with was to use girders from framework hills. But those were relatively small, and fastening them together would be difficult. In a framework hill like this one, the girders were already fused together. Rain coming through would be a problem, but they could figure that out later. Assuming the coming winter would be cold, insulating a smaller living space within the hill would also be problematic. But still, this was the best idea anyone had come up with.

"Sounds like a plan to me," Infinity proclaimed. "And with a plan comes purpose. Let's get out of here and find a water source."

"You already have a place to stay," President Millwright said. "All you have to do is return with us to our hive. You will be protected there. They won't hurt you."

"Yes," Alexander said, "it will be safe for all of us. They won't hurt us."

Everyone fell silent, and Desmond could scarcely guess what thoughts were going through the other refugees' minds.

"Who exactly are *they*?" Infinity demanded.

"You saw them," Mrs. Millwright said. "They are the hive. And they want us to come back. We are to bring you back with us. You don't need to be afraid."

"We told you—they're curious about us," Alexander said. "We can all stay there together."

Desmond gazed at Alexander through the framework. The man was awkwardly wedged between several angled girders. He was upside down, and his broken leg was dangling at a seemingly impossible angle. Yet he didn't seem to care.

"We're curious about them, too," Desmond said. "But from what we've seen so far, they intend to take over our minds as they've taken over yours."

"Do you even still know who you are?" Infinity asked.

"I'm Hayley Millwright, the former president of the United States. Yes, we know who we are. You need to trust us."

Isabelle spoke up. "Dad, you tried to drag me back to that swarm. You were rough, like you didn't care what happened to me. Something's wrong with you. And with Mom."

"We're different now, Izzy, but that doesn't mean something's wrong with us. We want you to come with us because we care about you." Alexander swiveled his head, scanning the group around him. "We care about all of you. And we need you to come back with us."

"We're wasting time," Gideon said matter-of-factly. "Does anyone here want to go back and become possessed by a swarm of gnats?"

Everyone stayed silent.

"Gideon's right," Infinity said. "Our two priorities right now are finding water and avoiding that swarm. Let's move."

AFTER TRAVELING another quarter mile toward the rocky hillside, the group encountered a pair of tiger beetles. The creatures came into view as the humans rounded the edge of a small framework hill. The creatures came after them, and the refugees had no choice but to scramble up the hill's slope and drop down into its interior. They cowered there for several minutes as the two predators climbed the hill and paced around on the girders above, searching unsuccessfully for openings large enough for them to enter so they could claim the soft, naked humans as their prey. Much to Desmond's relief, this was apparently another hill that contained no other threats. Eventually, the tiger beetles gave up, and the colonists cautiously emerged again.

Mr. and Mrs. Millwright had become relatively quiet since the anglerbeast attack, and they had become more cooperative, no longer resisting. Alexander obviously still had to be carried, but now at least he was allowing a person to assist him on either side, without anyone needing to resort to the fireman's carry. Mrs. Millwright was actually walking on her own now, although surrounded by several escorts. Desmond hoped all of this meant that the swarm's hold on their minds was wearing off, perhaps due to their increasing distance from the hive.

As the group gradually drew closer to the rocky hillside, Desmond's hopes that it would offer some miraculous solution to their problems began to fade. The hillside was mostly covered in moss interspersed with wide sheets of bare bedrock. Obviously the hillside was not conducive to the development of framework hills. There were few terrain structures that implied the possibility of caves or rocky shelves that might provide shelter. The larger hills beyond this one didn't look any more promising. The other refugees must have come to the same conclusion, because the group had become even more somber than before.

But then, when the group was several hundred yards from the base of the rocky hillside, everything changed. They came upon a stream. Clear water, sparkling in the sunlight, flowed over a mud-free bed of solid rock. The stream was perhaps ten yards wide and only about a foot deep. Desmond involuntarily licked his lips as he stared into the beautiful, life-sustaining water. He had managed so far to push aside his constant thirst, but now there was no denying it. He found himself consciously fighting the urge to throw himself into the stream immediately, letting it wash away the dirt from his wounds and the grime from his skin. Given the way the others were ogling the water, they must have been fighting similar urges.

Poppy Safran cleared her throat, breaking the spell. "I feel obligated to point out that there are inherent risks in drinking this water, although I'm sure you're aware. It could contain pathogens or toxins. Although under the circumstances, I don't see that we have any other choice. I'd suggest we filter it, and we could possibly use moss as a filter, except we have no holding containers."

"I should probably add," said Sarah Suzuki, "that our

wounds from the skitterbugs are showing signs of infection. It's possible these signs are merely inflammation, but I'm guessing there are bacteria here capable of colonizing our tissue. So it's possible infectious bacteria—or protists, or other microbes we don't even know exist—inhabit the water." She shook her head. "But...."

As usual, Àurea continued Sarah's line of thought. "But to be honest, we've already been exposed to any number of microbes. We have no way to avoid them. So, like it or not, we're either going to live here or we're going to die here."

"So, we might as well drink the water," Sarah concluded.

That was all it took. The group waded into the cool stream, guiding Mr. and Mrs. Millwright in with them. The stream bed consisted of smooth rock, which was easy on the feet. As Desmond stepped in, he saw several camouflaged, bottom-dwelling creatures dart away from his feet and come to rest a short distance away. They were each the size of his palm and looked like crustaceans—a potential food source?

He watched the others as they sucked in handfuls of water, and he noticed Infinity was also watching, perhaps hesitant after the doctors' warnings. Her eyes met his, and she shrugged. She then got on her knees and submerged her entire head. Desmond tucked his mandible weapon under one arm and did the same. The water felt amazing, although it made his skitterbug punctures and the two tiger beetle gashes on his scalp sting slightly. He pulled his head up and scanned their surroundings, like a deer watching for danger. He was surprised to see the Millwrights drinking eagerly. A few of the refugees had set Alexander down on his butt in the stream, and the lower half of his shattered leg was bobbing loosely in the current. He still didn't seem bothered by it. President Millwright splashed water on her face, washing off most of the blood from her futile fight against Infinity. But trickles of fresh blood were still flowing from her nose and a split lip.

Desmond submerged his head again, and this time he finally opened his mouth and drank deeply, all the while trying not to imagine thousands of tiny, unknown lifeforms flowing into his body. He was, of course, worried about contracting an infection, but he was comforted by knowing that none of the microbes were adapted specifically to infect humans. Or any kind of mammal, for that matter.

"I like that one," Sarah said when Desmond pulled his head up.

He wiped the water from his eyes and looked. She was pointing to a relatively small framework hill. It stood by itself at the foot of the rocky hillside and not too far from the stream.

Infinity got to her feet, her body now noticeably cleaner. "It's worth checking out. And the sooner, the better."

Everyone sucked in one more gulp, and then the group reluctantly prepared to leave the refreshing water. Lenny and Xavier shouldered Alexander's arms, and the colony began making their way toward the framework hill.

This mound was significantly smaller than many of the others, no more than fifty yards in diameter and perhaps twenty yards tall at its peak. If they could find the right material to cover it, they might feasibly be able to cover the entire structure.

The group stopped at the base, and Desmond gazed into the mound's interior. It was dark in the center, but he could actually see a few pinpoints of light shining through from the opposite side. It seemed unlikely a colony of skitterbugs would choose to inhabit this mound, but they would have to find out for sure.

Broken pieces of girder cluttered the lowest levels, but not nearly as many as Desmond had seen in some of the larger hills. If these hills did indeed grow like coral formations, with the amber-like material being secreted by the moss, then this hill was simply younger than many of the others. Presumably, over many years it would double or triple in size.

"Hot damn," Lenny said. "Nice digs. But some lucky mofo is gonna have to go in there and check it out."

They all looked around at each other or stared at the ground.

"I'll do it," Infinity said. She stepped closer to the slope and peered in.

Alarmed, Desmond started to insist on going with her, but President Millwright interrupted him.

"You need to let me do it."

"Good thinking, Hayley," Alexander said.

Infinity turned to her. "And why would we do that?"

"Because I'm not afraid. And I want you to trust me."

Desmond said, "We're not entirely convinced that you're no longer possessed by the creatures from the hive."

"We are not possessed!" Alexander exclaimed.

"You simply don't understand yet." President Millwright said. "We are influenced by the hive, yes. But in a good way. They will protect all of us."

"I want to know why you're not afraid," Infinity demanded.

President Millwright actually displayed a hint of a smile, which looked somewhat creepy with blood still flowing from her nose onto her mouth and chin. "The hive will protect me, even here."

Desmond and Infinity glanced at each other. He shrugged. "Why not let her do it?"

"Because she's the president," Gideon said. "We're supposed to be protecting her."

"I *was* president back home," Hayley said. "Here, I'm not. But I *am* the only one here who can crawl into this hill without fear. Let me go inside."

Desmond and Infinity turned to Gideon. He sighed and nodded.

"Very well," Hayley said. "This shouldn't take long." She stepped up to the mound and studied the openings. The girders at ground level were thicker than those higher up, making most of the openings too small for a human body to fit through. She stepped onto one of the girders and began climbing, prompting a swarm of the locust-like creatures to burst skyward from openings farther up the hill. She turned to the other refugees and said, "Those creatures are harmless. No need to worry about them." She then continued climbing.

When she was about ten feet up, she entered the hill. The entire group lined up along the mound's base to watch her as she made her way through the interior.

By the time she was perhaps three quarters of the way to the center, Desmond could only catch glimpses of her.

"Talk to us," Infinity called in. "What do you see?"

"There is nothing to fear here," she replied. "The oldest girders in the center are thinner and easier to break. You should be able to clear a chamber."

A few minutes later, she emerged again from an opening near where she had entered and descended to the ground. Several new bleeding scrapes adorned her arms and legs, but she didn't seem to notice.

"You will be somewhat safe here," she said, looking around at the group. "However, you would be much safer back at our hive. I beg you to return with us. But if you will not, I would like you to allow me to take my husband and return to where we belong. You have no right to hold us as prisoners."

"Mom, come to your senses!" Isabelle said. "I'm not going to that hive, and I can't believe you would think of leaving me."

Hayley gazed at her daughter without expression. "We belong there, honey. And so do you. You will understand soon."

"No!" Isabelle cried. "You're not leaving." She turned to Infinity. "We're not letting them leave, are we?"

Infinity faced the president. "Hell no we're not."

9

———

MOSSVIEW

SEPTEMBER 5 - MID-DAY

STILL unwilling to trust President Millwright, Infinity forced her to lead the way to the hill's interior. Alexander was now being relatively cooperative, making it fairly easy for the colonists to thread his body through the gaps in the latticework of girders.

Since Infinity's previous experiences inside these framework hills had involved narrow escapes from gruesome death, she had to overcome an annoying sense of agitation. But crawling through the lower levels of this particular hill turned out to be easier than expected, as it was reasonably well lit, with few broken girders littering the latticework.

At ground level, girders near the center of the hill were, as Hayley had said, thinner, presumably because these older girders had supported less weight when the hill had been smaller. Some of them were as thin as Infinity's pinky finger and were easy to break away using larger pieces of broken girder the other refugees had found. After several of the colonists had worked for about an hour, they had cleared out a space the size of a small living room, twenty feet in diameter and eight feet tall. They were now stacking the newly-broken pieces along the sides of the chamber. There was no live moss growing this deep within the structure, but a thick layer of loose, dead moss had accumulated on the ground. This dead moss had probably built up over the years as the moss growing on the outermost girders had died off and fallen through the framework.

Throughout the entire girder-clearing process, President Millwright and her husband had sat to the side. They had remained silent, except for the occasional annoying comment on how all this work wouldn't be necessary if the group would simply return to where they belonged—the hive. Unlike Desmond, Xavier, and Lenny, Infinity felt no biological fascination with the creatures of the hive. In fact, she never wanted to see the goddamn swarm again. Still, once the group was settled in their new shelter, she'd probably make another attempt to extract the three AWOL colonists. Assuming she could think of an extraction plan that wouldn't risk any more lives.

When the last piece of shattered girder had been cleared, the refugees gazed silently at their new shelter, unsure what to do next. With their water and shelter needs at least partially met, Infinity knew exactly what was next—they needed to find food.

"Well, it ain't a luxury mansion," said the guardsman Alfie Lewis. "But we gotta be safer in here than out in the open."

Several others nodded in agreement, their bodies glistening with sweat from the demolition efforts.

Lenny clapped his hands together. "We're the first humans on this world, and as such we must establish traditions for all future generations to follow. I propose that every new home deserves a fitting name. Isabelle, perhaps you would do the honors of naming this one."

Isabelle was kneeling beside her parents, watching Poppy examine her father's shattered leg. Isabelle looked up without smiling, but her eyes were gleaming nevertheless. "Well, *The Cuckoo's Nest* comes to mind."

Several refugees chuckled.

Isabelle then said, "But I think *Mossview* would be a more suitable name."

Lenny gave her a thumbs-up. "It's perfect."

"I think the rest of you need to see this," said Poppy Safran, still examining Alexander's leg.

Infinity kneeled at Poppy's side, and several of the others gathered around.

Poppy pointed to the man's leg that hadn't been broken. "His punctures and lacerations. Compare them to mine. And to yours."

The skitterbug wounds on Alexander's leg were pale. Likewise, in spite of massive bruising from internal trauma on the other leg, the surface wounds there also looked like they were beginning to heal. Everyone else's were still puffy and red, showing signs of infection.

"And compare them to this one," Poppy said, pointing to a cut on Alexander's abdomen. The tissue around this wound was swollen and angry.

"It's because of the isopod's saliva," Alexander stated with a sigh, as if he thought everyone should already know this.

Infinity studied Alexander's face. He was sweating and gritting his teeth, signs that he was starting to feel pain. Maybe this meant the swarm's grip on his mind was loosening. "What makes you think the isopod saliva has anything to do with it?" she demanded.

"He doesn't think it—he knows it," President Millwright said. "The isopods are protected by the hive. So it shouldn't be surprising that their saliva has beneficial properties."

"I was the one who wiped the saliva from his legs yesterday," Poppy said. She pointed to Alexander's knees. "This is definitely where it touched his skin." She looked up at Infinity, her eyes full of hope. "This is amazing. Everyone here is currently at risk of infection and possibly sepsis. We need more isopod saliva, enough to spread over every wound. The sooner, the better."

Infinity considered this. "We've seen several isopod herds today," she said. "The nearest herd can't be far."

"Just say the word and we're on it," Gideon said. "I'll take Emily and Alfie."

Infinity nodded. "I think we should do it."

Gideon said, "I don't exactly know how to convince those monsters to give us their spit, but we'll figure it out."

"Based on what happened to me yesterday," Alexander said. "Just allow them to investigate your skin. They'll taste you and realize you're not their kind of food, but they'll leave behind copious quantities of saliva."

Infinity gazed at Alexander, who seemed to be feeling his pain more every minute. "You're actually willing to be helpful now?"

He nodded with a grimace. "Why wouldn't I? I'm still convinced we all must return to the hive, but I'm feeling less... fixated on it."

"There is no doubt we should return to the hive," President Millwright said. "Eventually you'll all understand."

"We'll return there, alright," Gideon said. "But only to extract Steven, Tyrone, and Eagleton." He eyed Emily and Alfie. "You two ready for a mission to gather bug spit?"

"Let's get it done," Alfie replied. Emily nodded.

"You three be careful," Infinity said. "Stay as close as you can to the framework hills in case you need shelter."

The guardsmen departed through the maze of girders.

Infinity turned to Desmond. "It's time to go hunting. We need food."

Lenny stepped forward. "Now you're talking my language. Count me in."

Infinity, Desmond, Lenny, and Xavier waded slowly into the clear water, scrutinizing the smooth bedrock at the bottom of the stream.

Desmond pointed. "There's one." He lunged forward and thrust his hand into the water. But he came up empty. "Faster than I thought they'd be," he muttered.

Infinity saw one of the creatures scuttle away from her and come to rest a few feet to her right. When it stopped, it blended in with the rock bottom perfectly, becoming nearly invisible. "I got this one," she said. She carefully approached the spot where the thing had disappeared and readied the three-foot, sharpened girder she'd selected as a hunting weapon. She thrust the weapon, but the creature darted off to the side. She crept over to the creature's new spot and tried again. Still no luck.

For the next ten minutes or so they all attempted to catch the crab-like animals, trying every strategy they could think of, without success. The things were too fast.

Finally, Xavier groaned and said, "Okay, this is exasperating. And it isn't the least bit dignified."

"I have a better idea," Lenny announced. He pointed up toward the nearby rocky hillside.

At first, Infinity wasn't sure what he was pointing at. She

looked a few hundred yards up the slope and only saw a wide swath of bare bedrock. But then she noticed it. The rock face appeared to be shifting. She squinted. The rock was actually covered with hundreds of animals. They appeared to be very flat, each approximately the size and shape of a hubcap—far larger than the palm-sized crabs in the stream. "That's pretty far from the nearest shelter," she said. "We'd be visible and vulnerable."

"And well fed," Lenny retorted.

"We'd be more visible up there," Desmond said, "but we'd also have a better view of the area. We should be able to see tiger beetles or other predators approaching from miles away. I vote we do it."

That settled it, and the group began making their way up the slope. They walked on the soft moss when possible, but at times they had no choice but to cross sheets of bare rock, which was less kind to their feet than the smooth rock of the stream bed had been. They quickly discovered that the rock's surface had softer patches of an orange, crusty substance growing on it, which was, as Desmond pointed out, similar to lichens.

As the humans drew near, the herd of creatures ignored them and continued scuttling around on the rock. The things were gray, slightly darker than the rock beneath them, and were perhaps fifteen inches across but only six inches tall. Their backs were covered by one large protective shell, again reminding Infinity of hubcaps. She could see numerous small legs scuffling beneath the shells as the creatures moved across the rock.

The humans stopped at the edge of the rock sheet. The creatures still ignored them, even though the nearest were only feet away.

"Okay," Lenny said, "this should be a lot easier."

Infinity watched as the creatures moved about, noisily

scratching and chewing on one patch of lichen and then moving on to another. "Any thoughts about a strategy?"

Lenny blew out a thoughtful puff of air. "Not a clue." He stepped from the moss onto the rock sheet and slowly approached the nearest creature. When he was close enough to step on it, the thing noticed him and pulled its shell down against the rock with a clack. The other creatures near it immediately did the same thing, and this behavior spread in a wave across the entire rock, hundreds of shells clacking against the stone. The creatures then remained still.

Infinity and the others gathered around Lenny as he kneeled and tried to flip the nearest creature onto its back. But the edges of the animal's shell had conformed to the ridges and crannies of the rock surface, forming a tight seal. Lenny couldn't get his fingers underneath to pry the creature up. Infinity kicked the animal, assuming this would send it sliding across the rock, but still it didn't budge.

"Well, crap," Xavier said.

They each went to one of the creatures and tried moving it. The things were stuck tight, as if the edges of their shells were now cemented to the rock.

"I guess we know why they didn't bother to run away," Infinity said as she continued trying to get her fingernails under the shell of the creature before her. But of course her nails had been reduced to almost nothing when she'd bridged to this world.

Eventually, defeated, they all sat back on the rock and stared out over the plain. The nearest herd of isopods was milling about on the moss about half a mile to the south, but Infinity didn't see the guardsmen who had gone in search of the creatures' saliva. She scanned the rest of the vast landscape but still couldn't pick them out. The framework hills and moss seemed to go on forever, but in the distance—perhaps ten miles out—a large river wound through the plain from north to south. In spite of the horrors of this place, the view was really quite beautiful.

After a few seconds of silence, Desmond said, "If we can figure out how to stay alive, this world might not be so bad."

"That's the attitude I like to hear," Lenny said. "And we *will* figure out our place in this world. I'm happy to be here with you guys. The band is back together—the four musketeers."

"Sorry," Xavier said, "but you guys are in denial. This place is crawling with killer arthropods. And that's not even the scariest part. There are also swarms of flies with a unified intelligence. Not the collective, coordinated behavior of bee colonies—an actual *intelligence*. And it wants to possess all of us and make us slaves, or eat us from the inside out, or something even worse. This world is the stuff of nightmares."

Infinity considered admonishing Xavier for his negativity, but with just the four of them here, what difference did his comments make?

"About this intelligence," Desmond said. "I just can't believe it's really possible. I'm more inclined to believe that, when the flies engulfed Eagleton, his mind snapped. Suddenly he decided he was part of a hive mind that was speaking through his body. And then when the others became engulfed, they snapped too, and in their vulnerable states, they simply followed Eagleton's lead."

Xavier just shook his head.

"Not a bad hypothesis, Des," Lenny said. "But there's another, simpler way to avoid the collective intelligence theory. Perhaps the flies secrete some type of chemical when they engulf other creatures, a chemical that makes the creatures behave in ways that benefit the swarm. We've seen plenty of examples of that on our own world. There's an ichneumonid wasp in Costa

Rica that lays its eggs in the abdomen of an orb-weaving spider. After the wasp larvae hatch, they secrete a chemical that changes the spider's behavior. Suddenly the spider starts building a totally new kind of web, not like any web it's made before. But the web isn't for the spider. It's for the wasp larvae. It's constructed in such a way that it can support the larvae's cocoons after the larvae kill and eat the spider. Wicked cruel and wicked sci-fi, man."

Desmond said, "And since humans are so different from the life on this world, our minds might respond to this chemical in unpredictable ways."

"Like going crazy and thinking the swarm is actually talking through you," Infinity added.

Desmond nodded. "This chemical theory might explain why the Millwrights are starting to recover from the effects. It could be something that wears off over time."

Lenny rubbed his chin intently, like he was actually excited about this. "Which would explain why the chemical gave the Millwrights such a strong desire to return to the hive. It benefits the hive to continue re-administering the drug so that their slaves will continue serving their needs. That's why the isopods were so determined to go back to the hive."

Xavier shook his head again. "Sure, it could be a simple chemical effect, but that doesn't make it any less terrifying. And how can you explain the swarm congregating into a human shape and mimicking Eagleton's movements?"

This was followed by contemplative silence.

"I got nothing, brother," Lenny said.

Desmond shook his head. "Nothing."

Throughout this discussion, the disk creatures hadn't budged, perhaps sensing that danger was still near.

Infinity got to her feet. "We're wasting time." She moved to the rock's edge, where a chunk of the sheet had cracked off from the rest. She wrestled the stone back and forth until it came loose from the soil. She hefted it, estimating that it must weigh twenty pounds. She carried it back over to the creatures, raised it over her head, and slammed it down onto one of them, crushing its shell and splattering goo and bits of exoskeleton in every direction.

"Jesus," Xavier exclaimed, wiping something gooey from his cheek. "That may have been overkill."

Desmond stepped over, pushed the rock aside, and poked at the creature. Its shell was no longer glued to the bedrock, and he flipped it over. A dozen or so jointed legs, each the size of a pinky finger, were more or less intact, but the rest of the body had been pulverized together with bits of cracked shell. "Well, that's not going to be very useful," he said. He picked up the rock and moved to another creature nearby. "I'll try this with a gentler touch."

He swung the rock from the side, breaking the creature's grip on the rock and flipping it onto its back. Its legs clawed frantically at the air. In spite of its relatively wide shell, the thing's body was only the size of a partially flattened softball. Not huge, but certainly larger than the crab creatures they'd failed to catch in the stream. The creature began arching its back, bending its shell into a saddle shape as it tried to turn back over. Desmond grabbed it and held it down.

Infinity picked up her girder weapon and shoved the sharper end into the creature's body where she thought its head might be. Its legs stopped flailing. "We have to start somewhere," she said. "These things may not look appetizing, but they're abundant, and now we know how to kill them. They're going to be our first meal."

The others were staring down at the now-dead creature. "I can't wait," Xavier muttered dryly.

"And by the way," Infinity said, "I get to name this species. These things are hubcaps."

Xavier poked one of the creature's legs with his finger. "I suppose we're going to eat them raw."

Infinity shrugged. "Unless we can figure out how to make a fire. There's no wood to burn, but I have a few ideas worth trying."

The group repeated the process with the rock and their girder weapons until they had killed another fifteen hubcaps, with the assumption that they would each be able to carry four back to the shelter. Infinity then hurled the rock at the ground as hard as she could, hoping to create shards that could function as cutting tools. But the rock simply broke in half. She and Desmond then repeated this with the two halves until they had produced three hand-sized pieces that would work, although they could hardly be called sharp.

As the group was gathering up their dead hubcaps, Infinity looked up and saw a large creature approaching along the hillside. It was already less than a hundred yards away, and she cursed herself for having become careless.

"Everyone hold completely still," she ordered.

They all froze.

The creature was coming straight for them. It was the height of a large dog but was broader and looked much heavier. It walked on four jointed legs, with two additional strong-looking appendages held high near its head, like the front legs of a freakishly-muscular praying mantis. Its back was mostly black, but the color faded to rusty orange on the sides of its body. All six of the legs were glossy black. But the most distinctive feature was a single long, curved horn protruding from its forehead. Behind that, a row of upward-pointing spikes ran the length of the creature's back, becoming shorter near its hind end.

"It doesn't look like a fast runner," Desmond whispered. "Maybe we should make a run for it."

"Looks can be deceiving," Lenny said. "Think of the hippo—twenty-mile-an-hour sprinter."

"I say we kill the damn thing," Xavier said. "It's four to one, and we have weapons. It could feed our entire group."

Infinity studied the creature. It looked as strong as a horse. "No, it's not worth the risk. Just hold still."

The creature walked onto the sheet of rock less than twenty yards away, its feet clacking on the surface. It stopped in front of one of the still-living hubcaps, which, like the others, was still glued to the rock. The praying mantis creature lifted its two front legs and rammed them straight down onto the hubcap. The legs' sharp tips punctured the broad shell. The predator quickly raked the two claws outward, tearing the shell wide open. It then lunged forward and started consuming the creature's insides, making loud crunching and slurping noises.

"Wicked cool!" Lenny said. "It's adapted for eating hubcaps. Which means it probably doesn't eat anything else. We're safe."

"That sounds like an assumption that could get us killed," Xavier hissed.

The creature moved over to another hubcap and repeated the same process, again sucking and chewing the soft body after exposing it.

Infinity made a decision. "We're going. First, pick up your weapons and hold them ready. If it doesn't come after us, pick up your four hubcaps, but keep your weapons ready. Got it?"

They all nodded.

"Okay, slowly. Now."

Unfortunately, Desmond's mandible and Xavier's girder

were a few yards out of reach. They began moving to pick them up.

The creature suddenly stopped eating and raised its head. They all froze. Infinity couldn't identify any eyes, but the thing was obviously watching them. Abruptly, it charged.

"Grab your weapons now!" Infinity ordered.

Desmond and Xavier scrambled to their weapons and then darted back. The four gathered side by side as the creature closed in on them. The thing was like an armored tank with spikes, and Infinity suddenly realized standing their ground had been a mistake.

"Oh, shit," Lenny muttered.

Infinity braced herself. "Make your first hit count!"

But then the creature skidded to a stop, the tip of its horn only a few feet from them. It skittered a few steps to the left and then back to the right, perhaps a threatening gesture.

"It's just trying to scare us off," Desmond said. "Let's slowly pick up the hubcaps and back off."

As soon as they began moving, the creature became even more agitated, dancing back and forth and shaking its horn. But it still didn't come any closer. They slowly gathered their dead quarry and their three stone tools and started down the hillside. Soon the creature turned away and went back to puncturing, shredding, and eating hubcaps.

"I believe it's your turn to name an animal, Xavier," Lenny said when they finally turned their backs on the creature. "Remember, this is for future generations, so don't make it something stupid that will embarrass your grandchildren."

Xavier turned to take another look at the creature. "Despite the fact that it's highly unlikely any of us will live to have grandchildren, I'll choose the most logical name—*rhino*."

Lenny chortled. "That's all you got? *Rhino*?"

"Whose turn is it?" Xavier retorted.

Infinity glanced down the slope toward the group's shelter and realized she'd been careless again. At the base of Mossview's slope, she saw three black shapes. "Are those tiger beetles?"

"Looks like it to me," Desmond said.

They watched as one of the creatures rammed itself into the hill's girders. Even at this distance they could hear its mandibles clattering against the framework. The creatures obviously knew the refugees were inside.

"The madness never ends," Xavier said.

Infinity looked for alternative shelter. The next-nearest hill was to their left. "This way," she said, angling down the slope toward it. "If we're lucky, we can get in there to hide before they see us."

They weren't lucky. The tiger beetles spotted them almost immediately and all three headed toward the group, forcing them to run. In spite of carrying armloads of hubcaps, they all made it to the hill in time to shove their things through the ground-level openings, climb up to where their bodies would fit through, and get inside. When the creatures arrived, it became clear once again that tiger beetles had one single objective, probably driven by a pea-sized brain—kill anything that moves. The creatures slashed at the hill with their mandibles for a few seconds. Then they clambered up the slope to where the humans had entered and began trying to chew their way in, breaking a few girders. Finally, they gave up, returned to the ground and began pacing back and forth.

Infinity scanned the area below for any signs of skitterbugs or other threats emerging from within the mound. She then turned and silently watched the pacing tiger beetles for several minutes.

"Not too smart, are they." Desmond whispered.

Xavier said, "You may take that back if they wait long enough that we're forced to come out or die of thirst. Or if skitterbugs chase us out."

Infinity sighed and shifted her position on the girders to look back at the interior of the hill again. This mound was much larger than Mossview, and a thick layer of dead moss and broken girders had accumulated at ground level a few yards below them. She considered this and then glanced down at the dead hubcaps they'd shoved into the mound.

She started making her way through the framework toward the hubcaps. "No reason to sit on our asses wasting time," she said. "You guys find an open spot at ground level, big enough to hold a few people." She ignored the questions that followed and concentrated on getting to the hubcaps. Once the dead creatures were within her reach, the tiger beetles stopped pacing and started battering the framework again. They shoved their mandibles through the gaps and gnashed them, knocking the hubcaps back and forth as Infinity tried to get a grip on the shells. She managed to grab two and then made her way back to where the others were, about twenty yards into the mound's interior.

"This is probably the best we can do without going all the way to the hill's center," Desmond said, referring to a chamber next to him that was three feet across. He, Lenny, and Xavier had arranged themselves awkwardly around its perimeter, their arms and legs straddling various girders.

Infinity shoved the two hubcaps into the chamber and then crawled in. The ground here was cushioned by dead moss at least a foot deep. She pushed aside some from the top layer, which was dry, and then sat cross-legged on the damp moss she'd uncovered.

"You want to enlighten us fools as to what you're doing?"

Lenny asked.

"I'm going to try to make a fire. If it works, we'll have a way to cook our food. Hand me some of those broken girders. As many of them as you can reach."

They started passing pieces to her. She laid them out beside her until she had a variety of shapes and sizes to choose from. To start with, she selected a fairly straight piece that was only half an inch thick and a shard that was flat on the edge where it had broken.

She held out some of the dry moss from the pile next to her. "Now, I need you to pick out small fibers from this—only the driest pieces."

They each took a handful and started picking. Soon they had collected a fist-sized bird's nest of dry moss fibers, which she arranged on the flat shard. She held the thin girder vertically and pushed the lower end into the center of the bird's nest until it was pressed against the flat piece.

Xavier and Lenny both sighed, and Desmond said, "Hmm… I don't know. Without wood?"

She looked up at him. "If you have a better idea, spit it out."

Nobody said anything.

She placed her hands on either side of the vertical girder and rubbed her palms together rapidly, spinning the girder and moving her hands downward to increase the friction between the two pieces. When her hands got to the moss fibers, she quickly moved them back to the top and started again. After ten of these cycles, she pulled the vertical girder up and put her finger on the point of contact. It was warm. In fact, it was more than warm. She held it out to Lenny.

He touched the tip and quickly pulled his finger back. "It's wicked hot! You the man, Infinity."

She decided to ignore the comment and went back to work.

Actually, she was surprised so little effort had produced so much heat. It was sheer luck that this material happened to heat up easily with friction—a property that might be conducive to the colony's survival.

After another thirty rapid cycles, a tendril of smoke started rising from the bird's nest.

Without looking away, Infinity said, "Desmond, gently push the moss against the friction point."

He compressed the moss with two fingers while she kept spinning the girder. "Now blow on it. But gently!"

He had to pull one leg through the framework to be able to get close enough. He started blowing, and Infinity spun the rod even faster. A red ember began to glow.

And then the entire bird's nest exploded into flame.

"Ow!" Desmond pulled his hand back.

Some of the burning moss clung to his fingers. He shook his hand, flinging the flames into the pile of moss at Infinity's side. The pile immediately caught on fire, searing Infinity's knee. She slapped at the fire, trying to extinguish it, but this only made it spread faster. Desmond, Lenny, and Xavier tumbled backward from their perches while trying to back off.

"Get out of there, Infinity!" Desmond cried. He reached into the open cavity for her hand.

She ignored him and climbed through a larger opening to his side, the flames licking at her body.

The fire kept spreading, moving beyond the small chamber faster than should have been possible. Within seconds it was going to consume them.

"Go! Get the hell out," she ordered. They had to vacate the mound, regardless of the tiger beetles.

Infinity scrambled through the framework amidst grunting, cursing, and the fluttering of wings from swarms of escaping bugs. The smoke and heat of the spreading fire made it almost impossible to breathe. Infinity could no longer see the others, but their panicked voices confirmed they were at least still alive. If one of them got stuck, there would be no time to provide help.

Infinity's skin felt like it was going to boil. With her eyes clenched shut against the smoke, she pushed herself through another opening and then realized there were no more girders above her. She had made it to the surface.

"I'm out!" she heard Desmond cry. He was perhaps ten feet away, but she didn't dare open her eyes.

"Get off the mound!" she shouted as she threw herself onto her belly and slid down the slope. She hit the ground hard and then rolled away. The heat was still intense, but every foot of distance from the hill made it more tolerable.

"I can't see!" she heard Xavier shout from perhaps five feet away.

Infinity wiped her eyes and forced them open. Trying to blink away the stinging, she stayed low and crawled to Xavier. She grabbed his arm. "This way. Move!" She crawled away from the burning mound, guiding him.

"Infinity!"

She looked to her left and saw Desmond helping Lenny crawl through the smoke. She pulled on Xavier's arm to let him know she was changing course and heading toward the others. If the tiger beetles were waiting for them beyond the smoke, it might help to be together. Then again, it might not. While weighing the pros and cons of each scenario, she realized she'd left her weapon in the mound.

Soon they were emerging from the smoke about fifteen yards out, where the heat was tolerable. Her vision was still distorted by the debris and tears in her eyes. But she didn't see the tiger beetles.

The humans crawled a few more yards and then stopped. They sat there on the moss, rubbing their eyes and inspecting their burns. Infinity still didn't see the predators. She glanced at Desmond.

"I don't see them either," he said. "The fire must have scared them away."

"It's the freaking oxygen level," Lenny said. "It's high enough in this atmosphere that fire burns like a match to a fart."

"He's right," Xavier said. "Our own world's air is twenty-one percent oxygen. Even a small increase to twenty-three percent would cause fires to burn more readily. We should have cleared the area around you before you started the fire, Infinity."

"This could even explain why there aren't any trees here," Desmond added. "Fires from lightning strikes might prevent any type of larger, combustible plants from taking hold in any large-scale way."

Lenny said, "Then why do these mounds have dead moss in them at all? Lightning strikes should burn every one of them."

Desmond shook his head. "Not really. This isn't like a continuous prairie or forest. These mounds are isolated from each other by distance, so fire won't spread between them. The chance of lightning striking one particular mound during, say, a hundred years, is actually slim. But the chance of lightning striking somewhere in a hundred square miles of prairie is quite high."

Infinity turned back to the mound. The fire was already burning down. The dead moss had been consumed at an unbelievable rate. The girder framework hadn't collapsed, which was somewhat surprising. She had assumed the translucent material might melt at high temperatures. Their sixteen hard-earned hubcaps were surely gone now. And so were their three rock tools, although they might be able to retrieve those after the mound cooled. This made Infinity think of the girder weapon she'd left in the mound. She shot a glance at Desmond. His mandible weapon was still at his side, his ash-stained fingers gripping it tightly. Again she felt careless, this time for having left her own weapon behind.

Desmond noticed she was looking at the mandible and shrugged. "Not sure how I hung on to it."

INFINITY, Desmond, Lenny, and Xavier returned to Mossview empty-handed. After explaining the fire and the loss of the potential food they'd caught, Infinity noticed that Gideon, Alfie, and Emily still weren't back. She asked about them. Chloe explained that the guardsmen had already returned with as much isopod saliva as they could carry smeared on their skin and cupped in their hands. They'd gone back out to get more but hadn't returned yet.

Infinity then suggested her team try again to procure food and tools. It had now been forty-eight hours since anyone had eaten, and the already-abysmal morale would soon deteriorate. So the group of four left the mound again. In a fraction of the time it had taken before, they spotted the herd of hubcaps, climbed the hill, and killed another sixteen, this time without being impeded by a rhino or tiger beetles. Instead of detouring to the burned-out mound to retrieve their stone tools, they found another rock on the hill to break, resulting in four reasonably-sharp cutting or scraping implements.

Back in Mossview's center chamber, Lenny and several of the doctors set to work scraping the edible body tissue from the underside of the hubcaps' shells. It quickly became obvious the empty, bowl-like shells would be immensely useful. The group placed all the softer tissue into two of the inverted shells and used the rocks to mash it into sludge. Several refugees suggested they could simply eat this stuff raw, but Infinity now had bigger plans. She sent Aurea and Sarah to the stream to fill two shells with water after giving them a pep talk about running back at the first sign of predators.

Infinity then instructed the refugees to clear out every last shred of moss from the ground in the chamber. This created a bare area twenty feet across, with the nearest combustible material ten feet away. With no breeze to carry embers, she was reasonably sure there was little risk of another unintentional inferno.

She addressed the entire group. "Some of you may want to get up to the surface so you can quickly get off if something goes wrong."

"Does that include me?" Alexander asked.

Infinity studied his face, still unsure of his mental state. All she could determine was that he was pale, perhaps close to shock. "You want us to carry you out?"

He actually smiled a bit and shook his head. "Of course not. But I'd like you to allow Hayley to move to safety."

"I'm not leaving his side," President Millwright said. "Make your fire."

No one else made a move to leave.

Infinity and Desmond sat in the center of the clearing and started building a fire. Using two girder pieces they'd picked out and the same approach as before, it took only a few minutes. When the initial mass of dried moss exploded into flame, she had Desmond add one handful of dried moss at a time. This was burning too quickly, so they began mixing wet moss with the dry until they got a burn they could keep up with.

Celia brought over several girder pieces and stacked them six inches high around the fire as a support for the bowls. Lenny took one of the bowls the doctors had filled with water and poured some into a bowl of mashed hubcap tissue, which he then carefully placed on the support. Infinity continued feeding handfuls of moss through an opening in the support. Minutes later, steam started rising from the mixture.

Infinity added some wet moss to slow down the burn and finally allowed herself to relax. She gazed around the chamber at the refugees. Most of them were now sitting in a circle around the fire, staring silently at the food, as if they couldn't quite believe such a miracle was possible.

"It actually smells good," Richard Hussain said softly.

The light in the chamber was fading as the sun outside neared the horizon. Infinity realized it was probably close to 7:00 PM, thirty-six hours since the group had bridged in. Normally, she would be bridging back around this time. But this time there would be no bridging back. And it was possible there was nothing to bridge back to.

She wanted the meat to cook for a while longer, so she scooted over a few inches until her leg touched Desmond's, prompting him to put a hand on her knee. He would have to get up soon for more moss, but something about this moment made her want to be near him. This pot of food was symbolic, a break-through. One of their group was dead, three were apparently under the control of a chemical secreted by a swarm of flies, and three others hadn't returned from what should have been a short mission. But thirteen colonists were here in the chamber, about to eat their first meal on a completely unfamiliar world. There was actually a chance they might survive.

"You did this. You are the driving force behind everything we've accomplished. You're the shining light of this colony. And I love you."

Infinity shot a glance at Desmond's hand on her knee and then looked up at his face. He had silently sent these words directly to her mind. She tried to smile—she wanted to smile—but it was too soon for it to feel right.

"Hey, colonists! I'm coming in."

Infinity snapped her head up. The voice was Gideon's. The guardsmen were back.

"I may need a hand," Gideon said. "I'm hurt."

Infinity jumped to her feet and climbed up through the framework as quickly as she could, with Desmond and several others close behind. She spotted Gideon at the base of the hill, slumped over. She descended and then dropped the last few feet to his side. He was bleeding from several wounds, including a laceration on his shoulder so deep that it exposed muscle and bone. And he was alone.

"Gideon," she said, "what the hell happened? Where are the others?"

He was breathing hard, drenched in sweat, and covered in blood and grime. "They're gone," he panted. "It was Tyrone and Steven. They came after us. To take us back to the hive."

"Tyrone and Steven came after you?" Desmond asked as he slid down and stopped beside Infinity.

Still panting, Gideon lifted his head and nodded. He looked from Desmond to Infinity. "And there's something else you need to know. They had a tiger beetle with them. I mean it was *with* them. Like a goddamn hunting dog. It killed Alfie. Then it tore into me and Emily pretty bad. I got away, but those sons of bitches dragged her off."

Infinity stared at him, trying to process this. "Shit," she muttered.

10

ISOPOD

September 6 - Early Morning

Desmond lay on his back, staring up at the chamber's framework ceiling. A few stars twinkled through the gaps, and the moon was visible to the south, creating a halo of illuminated girders around it. He had no way of knowing exactly what time it was, but he sensed that dawn's first light would appear soon.

Sleep had not come easily this second night on their new world. And the restless movements and whispering he'd heard throughout the night suggested that sleep had been elusive for the other refugees as well. Desmond, like the others, had created a reasonably soft bed of dead moss. But he'd discovered that numerous small arthropods inhabited the moss, and although none of them seemed to bite, they had frequently crawled out of the bed to explore his body, which had made falling asleep especially difficult. And he hadn't been able to get his mind off the real possibility that a swarm of skitterbugs or other small, unknown creatures could suddenly invade the mound.

Now, on the other side of the chamber, he could hear Lenny and Isabelle whispering to each other. Actually, Lenny was doing most of the talking. Isabelle had obviously been traumatized by her parents' ordeals, so perhaps she simply needed someone to talk to. But Desmond was surprised that the two had already progressed to a whispering-in-the-dark stage.

He rolled onto his side to face Infinity. A single shaft of moonlight faintly illuminated the faded painted bunting tattoo on her chest. He reached out and traced the bird's outline with the tip of his finger.

"We're taking back our people at first light," she said.

He started. "I thought you were asleep."

"We're not losing any more colonists."

He nodded into the darkness. "Okay. What's the plan?"

She was silent for a few seconds. "I don't know, dammit. Other than brute force. But the tiger beetle changes that."

"Then we'll come up with a new plan."

Abruptly, she sat up. "How many of you are awake?"

Most of the refugees quietly replied.

"Leave those who are sleeping and gather around over here. Madam President, are you and Alexander awake?"

"I am," the president replied in the dark. "I'd prefer not to wake Alex."

"Are you willing to help us rescue our people from the hive?"

President Millwright sighed, but Desmond could hear her getting up. Her figure moved through the darkness and she took a seat beside Infinity. Soon everyone who was awake was seated nearby. Desmond couldn't tell how many, but it had to be most of the group.

"The way I see it," Infinity started, "we have two choices. One: we leave our people behind at the hive and move as far from it as possible, far enough that there's no chance they'll continue to ambush us. Or two: we do what it takes to extract them from the hive and hope they don't turn on us."

The group remained silent.

"Mrs. Millwright," Desmond said, "can you give us your honest thoughts on this?"

After a hesitation, Hayley said, "First of all, I'm tired of being called Mrs. Millwright or Madam President. I'm not the president here, and my name is Hayley. Please call me that from now on." She sighed, as if she were thinking. "I don't know. I'm so tired that my judgement is questionable. And you probably won't believe me anyway. But for the record, I still believe the hive does not intend to kill us."

"That's funny, because Alfie is pretty damn dead," Gideon said.

Desmond hadn't even realized Gideon was awake.

"And I'm as distressed about that as you are," Hayley said. "You need to understand something, though. Yesterday, after the hive influenced my mind, I knew that they didn't intend to hurt us. At the same time, I had an overwhelming need to do whatever they wanted of me. And they made it clear that they wanted all of you to come to them. They're curious about us. They did not provide specific strategies for me to bring you to them. They only provided the desire to help them achieve that goal. I did not become violent, although I know my husband did. I can't explain why. Perhaps it was some previously-hidden aspect of his personality. Some people are naturally more inclined to do harm, even if they don't know that about themselves until they are in certain circumstances. Perhaps Tyrone and Steven also have such latent tendencies."

"And even Reece Eagleton?" Gideon said.

"Perhaps," Hayley replied. "I'm simply telling you what I

believe. The hive makes you want to help them. It doesn't tell you how. Those men turned to violence of their own volition. Including Alex. Perhaps it's a trait shared by men. Or certain men."

The chamber became quiet as everyone considered this.

"You want my honest opinion?" Hayley said. "Until you remove our people from the hive's influence for an adequate amount of time, they're never going to stop trying to help the hive. The hive has no desire to hurt us. But that doesn't mean our own people won't."

"So how do we extract them?" Infinity asked.

"I don't know. By force, I suppose."

Desmond said, "How do you explain the tiger beetle that was apparently working with Tyrone and Steven?"

"I don't know anything about that. Perhaps the creature was also under the influence of the hive, cooperating with Tyrone and Steven to achieve the same purpose. As for it killing Alfie Lewis, well, it shouldn't come as a surprise that tiger beetles have violent tendencies."

Again the chamber was silent.

Xavier's voice penetrated the darkness. "I've been mulling an idea around in my head. It might seem crazy, but this may be the appropriate time to share it."

"Then spill it, brother," Lenny said.

Xavier took a deep breath. "The isopods, which seem to be deeply connected to the hive, have the ability to create a safe zone around themselves, repelling predators."

"A major benefit of being deeply connected to the hive," Hayley interjected.

"Interesting that you should say that," Xavier said. "Because it provides support for my idea. See, I started to wonder about the mutualistic relationship between the isopods and the hive.

Are the isopods useful to the hive because isopods happen to repel predators? Or are the isopods attracted to the hive because the hive actually *makes* isopods repellant to predators?"

Desmond sat up straight. He hadn't seriously considered the possibility, as it had seemed so far-fetched. But now he was starting to see the implications Xavier had been contemplating.

Xavier continued. "Let's assume the latter—the isopods get this ability from the hive. What got me thinking about this was that, as of yesterday morning, we know there are other hives. We saw them." He paused, either thinking or letting this sink in.

"Wicked-keen cogitation, Xav!" Lenny said. "If the other hives also have their own isopods—"

"Then those isopods may have their own unique defense pheromones," Desmond said.

"Which would also repel predators, including any predators controlled by another hive," Lenny said.

Desmond could almost see Xavier nodding. "Exactly."

Gideon said, "You want to explain that in plain English?"

Desmond beat Xavier and Lenny to it. "If we can get an isopod from another hive—or just the chemical from the isopod that creates the safe zone—then we'll have a defense from predators controlled by the hive that has our people."

"There are a lot of *ifs* in that statement," Infinity said.

Desmond agreed—it was a long shot. Still, it was a possibility. "Yes there are," he said. "So that's idea number one. Who has idea number two?"

The group fell silent again and remained that way for several contemplative minutes.

"We could burn the hive's framework mound," Infinity said.

"No!" Hayley said. "You can't do that. It's an intelligent species!"

"Alfie was intelligent," Gideon said coldly. "I say we draw

our people out while someone enters from the opposite side of the hive and torches the whole damn thing."

"Please don't do that, Infinity!" Hayley begged. She sounded like she was actually crying.

Infinity sighed, and Desmond could already tell she was going to side with President Millwright. He knew that Infinity respected the woman, or at least she had before they had encountered the swarm.

Desmond glanced up. Specks of sunrise orange were showing through the framework. "If yesterday was any indication, then the hive creatures will soon emerge from their mounds for their morning ritual, whatever purpose that serves. We should still be able to spot a hive and get to it before its isopods take off for the day."

"I vote we try this idea," Infinity said. "But if anything goes wrong, I say we go back to my idea of torching the hive. How many of you agree?"

Seconds later, it was decided.

Desmond, Infinity, and five other colonists chosen for the team were sitting atop the girders that made up Mossview's peak. They were watching the sunrise when the first swarm started rising like smoke from a mound several miles away. Within minutes, several others appeared, including one due east that everyone agreed was the swarm that had possessed their fellow colonists. Unfortunately, that one was the nearest, about a mile away. But soon another plume appeared about half a mile to the south, near the base of the rocky hillside that was to their backs. They could probably walk there in fifteen minutes, assuming they didn't encounter trouble.

The team of seven was already prepared to leave. In addition to Desmond and Infinity, it included Xavier, Chloe, Àurea, Sarah, and Gideon. In spite of Gideon's substantial injuries from the previous afternoon, he had insisted on coming. He had argued that he needed access to isopod saliva as soon as possible, and since the wounds of those who'd applied the stuff yesterday were already looking better, it was hard to argue with this.

The plan? Capture an isopod from the new hive, take it to the original hive as protection against the tiger beetle, and then isolate and capture at least one of their possessed companions. And then repeat. The details? The variables were far too numerous to allow for a detailed plan. They would have to play it by ear—remain wicked frosty, as Lenny had put it.

Five colonists, including Lenny, were staying behind to make sure Alexander and Hayley didn't try to escape. Although Desmond was now confident the Millwrights had pretty much recovered from the hive's disturbing mental grip, Infinity was still insisting on being cautious. Altogether, the group remaining behind consisted of three men and four women. Although Desmond hadn't heard anyone say so aloud, it seemed to have been understood that this would still leave a viable human colony if the entire team were killed during the mission. If it was even possible seven people could be considered a viable colony.

As the team descended Mossview's slope, Desmond made mental notes of a few visible landmarks on the rocky hillside above the new hive. Once on the ground, they shouted a few details about the new hive's location to Lenny and the others within the mound, and then they embarked, carrying nothing with them but Desmond's mandible and several girder weapons.

The swarm was still flying above the new mound as the group approached, so the hillside landmarks ended up being unnecessary. As the team cautiously rounded the edge of a framework hill a few hundred yards from the new hive, Desmond was almost surprised to see that a herd of isopods actually was gathered around the base. Xavier's idea, at least this first, small part of it, was turning out to be feasible. The monstrous isopods were just waking up, slowly unrolling and getting to their numerous feet. Some of them wasted no time and immediately began rubbing against the mound's girders.

The team huddled against the nearby mound and watched as the swarm of millions of tiny winged creatures began to descend, the cloud gradually flattening out and spreading down the slopes to feed on the isopod-secreted nectar.

"Well, at least *some* things on this world are predictable," Desmond said.

"Now all we have to do is capture one," Xavier said. "I don't know what the hell I was thinking. Those things weigh a couple thousand pounds."

Sarah Suzuki pointed. "It looks like some of them are only half that size. Not that it makes much difference."

"We don't need the whole animal," Infinity muttered.

Desmond gazed at the isopods, many of which were now completely covered by the feeding swarm. Infinity was right, in theory, but how could they know which part secreted the predator-repelling pheromone? And what if it wasn't even a pheromone at all. Maybe it was a sound the isopods created, at a frequency humans couldn't hear. Or maybe it was an electromagnetic field. Heck, it could even be a form of thought projection, something Desmond used to dismiss as impossible but now, for obvious reasons, couldn't.

The minutes passed slowly as the swarm fed. Finally, the isopods' color began transitioning back to olive green as the flies gradually left them and returned to the mound's interior. The isopods milled about for a few more minutes and then gathered on the north side of the hill. Responding to some unknown cue, they all began moving to the east. It was time to act.

Infinity got to her feet. "We'll circle to the northeast to avoid the hive, then we'll cut south and intercept them."

The group headed to the northeast and made their way around two more framework hills, but then they were delayed when Chloe spotted a pair of tiger beetles to the east. The predators didn't spot them and continued on their path to the north. Once the tiger beetles were out of sight, the humans moved on and converged with the isopod herd.

"That's the one," Infinity said when they were fifty yards away. She pointed to the rear of the herd, to a beast that was substantially less gigantic than the others, although it could probably tip the scales at over a thousand pounds. The creature seemed to be struggling to keep up due to some kind of problem with its legs. This specimen was definitely the right choice—it would be easier to convince the refugees to kill and butcher an already injured isopod. If it came to that.

The creatures were moving slowly, so the colonists simply walked up to the selected isopod and encircled it. The beast briefly explored their feet with its antennae and then went back to shuffling along, tapping and tasting the moss. The colonists raised their eyebrows at each other over the creature's domed back. Desmond's eyes met Infinity's.

She shrugged. "I guess we just see if we can guide it away from its herd and then all the way to the other hive."

As unlikely as this seemed, it was at least a plan. The group gathered into a half circle around the isopod's right side and started pushing. The creature responded by changing direction. Slowly, they turned it to the north, the idea being to intersect the east-west path between Mossview and the original hive. From there they'd have a better idea of how to get to the hive, where they hoped to find Eagleton, Steven, Tyrone, and now Emily, still alive.

Desmond was surprised the creature was actually cooperating with them. So far, the second step of the plan was turning out to be as easy as the first had been. But suddenly, for some undiscernable reason, the isopod turned back. The humans pushed on its side, all of them at once, which slowed it down. But it dug its numerous feet into the moss and used brute force to continue moving slowly back toward its herd.

Infinity growled in frustration and stepped back from the creature. "Time to kill the damn thing." She moved around to its head and raised her girder weapon.

"Wait," Desmond said. "Once it's dead, it might not repel predators."

"But then again, it might," she said.

Desmond moved between Infinity and the creature, although they were still keeping pace with the thing's plodding movement. "I realize we probably have no choice," he said. "A small chance for protection is better than no chance. But what are we going to do with it once it's dead? What if the defense chemical is contained in only one part of its body?"

"Then we take as much of the body as we can."

Desmond sighed. The chances of this plan working seemed abysmal.

Xavier said, "If you don't kill it instantly, it will almost certainly conglobate."

"What?" Infinity demanded.

"It'll roll up into a protective ball," Xavier replied. He shrugged. "I've never had a chance to use that word, so...."

"He's right," Desmond said. "If we're going to do this, it has to be quick and devastating."

"So we do it together," Infinity said, tilting her head at

Desmond to encourage him to get out of her way. "We're wasting time."

They all gathered around the isopod's head, which was partially hidden by the anterior-most plate of the exoskeleton. Two soccer ball eyes dominated most of what was visible. Between the eyes was a featureless area of leathery exoskeleton about ten inches wide.

"We're going to stab instead of swing," Infinity instructed them. "Thrust hard, like you're going to ram your weapon all the way through and into the ground. On three. Everyone ready."

Desmond took a deep breath and got his mandible ready to strike. From the corner of his eye, he saw several others nod.

"One... two... three!"

They all lunged in, thrusting their weapons. Desmond felt a few inches of his mandible enter the creature's head, but the weapon had a forked tip and stopped at the second tine.

The isopod flopped onto its side, nearly knocking Sarah and Xavier to the ground. A split second later it had rolled into a tight sphere.

Panting and trembling, the humans stared at the immobile creature.

"That didn't work so well," Xavier said.

Desmond stepped closer and tried forcing his weapon into a seam between two of the exoskeleton plates. There wasn't room, and the plates wouldn't budge. He stepped back and shook his head.

Abruptly, the creature's tight posture relaxed. The sphere opened a few feet, revealing the head and underside, and then the isopod became still again. Milky fluid oozed from numerous punctures in its head.

"Damn if it ain't dead," Gideon said. "Nice work, people." He kneeled by the creature's head and plunged his hand into its mouth. He pulled it back out covered in saliva and started rubbing the stuff into the gash on his shoulder. "Should be plenty here for everyone," he said.

After they had all applied saliva to their wounds, they worked together to pull the shell open a few more feet. Twelve legs, each about the size of a human arm, hung loosely from a pink, complexly-jointed belly. It was obvious that there should have been fourteen legs, but the two hindmost legs on the left side had recently been torn off. Perhaps there were some large predators out here that weren't inclined to honor the isopods' safe zone. If so, then the plan wasn't as likely to work as Desmond had hoped.

Infinity moved in and used her weapon to puncture the creature's underside, which was relatively soft. She then dragged her weapon lengthwise, ripping the hole wider, revealing muscle tissue and internal organs. She looked at Desmond and then Xavier. "Your best guess. Which parts are most likely to do the trick?"

Xavier shook his head and shrugged.

Desmond thought for a few seconds. "In some insects, pheromone glands are concentrated near the anus, or sometimes near the mouth. With this thing, they could be anywhere. But since we have to choose, I'd say our best bet is to take tissue from the head and from the posterior abdomen."

Infinity turned to the others. "We're going to remove and carry what we can. But that's not all—and you might not like this part—I also want you to cover yourselves from head to foot with isopod."

11

SHIMMERMOTH

SEPTEMBER 6 - MID-MORNING

INFINITY CURSED and wiped the sweat from her face, frustrated by their lack of progress. Opening the isopod's abdomen had been easy. Detaching and removing body parts—that was proving to be a different story. The thing had a massive internal skeleton, which appeared to be composed of a material similar to that of the framework hills' girders. And it seemed that every muscle, internal organ, and segment of exoskeleton was attached to some portion of the skeleton by tendons or connective tissue as difficult to cut as steel cable. Crude girder weapons were hardly the tools for such a job.

So far, she and the other refugees had managed to remove two gland-like structures near the anus and two more at the base of the head, but there was no way of knowing whether these had anything to do with repelling predators. Exasperated, Infinity turned to Desmond. "We're wasting valuable time."

He nodded. "Yeah. It's time for plan B." He pointed to some

ooze that was still dripping from the punctures on the isopod's head. "This will be my region. I'll smear this fluid all over my body." He pointed to a spot at the base of the creature's neck. "Sarah, this is your region. Try to use fluids you find on or near the body's surface, as anything deep inside won't be a good candidate. Cover every inch of your skin."

He went on and assigned a different section of the beast's carcass to each team member. Soon they were all smeared with different types of isopod goo, each with a slightly different color, consistency, and smell. With a little luck, at least one of these substances would repel the tiger beetle that had killed Alfie Lewis.

The group gathered their weapons and the four fist-sized glands they'd hacked from the creature's body and headed back toward Mossview. Once they were close enough that Infinity was confident she could navigate to the original hive, they cut to the east.

They were about halfway there when Infinity spotted a naked human figure coming around the edge of a framework hill about a hundred yards away, walking directly toward the group. She and the others stopped.

"That's Reece Eagleton," Desmond said.

Tyrone and Steven emerged from behind the hill, following Eagleton. And then Emily Sanchez.

"Would you look at that," Gideon said. "She's cooperating with them, as if she couldn't care less that they killed Alfie."

A large, black shape emerged next, and Infinity felt adrenaline surge through her body. The tiger beetle was near enough to Emily that its relative size provided an all-too-clear reminder of how massive the creatures were. It was following Emily and the others as if stalking them. But the truth was actually worse—it was working with them.

Another creature rounded the hill.

"What the hell?" Gideon muttered.

Infinity's adrenaline kicked into overdrive. The thing was the size of a horse. At first glance, she had thought it was much larger because of the two triangular, wing-like appendages attached to its back. They were held vertically like butterfly wings. The most striking thing about these appendages, though, was that they shimmered in the sunlight with shifting patterns of green, pink, and brown. They would have been beautiful if they hadn't been attached to the most vicious-looking creature Infinity had ever seen.

Eagleton was still coming directly at them. He waved at the team as if he were simply greeting some friends.

"What do we do?" Chloe asked.

"I think we need to move to the nearest mound," Desmond said. "You know, in case our plan doesn't work."

Infinity nodded. "Definitely."

They began moving toward the nearest hill on their left, which wasn't as close as Infinity would have liked.

"Colonists!" Eagleton shouted.

Infinity looked. The tiger beetle and the other creature were now ahead of Eagleton, sprinting straight for the team.

"Run," Desmond said. "But stay in a tight group."

Infinity could already see they weren't going to make it. She considered ordering the team to stop but realized that might cost all of them their lives. If they kept running, perhaps a few would make it while the creatures were busy attacking the others.

The tiger beetle overtook them first, darting in front of them, cutting off their path to the mound. It rushed at them, prompting fearful shouts. Several refugees tripped while trying to back up.

"Weapons!" Infinity shouted. She stepped in front of the others and braced herself against the oncoming beast.

The tiger beetle skidded to a stop less than ten yards out, gnashing its mandibles and kicking up tufts of moss.

"It's actually working," Desmond said. "At least one of us is creating a safe zone."

The other creature caught up and positioned itself on the opposite side of the team from the tiger beetle. It was at least twice the tiger beetle's size, perhaps close to a thousand pounds. It was mostly tan in color and stood on four legs, but it had two additional wicked-looking limbs on the front of its body, each the size of a human leg and equipped with fierce pincers. Its stump-shaped head was mostly mouth, with no eyes Infinity could identify. Its shimmering butterfly wings constantly shifted angles but always remained perpendicular to the humans. These had to be some kind of sensors, like the anglerbeasts' flat, leaf-like structures.

"Colonists," Eagleton said again as he drew near. "You needn't fear us. We only wish the best for our colony. The hive will help." He walked right up beside the tiger beetle and stopped.

Steven, Tyrone, and Emily approached, spreading out and surrounding the team.

"You're coming with us," Tyrone said.

"We ain't going anywhere with you," Gideon snarled.

Infinity saw movement to her left and turned. Emily had grabbed one of the legs of the larger beast and was trying to push the creature toward the team.

"Something's wrong," Emily said. "It won't go any closer."

Eagleton stepped behind the tiger beetle and started pushing. The black creature resisted and stepped back even farther, forcing Eagleton aside. Eagleton frowned and turned to Infinity and the rest of the team. "What have you done?"

"Here's the deal," Infinity said. She waved to the others on her team to follow her, and they all started moving toward Eagleton. "We'll go with you to the hive. *If* you can convince us the hive isn't going to hurt us."

As Infinity had hoped, the tiger beetle continued backing off as the team moved closer.

Eagleton glanced at the retreating creature and turned back to the team, frowning. "I swear that the hive won't hurt you. You can trust me."

"Just come with us," Tyrone said from behind the team. "You'll understand then."

Infinity kept her eyes locked on Eagleton. "Okay, Reece. We're willing to give it a chance. There must be a good reason you guys are so convinced." She hoped the others understood what she was attempting.

Eagleton looked like he might flee at any moment, which was not what Infinity wanted. She quickly added, "But here's the deal. First you take just me. If I find that you're telling the truth, I'll tell the others, and they'll come too." She glanced back at Desmond. "You guys will come if I find out it's safe, right?"

He nodded. "If you're convinced, we'll be convinced."

She took two more steps toward Eagleton.

Eagleton studied each of the refugees and then nodded. "That sounds reasonable. Come with us, then. We'll take—"

Infinity swung her girder weapon into the side of Eagleton's head. He crumpled to the ground. She spun around, assuming at least one of the guardsmen would charge in to attack. But they were keeping their distance, staring back cautiously. Eagleton moaned, holding a hand to his head. He was conscious and would likely be able to get back on his feet soon. The opportunity to capture a second possessed refugee would be brief. And the team couldn't split up because they didn't know which of them was repelling the predators.

"What do you think you're doing?" Emily asked. "We're trying to help you!"

Desmond broke away from the team without warning and charged Emily, raising his mandible. Tyrone and Steven darted over to stop him. Instead of continuing toward Emily, Desmond turned and swung at Tyrone, driving one of the weapon's tines into the guardsman's arm as Tyrone and Steven tackled him.

Infinity nudged Sarah and pointed at Eagleton. "Pull him over to the rest of us. Hit him again if you have to!" Without waiting to see that Sarah understood, she ran to help Desmond. But this was hardly necessary. Gideon, Xavier, and Desmond now had Tyrone under control. Steven had broken away from the fight, and he and Emily were retreating, apparently aware they were outnumbered.

Infinity spun around and assessed the entire situation. The two predators were still keeping their distance, pacing back and forth at the safe zone's perimeter. Eagleton was starting to struggle as Sarah and Àurea dragged him by his ankles toward the rest of the team. Chloe was standing to the side, ready to help if needed. Dragging Eagleton and Tyrone to Mossview would be a challenge for the team of seven. Capturing Steven and Emily would have to wait.

Steven and Emily, now over fifty yards away, stopped fleeing and turned to the team. "You're making a mistake," Emily shouted.

"We won't survive without the hive's help," Steven added.

Infinity shook her head. "You two sound like a goddamn broken record. You can either come with us peacefully now, or we'll come back, beat you into submission, and drag you back by your heels. It's your choice." She turned her back on them.

By the time the team had carried and dragged Eagleton and Tyrone within sight of Mossview, Infinity was doubting whether the two men were even worth the effort. Threatening them with violence had proven useless, as they didn't seem to feel pain. Infinity had suggested knocking them senseless or choking them out. But the two doctors had protested, explaining that either of these strategies involved the risk of permanent brain damage. Infinity had relented, but she'd silently mused that risking brain damage would be worth it to get the men to shut the hell up.

When they finally arrived at the edge of Mossview's slope, several of the colonists came out to meet them, including Hayley and Lenny.

President Millwright descended to the ground and stood before Eagleton, who was still struggling and had to be held in place by three colonists. She looked the man up and down, frowning. "Reece," she said, "you don't understand right now, but you will by tomorrow. I know as well as you do that the hive has no intention of hurting any of us. But if you think it's okay to kill, maim, and force these people to go there, then clearly the hive is influencing your ability to reason."

Eagleton glared at her without speaking.

Infinity's team dragged the men up the slope and into the hill's interior. Forcing them through the latticework of girders was even more of a challenge than carrying them on flat ground had been. Infinity finally ended up telling them matter-of-factly that she was seconds away from choking them into unconsciousness. This resulted in a bit more cooperation but did little to shut them up.

Once everyone was inside the center chamber, the colonists gathered around Eagleton and Tyrone and forced them onto their stomachs on the ground. Without rope to tie them up, it was going to take most of the group to keep them safely restrained. There was no way Infinity's rescue team could leave again until the two men became more docile. It might be several days before they could go after Emily and Steven.

"The way I see it," Lenny said once the group had settled themselves on and around Eagleton and Tyrone, "each of these challenges serves the purpose of strengthening our resolve. Losing some of our members has made us understand how important each of us really is. Having our members become possessed by demon gnats is making us understand to what lengths we're willing to go in order to help each other."

Eagleton grunted and lifted his head. "You've got that back-wards. Soon you'll see that *I'm* the one who has gone to great lengths to help *you.*"

Isabelle moved to Eagleton's side. She put her hand on the man's shoulder for a moment as if trying to calm him. "Mr. Eagleton, I'd like to tell you a story. Do you mind?"

He stared up at her without answering.

"Forgive me if this seems unrelated," she said. "It's a story of one of my experiences in college. As was expected of me, I was in a sorority. But I was one of those girls who always felt awkward. I was never quite sure how to fit in. During my junior year I discovered the prescription drug Adderall. Well, suddenly I became comfortable in almost every social situation. Perhaps even vibrant. I was happier than I had been since starting college. But, of course, when I told my sorority sisters why I was happier, they warned me about the dangers of long-term use of the drug. But you know what? I didn't care. I was happy, so why would I? Just about every day for the rest of that school year I would tell my friends that they should be using Adderall too. I couldn't understand why they refused—it had improved my life that much." Isabelle paused, perhaps because her story was finished.

Eagleton glared at her. "You were right—your story is unrelated."

Isabelle glanced over at her mother and displayed what appeared to be a forced smile. "Well, to this day I don't fully understand why my friends didn't listen to me. I still believe they would have been happier if they'd taken my advice. But I've come to believe that my opinion is simply that—my opinion. They had reasons for ignoring my advice. Reasons that were important to them. Perhaps they feared Adderall would affect them differently. I don't know, and it really doesn't matter, because I still love them all."

"You're going to make a point now, I suppose," Eagleton said.

She smiled. "Of course I am. You're part of my family now. So I love you, even though you want me to do something I prefer not to do." She tilted her head toward a few of the other colonists. "They love you as well, even if they don't say it or act like it right now. And even if you don't say it, you must love all of us. Why else would you try so hard to convince us to do something you believe will help us?"

Eagleton stared at her a few more seconds. Then, whether due to Isabelle's words or to his own fatigue, he closed his eyes and lowered his head back to the ground.

EVENING

THE THICK AIR hanging in Mossview's central chamber smelled of wet moss and boiled hubcap flesh—which was actually pleasant. It had rained briefly several hours earlier, and then Infinity and the other three members of the now-official hubcap-hunting team had killed and carried back another sixteen of the creatures. A few of the other refugees had used water from the stream to boil the hubcaps in their own shells—a concoction that could pass for very plain crab soup. A little salt and pepper would help, but both were as unobtainable here as a microwave oven.

Infinity sat cross-legged, her eyes closed, trying to meditate. But with several conversations going on at all times, she was struggling to focus. Finally, she gave up, taking one last deep breath and opening her eyes. Close-quarters living was going to take some getting used to.

She gazed from one colonist to the next. Some of them were busy cleaning the bowl-like shells from the day's harvest of hubcaps, scraping out the softer tissue with stone implements. The group had brainstormed potential uses for these shells. Chloe had come up with one of the more creative ideas, suggesting that they could be used as roofing shingles, perhaps even covering Mossview entirely.

The shells might also serve as material for building walls within the mound. If the coming winter turned out to be cold, heating small compartments with controlled fires would be more feasible than heating the entire dome. But Infinity was starting to suspect that the winters in this area were mild, or perhaps even nonexistent. The two nights they'd spent here had been surprisingly warm. And Desmond had explained that at least some of the moss would likely die in subfreezing temperatures, eventually creating a thick layer of organic matter and soil beneath the live moss in the open areas of the plain. Instead, the plain was covered only by a three-inch layer of live moss directly over a very thin layer of soil.

Eagleton and Tyrone had fallen silent, probably because they had finally realized their arguments simply weren't going to work. Tyrone appeared to be sleeping now, and Infinity hoped this was a sign that the hive's grip on his mind was loosening.

Desmond, Lenny, Xavier, and Gideon were discussing possible strategies for capturing Emily and Steven. Once they had reached the point of rehashing the same basic ideas, Infinity had tried tuning them out. But having given up on meditation, she now got up and moved to Desmond's side.

"Infinity, here's what we've got," Lenny said. "First we make sure Steven and Emily are at the hive mound. Then we approach the hive with a burning torch, with the apparent intention of incinerating the holy crap out of the entire mound. If that doesn't bring those two out to play, nothing will—right?"

She considered this. "How will we make a torch that can stay lit until we get there?"

Lenny shrugged his shoulders. "Details. Anyway, they'll come right on out past the magical mystery line—the line the swarm won't cross for whatever reason. From that point on, it's your show. You knock the everloving sense out of them and we haul their asses back to Mossview. Job done."

Infinity nodded. "If you can create a slow-burning torch, I'm in." She shot a glance at Eagleton and Tyrone. "It'll be at least morning before we can leave those two behind with so few guards to restrain them."

"Life would be significantly easier if we had rope," Desmond said.

Lenny gave a thumbs-up. "I've got some ideas for that. We need to go back to the isopod carcass. Tendons, skin from its belly, maybe even intestines, assuming it has intestines—those, brother, are the raw materials for rope."

"He's right," Infinity said. "But let's focus on getting our people back first."

"Actually," Desmond said, "we probably need to go back to

the carcass *before* we try grabbing Emily and Steven. To re-apply its body fluids. To be safe, we may even want to kill another one. Chances are, the substance is more effective when it's fresh."

Xavier spoke up. "If the carcass is missing or chewed up tomorrow, we'll know the safe zone disappears as the dead body decays."

Infinity turned to look at Eagleton, and their eyes met. He had obviously been listening to the conversation. He shook his head at her, like he was disgusted with the stupidity of their plan. But he kept his mouth shut.

Desmond groaned softly and shifted his position.

Infinity frowned at him. "You okay?"

"Yeah. It's just... well, now that I've eaten two meals, it's finally time for me to go see a man about a horse."

Infinity shook her head, confused.

"That's guy talk," Lenny said. "What Desmond means is that he needs to pinch a grumpy. Stock the pond with brown trout. Release the kraken. Let the dogs out. Pump a clump of dump out of his—"

"Okay, guy talk," Infinity said. "I get it. And I'm betting Desmond's not the only one who needs to see this man about some horse. But no one goes out alone." She looked at the sun peeking through Mossview's girder framework. It was now low to the horizon. "Desmond, I'll go with you, and then the others can go in pairs or in larger groups. It'll be dark soon, so everyone needs to get the job done fast."

Desmond frowned but then got to his feet. "As long as you turn your back."

Infinity quickly got those who hadn't heard the conversation caught up. Alexander Millwright was still sleeping, and she decided to wait to deal with that problem when it actually became a problem.

She and Desmond picked up their weapons, and she followed him up and out, and then down to the ground. He immediately headed for the stream.

"You think it's a good idea to contaminate our water source?" she asked as she caught up with him.

"The current will remove our waste. And obviously no one lives downstream."

Infinity stopped ten yards from the stream and turned her back as Desmond entered the water. "Be quick," she said. "All this talk has made me need to take my turn." She scanned the area in front of her for predators.

"Um, how about you cover your ears. I'm having trouble relaxing with you here."

She sighed, tucked her weapon under one arm, and plugged her ears. After about a minute, she heard faint splashing.

"Okay, done and cleaned up."

She pulled her hands from her ears. Suddenly, she heard more splashing, frantic this time.

"Oh, shit—tiger beetle!" Desmond cried.

Infinity spun around in time to see the monster running full speed up the center of the stream, throwing water out in every direction. It was close—too close for them to be able to make it back to Mossview. Infinity heard something else behind her and spun around again. Steven and Emily were charging straight at them, followed closely by the massive predator Desmond had named the shimmermoth. Somehow they had all managed to approach unseen.

Infinity jumped into the stream and rushed over to Desmond. "Back to back!" she said. Standing in the knee-deep water, they got into defensive positions just as their attackers closed the last few yards.

The tiger beetle struck immediately, knocking Desmond into

Infinity and toppling them both into the water. Infinity's head went under and she felt a massive pressure crushing her into the stream bed. The pressure let up as Desmond was pulled off of her. She sputtered to the surface in time to see him being dragged from the stream by the tiger beetle. The creature kept backing up, its mandibles clamped onto Desmond's neck and one of his arms. His feet were kicking wildly, but the black, armored creature was far more powerful.

Infinity floundered for a moment as she got to her feet.

"If you had cooperated from the beginning, this would have been so much easier."

She spun around. The voice had been Steven's. He and Emily were standing in the stream, only a few yards away. And beside them was the shimmermoth, its multi-colored sensor panels shifting up and down, appraising her.

Infinity glanced at Desmond, who was still kicking as the tiger beetle dragged him eastward, in the direction of the hive. She bolted, leaping onto the stream bank and then sprinting after Desmond. Before she had made it ten yards from the stream's edge she heard the shimmermoth splashing through the stream and then clomping on the moss in pursuit. She didn't look back, she just sprinted as fast as she could. If she could somehow free Desmond from the tiger beetle, maybe they could make it to Mossview and climb inside.

The creature struck her shoulder and she went down hard, her face slamming into the moss. She flipped over and swung her weapon at the shimmermoth, but the girder just bounced off one of its legs, inflicting no harm.

The creature pinned her to the ground with its pincers, pushing on her chest until she could hardly breathe. One of the pincers clamped down tight against her skin, threatening to slice her open if she tried to struggle. The creature's eyeless head, about two feet wide, seemed to have only one purpose—to provide a location for its mouth. At least four pairs of jaws, obviously for ripping and chewing, gnashed open and shut. Dark saliva oozed out, hanging in long threads before splattering onto Infinity's skin. The two shimmering sensor panels angled inward as if they were scanning her body.

Her weapon was wrenched from her hand, and then Steven's head appeared from the right, sneering down at her. "Stupid thing don't even know why it's doing what it's doing," he said. "Just wants whatever the hive wants. You see, that's how this works. Once we all get properly motivated to achieve the same thing, then we'll get along just fine. No more need for all this fighting."

Infinity craned her neck to see Desmond. He was now at least a hundred yards away, and his kicking appeared to be diminishing. Infinity then saw Emily, who was running to catch up with Desmond and the tiger beetle. "It's going to kill him!" Infinity snarled at Steven.

"These creatures seem to have gotten over their reluctance to get near you all," Steven said. "I'm not sure how you accomplished that earlier." He shook his head. "The trouble some people go to just to avoid doing what's really best for them."

"Dammit," gasped Infinity, "make the tiger beetle drop him!"

"See, that's the thing," Steven said. "These animals aren't pets. I can't just tell them what to do."

The shimmermoth suddenly released her chest and spun around, stepping over Infinity's body. Before Infinity could get up, it clamped both its pincers onto her right ankle and started dragging her beneath it in the same direction the tiger beetle was dragging Desmond. On either side of her, the beast's thick legs pounded the moss as it walked.

"Colonists!" Infinity screamed. "Gideon! We need help!"

Steven dove toward her, forcing the shimmermoth to break its gait as it continued dragging her. He clamped his hand over her mouth. "I doubt they can hear you from here. But still, we don't want to bother them now. We'll come back for them later."

Infinity grabbed his ear, pulled him closer until she could get her other arm around his neck, and then started throwing rapid jabs into his face, one after another.

He cried out and began kicking and throwing his own punches. The shimmermoth tripped over their flailing bodies and tumbled onto its side, releasing Infinity's ankle in the process.

She leapt to her feet. As Steven was struggling to get up, she landed a solid kick to his face. He went limp, falling back onto the moss. The creature, having regained its bearings, swung around and lunged at Infinity.

She jumped back to avoid its pincers and started sprinting toward the nearest framework hill. Which unfortunately was in the opposite direction of Mossview. She looked back over her shoulder and realized the beast wasn't chasing her. Instead, it was standing over Steven, its wide, flat sensors appraising him as he lay there moaning, still disoriented from the kick to his head. The creature slowly rotated one of its sensors toward Infinity. It abruptly abandoned Steven and began running after her.

Now with a decent lead, she ran all-out and reached the base of the mound ahead of the shimmermoth. Without slowing down, she leapt and slammed into the slope. She scrambled higher to an opening large enough for her to drop through. Seconds later, as she was descending into the framework, the shimmermoth threw itself onto the mound. Its momentum and weight shattered girders until it came to a stop several yards in. It began flailing wildly, trying to free itself. Infinity was about ten feet farther in than the creature, and she could see that several of the broken girders had impaled its body. As it continued to struggle, more girders snapped, causing it to sink even deeper into the framework.

She searched in the direction of where she'd last seen Desmond, but the hill's girders were blocking her view, and the evening light was fading, making it impossible to see much of anything. The shimmermoth was still fighting to free itself and might succeed at any moment. Infinity climbed back to the framework's surface but then paused. She considered running back to Mossview for help, but by that time Desmond might be dead. And even if he were still alive, the tiger beetle would have dragged him halfway to the hive. She had to go after him alone, and she had to do it now.

Something stabbed her hip—a skitterbug. Below it, hundreds more were clambering up the girders. She hadn't even heard them coming over the clatter of the struggling shimmermoth. She snatched the creature from her hip, ripping its dagger-like claws from her flesh, and flung it away. Another skitterbug stabbed at her leg as she crab-walked over the girders to her left until she could slide down the slope without falling into the collapsed area with the shimmermoth.

As Infinity hit the ground, the skitterbugs began swarming over the shimmermoth, and its flailing became even more frantic. A few skitterbugs emerged from the mound and went for her ankles, so she turned her back on the desperate shimmermoth and started running east toward the hive.

She shot a glance at Steven and then stopped short. He was recovering from her kick to his head and had gotten to his knees. Dozens of skitterbugs were emerging from the mound to follow her. If she ran off now, they would probably go after him.

"Goddammit!" she growled. She continued east just long enough to outdistance the skitterbugs. When the creatures gave up on following her, she changed directions and headed straight for Steven.

"You comin' wit me, wot gu hive," Steven slurred as she approached. He was trying to get to his feet but was having difficulty.

"Get up!" She grabbed his arm and pulled him to his feet. "I'm saving your miserable life, so just keep your mouth shut." She began guiding him toward Mossview.

He mumbled something else about the hive but allowed her to lead him.

Infinity glanced back at the shimmermoth. In the fading light she couldn't see anything but the outline of a writhing mass of attacking skitterbugs.

When they were fifty yards from Mossview, she shouted, "Colonists! Lenny! Gideon!" She heard a faint reply. As she and Steven reached the slope, three figures emerged from the mound and scrambled down.

"What happened?" Lenny asked, Gideon and Xavier at his side.

"No time to explain. I'm going after Desmond. Get Steven secured in the shelter." She released Steven's arm and took off to the east.

"Where is Desmond?" Xavier shouted. "You're going alone?"

"Get him inside," Infinity heard Gideon say to Lenny and Xavier. Then she heard him grunting as he ran to catch up with her.

She didn't slow down.

"We're going to the hive?" Gideon said when he was almost beside her.

"Not if we catch up to them before they get there."

"Infinity, we can hardly even see. You sure this is wise?"

She ignored him, saving her breath for running. Then her foot hit something, and she went down. Gideon stopped and picked up the object that had tripped her—Desmond's mandible weapon.

She got to her feet. "Give me that."

He handed it over. Without another word they both started running again.

After several hundred more yards, Gideon grabbed her arm, almost yanking her off her feet.

"Stop!" he hissed. "There." He pointed south.

Infinity saw two faintly-glowing orbs. They were moving, bobbing gently in the dark. And they were definitely getting closer, glowing like the headlights of an approaching car. A massive dark shape became visible behind the two lights.

"Oh, shit!" Infinity muttered. "Not now. Any time but now." It was an anglerbeast. She could now hear its heavy feet stomping the moss as it galloped directly toward them. "We'll just outrun the damn thing," she said, breaking free from Gideon's grip and taking off again.

Seconds later it became clear they weren't going to outrun the monster. They had no choice but to angle north toward the closest framework hill. With the elephant-sized anglerbeast pounding along less than ten yards back, Infinity tossed the mandible weapon into the mound and dove headfirst into an opening that was barely large enough to accommodate her shoulders.

"Get inside!" she shouted to Gideon as she strained to pull her hips through.

"I'm working on it," he grunted, apparently also stuck.

Infinity got through and came to a stop entangled in girders. Suddenly she felt dizzy. She blinked and shook her head, trying to clear her thoughts. She then turned and looked out as the two glowing orbs came to a stop only a few feet from her face. The creature heaved the front half of its body up onto the mound, its forelegs cracking a girder directly above her head. Her left leg was stuck, so she grabbed her knee and pulled it free and then wriggled her way downward until she felt the dead moss on the ground. She tried pushing her way toward the center of the mound but was restricted by broken girders and the mound's tight framework. The anglerbeast's head was now no more than four feet above her.

The creature's orbs kicked into high gear, illuminating the interior of the mound around Infinity and Gideon. The beast kept lowering the glowing orbs into the framework until one of them actually bumped Infinity's scalp.

Again she felt a wave of dizziness, and she shook her head, trying to think straight. What the hell was wrong with her?

"Oh, you've got to be kidding," Gideon said. "Do you hear that?"

Infinity paused. A low, thrumming buzz that hadn't previously caught her attention was now rising, becoming an overwhelming presence. It seemed to be resonating with her brainwaves, making it difficult to focus. A raw, gripping fear rose from deep within her.

They were inside another hive.

12

———

HIVE

September 6 - After Dark

"IF YOU'D STOP FIGHTING, this would be a lot easier on you."

Desmond couldn't respond to Emily. It was hard enough sucking in enough air to stay alive. He'd already passed out twice, only to wake up still in the tiger beetle's mandibles. He felt blood dripping from his neck and arm, but he couldn't even use his one free hand to assess his wounds because it was busy gripping the mandible at his throat to prevent the serrations from cutting a major artery.

For what seemed like an hour but had probably only been fifteen minutes, the tiger beetle had been dragging Desmond over moss and the occasional patch of bare rock. All he could do was struggle to avoid suffocating.

"Well, that's a beautiful sight, even in the dark," Emily said.

The tiger beetle was holding Desmond so that his back was facing forward, so he couldn't see anything but the creature's monstrous face, but he was pretty sure Emily was referring to the hive. He could hear the familiar thrumming of millions of tiny wings.

She leaned over the tiger beetle so that he could see her face, although the darkness didn't reveal much about her expression. "Desmond, you're about to get the mother of all attitude adjustments. I know you're frustrated with me right now, but soon you'll understand."

Still, he couldn't reply. He couldn't even spit in her face.

The tiger beetle continued dragging Desmond forward, and he glimpsed a huge isopod curled into a ball to his side. The tiger beetle then leapt into the air, nearly breaking Desmond's neck. Its feet began scrabbling as if climbing, and Desmond realized he was being dragged up the slope of the hive's mound.

"This is good enough," Emily said. "Stop here." Apparently she was climbing the slope alongside the tiger beetle.

The creature didn't stop.

"I said stop!"

In his peripheral vision, Desmond saw her lean in and push on the creature's head. This time it stopped. He felt Emily tugging his legs to the side and then pushing them down into an opening between the girders.

"Now let go. Jesus, don't you listen to anything? Let go!"

The tiger beetle's mandibles started jerking from side to side, presumably because Emily was yanking on one of them. The mandibles opened abruptly, and Desmond collapsed into the framework, coming to a jarring stop against several girders. He gasped for breath, rubbing the wounds on his neck and shoulder where the mandibles' serrations and tines had chewed his skin raw.

He heard the tiger beetle retreating down the slope, and then Emily's voice sounded from above. "You're really quite lucky," she said. "I wish I could relive what you're about to experience. But I guess it's like sex. You can only have one first time."

Desmond coughed a few times and then spat. His mouth tasted like blood. "You've become psychotic, and you don't even realize it," he said. He painfully tilted his head back and stared up at her. He tried maneuvering his legs to start climbing, but every muscle burned from bruising and fatigue.

"Listen, Desmond," she said. "Do you hear that?"

He paused. The thrumming was getting louder. Now that he was less focused on struggling to breathe and protecting his throat, his fear of what was coming surged to the point of panic. "No!" He put all his energy into pulling himself up with his arms until his legs came loose from the framework and he was able to position them beneath himself. He started climbing.

"I can't let you leave quite yet," Emily said. She was sitting on the girders, her feet held ready to kick him if he came up any farther.

He reached up and grabbed one of her ankles, but she easily kicked his arm away with her free foot. The swarm's droning had risen to an almost deafening roar, making it hard for Desmond to think. "Get out of my way!" He pushed himself up, intending to plow right past her.

She kicked him viciously in the forehead. He lost his footing and dropped back down a few feet. And then he felt it—the tiny flies of the swarm alighting on his legs, arms, and torso. And then on his face.

"You lucky bastard," Desmond heard Emily's voice say through the swarm's noise.

He began swatting at his torso and legs. "No. No!" With each swat he crushed thousands of nearly-microscopic creatures against his skin, creating a moist, gritty layer. But he was fighting a losing battle, the creatures were swarming onto his body too quickly for him to keep up. They began covering his face, forcing him to use both hands to keep them out of his nose and mouth. His arms were actually becoming heavy from the creatures' weight.

Desmond tried holding his breath, but seconds later his burning lungs would no longer be denied. He cupped his hands over his mouth before inhaling, but each of his gasps swept more flies into his throat. He coughed and spat, but the creatures kept making their way inward.

Abruptly, he realized the creatures were no longer on his face, as if he had blacked out and they had dispersed while he was unconscious. The rest of his body was still covered by the swarm—he could feel the creatures' weight—but now he somehow felt less concerned about that. He relaxed.

"You... are... different."

The words had come from his own mouth. He had felt his mouth moving, pronouncing each word, but he hadn't willed himself to speak them.

"We... are confused."

Again the words had come from his mouth, but he hadn't made the choice to speak them.

"Who are you?" he said. This time the words were his own, spoken willfully.

Several seconds passed.

"You are not like the others," his mouth said. "With you... it is like speaking to two people. Why do you speak in two ways?"

Desmond felt his mouth frown. Was it his frown, or was he being forced to frown? "I don't know what you mean."

Again, his own mouth formed a response. "You speak to us like the others do. But there is something else within you. It speaks to us in a different way, although we can hardly detect it. We are curious."

Desmond felt himself frown again, and he felt more confident this time that the gesture was his own.

"What is the hive talking about?" Emily demanded from above.

Desmond ignored her. He now felt the sensation that had apparently overcome the other possessed refugees, truly believing that the hive did not intend to harm him. But there was also a part of his consciousness that understood that the hive was dangerous to him and the other colonists, even though it intended no harm. This portion of his awareness seemed fleeting, as if it were steadily slipping away. For the sake of the colony —for his friends, his family—he had to hold on to this fleeting part of himself. The hive is dangerous. The hive is dangerous. He repeated the thought in his mind, hoping it would stay.

"We are curious—there is something else within you," the hive repeated through Desmond's mouth.

"I don't know!" he replied. Why did the hive think he was different from the others? Abruptly, something dawned on him. He *was* different. He had been since his last bridging mission to the world of the mongrels. Abel, a strange creature of that world, had given him the ability to project his thoughts to others through physical contact. Perhaps that was what the hive was referring to.

Desmond concentrated on projecting his thoughts. He formed the words in his head, "Is this what you are referring to?"

The hive's droning suddenly intensified, and the flies covering his body shifted as if they had become agitated.

"Yes," the hive said through Desmond's mouth. "Yes, yes, yes. Something else is within you, and now it speaks to us. You are not like the others."

Desmond decided to stop competing for control over his vocal cords and simply speak to the hive by projecting his thoughts. "This is still me. I'm just talking to you in a different way."

After several seconds, his voice said, "You are not like the others."

"No, I suppose I'm not," he replied silently. "I am confused by you. I don't understand what you are."

"We are a hive."

"I know that. But I don't understand how you can talk to me."

Again, several seconds passed before Desmond's mouth spoke. "We understand the words you use—your language—because you are becoming a part of us. Soon you will understand more. And we will understand more."

"I don't want to become a part of you. I want to be myself. I want to live with my own people."

"Soon you will understand," his mouth repeated. "We like talking to you. We will keep you here and talk to you often. Your mind is different. It is interesting. We will keep your mind."

Desmond considered this. He knew he should be fighting to get away, but now he didn't really care to bother with that. The hive didn't intend to hurt him. He remembered thinking moments ago that the hive was dangerous. But why had he been thinking that? His body was covered with the creatures, and they weren't hurting him. He had even sucked thousands into his nose and mouth, yet he was fine. Why had he thought they were dangerous?

"We are happy you are a part of our hive," his mouth said. "We will talk to you often."

"Finally, we're making some progress," Emily said from above.

"I'm happy, too," Desmond said with his mind. And he meant it. In fact, he felt tears forming in his eyes and running down his cheeks—tears of absolute joy. He felt so lucky that the hive had come for him and taken him in.

"Would you like to know more about us?"

"Yes, of course I would," Desmond said silently.

His surroundings suddenly changed. He was no longer covered in flies. Instead, he *was* the hive—the collective consciousness of billions of creatures. And as the hive, he understood that this consciousness was possible because the creatures were in close proximity to each other. He could feel countless individual mental connections, connections that could only function when the creatures were infinitesimally close. Furthermore, because he was the hive, he also knew the connections would be severed if the creatures dispersed. If they were to spread out and leave the hive, they would become nothing more than individual specks with scarcely enough neural function to find their way back. Dispersing meant death to the hive's mind.

Abruptly, Desmond became the mind of a different hive. No, it was actually the same hive only much, much younger. The hive was self-aware but hadn't yet developed most of its current abilities. This young hive was the first hive to become self-aware, at least the first that it knew of. The hive at this earlier time consisted of individuals that were larger than those of the current hive, large enough to sustain neural functions that allowed them to venture away from the hive. The individuals would go out on their own to collect food, severing their connection to the hive mind. They would locate isopods—which were much smaller then, those many, many years ago—and would stimulate the isopods to secrete nectar. They would gather this nectar in the hairs along their abdomens to be transported back to the hive as food for the others. Altogether the hive consisted of members of dozens of different castes. Each caste was responsible for certain jobs. There were separate castes for reproduction, for rearing the young, for hive defense, and for processing and storing nectar. In return for the isopods' nectar, the flies would meticulously clean the crevices and seams of the beasts' exoskeletons.

Another abrupt shift and Desmond became an older version of the hive. Many thousands of years had passed. The individuals of the hive were now smaller than those of the previous, younger hive, allowing more of them to exist in the same space with the same quantity of food. More individuals meant more neural connections, which meant more sophisticated thoughts. This older hive still relied on isopod nectar. But now, instead of using precious time cleaning the isopods' comparatively-monstrous bodies, the hive provided a more useful service—they secreted a chemical onto the isopods that repelled nearly all other creatures, especially predators. The isopods' safe zone allowed them to wander the plain all day, feeding upon moss without risk. Over time, this had resulted in a steady increase in the isopods' body size.

Desmond became yet another hive, again of the same lineage. And again, a vast amount of time had passed. This was the hive he was now overjoyed to call his own. Over centuries, the individual creatures had gradually become so small that they were incapable of leaving the hive. And they had no reason to ever leave the hive anyway, as the hive had become increasingly proficient at influencing the behaviors of other animals. Isopods were particularly useful, but a wide variety of other animals were also made to provide for the hive's needs.

Smaller individuals had resulted in a still-larger hive population. This, combined with the fact that the hive's individuals never dispersed enough to break their neural connections, had resulted in exponential development of the hive mind's cognitive functions. Over many millennia, the hive had become an intelligent entity in a way that Desmond had never thought possible.

Desmond was suddenly himself again. He smiled, feeling warm and comfortable. The fact that the hive was capable of delivering this lesson about their long history in such a compelling way was just one more reason for him to feel overjoyed. How could anyone feel otherwise?

"You will now come to the heart of our hive," his mouth said. "We like the way you talk to us, so we will keep you. You will talk to us often."

"Yes, I would like that very much," Desmond projected with his mind. The winged creatures then began leaving his body. Within seconds they were all gone, having returned to the heart of the hive. He felt a twinge of sadness, longing for them to return.

He looked up at Emily, who was still sitting on the girders above him. All he could see of her face was a pale shape in the darkness, but he could tell she was watching him. "Please," he said aloud, "guide me to the heart of the hive."

She offered a hand. "That's what I like to hear. The easiest way is to go in through the top of the mound."

Desmond took her hand and climbed out, and together they crawled up the moss-covered girders to the mound's peak. In front of them was a large opening, about five feet wide. Desmond presumed the swarm used this opening when they emerged from the mound at first light each morning. This ritual was one of many aspects of the hive Desmond couldn't wait to learn more about. He had so many questions and so much he wanted to share.

They descended into the opening and began making their way straight down. As they approached ground level, the space became wider, and the hive's soothing thrum grew to a magnificent, all-consuming symphony.

Finally, Desmond's foot touched the ground, and he stepped off the framework and turned around. He couldn't see much in the darkness, but the faint outlines of several large objects were visible on the ground nearby. The open space here was almost as wide as the chamber he and the other colonists had cleared at Mossview. And before him, in the center of the chamber, was a dark, throbbing mass—the heart of the hive.

The hive's heart consisted of millions—perhaps even billions —of winged creatures, congregated on and around a pillar of girders. It was most of the hive's population. Separately, each individual was incapable of even the most basic cognitive functions. But together, interconnected by some mysterious link between each member and those closest to it, these creatures formed something unimaginably rare and precious—a sentient, curious, and compassionate being.

Desmond stepped forward and held his arms out. A dark, smoke-like wisp drifted out from the mass and began covering him. He sat down on the ground. He was aware of crushing many individuals with the motion, but he was also aware that killing a few thousand didn't really matter, not even to the hive. He crossed his legs and closed his eyes as the creatures continued covering every inch of his skin. They entered his ears, his nose, and even his mouth. But this was okay, as the hive was curious about him.

In that moment, Desmond felt safer and more serene than he had ever felt in his life.

13

———

ORB

SEPTEMBER 6 - After Dark

THE THRUMMING BUZZ of the new hive was all Infinity could hear. Within the next few seconds, the creatures would overtake her and Gideon. They needed to get out of the mound now.

But the damn anglerbeast was still right above her. One of the creature's glowing orbs bumped the top of her scalp again. The monster was trying to lure her out as if she were a skitter-bug. Infinity punched the orb, hoping this would encourage the creature to back off. No effect.

She scanned the area immediately around her, which was well lit by the orbs. Desmond's mandible weapon was within her reach. She grabbed it and maneuvered it until it was by her side. Serrations lined an eight-inch section near the weapon's forked tip. She thrust her other hand up and grabbed the living cord that attached the glowing orb to one of the anglerbeast's sensor panels. The creature immediately tried to contract the cord and pull its orb back, but Infinity held it tightly. She raised the mandible and started sawing the cord with all the strength she could muster.

The creature pulled back, actually lifting Infinity toward the mound's surface. Her shoulder rammed painfully against a girder but she ignored this and sawed even harder. The angler-beast stepped back and lowered its forelegs to the ground. Infinity almost dropped the mandible as she was pulled up and out of the mound. Still hacking furiously at the cord, she locked her legs around a girder to keep herself from being dragged down the slope. Finally, the mandible severed the cord, and Infinity fell back through the gap in the girders. She came to a stop entangled in the framework, still gripping the orb by the six inches of cord attached to it. The orb continued glowing, now even more brightly than before.

Infinity thought she heard Gideon yelling, but the incessant buzzing was so loud she couldn't be sure. She held the orb out in his direction and glimpsed him through the framework, wildly slapping at flies as they swarmed his body. "Gideon!"

She couldn't tell whether he'd heard her—either way, there was little she could do. He was fighting a losing battle, and soon his entire body would be covered by the swarm.

She suddenly realized the flies buzzing around her were keeping their distance. Why? The only possible reason she could think of was that she was holding the glowing orb. She raised it over her head. The mass of flies above her surged upward, apparently repelled by the orb. It was about time she caught a goddamn break. Holding the orb in one hand, she scrambled up and out and then made her way over to Gideon's position. She crawled headfirst down toward him.

By the time she reached him he was starting to choke on flies that had entered his mouth. Infinity thrust the orb out and held it within inches of his head. The swarm quickly abandoned him.

He gagged a few times and then spit out a mass of dark goo. He looked up at Infinity with a terrified expression, his face covered in smashed bugs.

"Damn things were getting into my head, taking over my thoughts," he said.

"Yeah," Infinity replied. "We're getting the hell out of here. You good now?"

He nodded. "Good enough."

She backed out of the hole, and seconds later she and Gideon were sitting on the mound's surface. The swarm had encircled them entirely, staying back about four feet. The orb in Infinity's hand illuminated the flies, making it look like the two humans were enclosed in a pulsating sphere. The bugs were so thick that Infinity couldn't see beyond them. She had no way to know whether the anglerbeast was still waiting below.

Regardless, it was time to go—the glow of the severed orb would surely start diminishing soon. Infinity grabbed the mandible weapon and handed the orb to Gideon so she'd have a free hand to climb with. "You really don't want to drop that," she said.

He thrust the orb out to arm's length and watched the swarm shift in response to its proximity. "Damn straight."

She and Gideon made their way down the slope to the ground. The flies followed but never ventured any closer to the orb. When they had walked about ten yards from the mound's base, the swarm lifted and returned to the hive. For whatever reason, the creatures were unwilling to go any farther.

Infinity scanned the area and saw no sign of the anglerbeast. She then turned back to get a look at the mound and realized this hive wasn't surrounded by balled-up isopods. Perhaps it was inhabited by a different species of fly? She shook her head and turned to Gideon. "Are you yourself now?"

He spat on the ground and then wiped his mouth. He nodded. "I was about gone. A few more seconds and they would've had control of my mind. So... thanks."

"Don't thank me yet. We're not done. We're still going after Desmond." She held her free hand out for the orb. After he handed it to her, she started walking east.

He followed behind her. "Do we have a plan?"

She raised the orb. "If this thing's still glowing when we get there, then yes."

INFINITY AND GIDEON stood ten yards from the hive mound that had possessed the others. In the dark, its looming shape appeared similar to that of every other framework mound. But the dark shapes of the sleeping isopods around its base and the pulsating thrum from within confirmed they were at the right mound.

They had already circled the entire hill at a safe distance and had seen no signs of Desmond, Emily, or the tiger beetle. Infinity could only assume Desmond was somewhere inside the mound. It was possible he had been killed before making it here, but she sure as hell wasn't leaving until she either had confirmed he was dead or had extracted him from the mound alive.

Before approaching the hive's mound, she and Gideon had gone to one of the other nearby mounds, where she had instructed him on how to make a contained fire with girder pieces and dead moss. They had then twisted handfuls of dry moss together with older, wet moss to make two serviceable torches that would each burn for several minutes. If things went south, Gideon was to quickly make a fire and light one of these torches.

Infinity looked at the orb in her hand. Its glow was now less intense than before. There was no time to waste. She turned to Gideon. "Let's do this."

"You sure you don't want me to go in instead?"

She shook her head. "I'm smaller. I can get in and out faster. And I know Desmond better than you do. I might have an easier time talking sense into him if the hive is influencing his mind. I need to do this."

Gideon nodded. "I'll be within earshot. Holler if you need help. But fair warning—if you tell me to burn that mound while you're still in it, I'm not sure I'll be willing to do that."

She nodded once. "I may not need you to burn it, but I will need you to be *ready* to burn it. The danger needs to be imminent and credible."

"Understood."

She left the mandible with him and strode to the base of the mound, passing between two balled-up isopods. Holding the orb in one hand, she used her free hand and her feet to begin climbing the slope. When she was halfway to the peak, she paused. The sound of the humming swarm within wasn't changing. Perhaps the creatures were still unaware of her presence. She had half-expected Emily—and perhaps even Desmond—to be guarding the place, but they were still nowhere to be seen. As much as she wanted to be wrong, she had no choice but to enter the mound.

She continued climbing. The main source of the humming sounded like it was coming from directly beneath the peak. She figured that would be the best place to begin. When she reached the summit, she was surprised to find a large opening. The hive's thrumming was coming from directly below.

Infinity shook her head, attempting to shed her fear. She then began descending the open shaft, grasping girders with her free hand. After she had descended about ten feet, she paused to look down. The surrounding framework was illuminated by the pinkish light cast by the anglerbeast's orb, but beyond a radius of about eight feet there was only darkness. The swarm's humming sounded close now, but she still couldn't see its source. She continued downward.

The shaft gradually widened to about twice the size it had been at its opening. Finally, something came into view at the edge of her sphere of light. Like the background beyond, the shape was black, but it reflected enough light to show that it was more than just empty space. It was shifting and pulsating.

Infinity continued descending until she was at the same level as the shape behind her. She turned to look again and could now see that the black mass was a cylindrical column, perhaps five feet in diameter. It almost appeared to be solid, but she knew it was composed of countless winged creatures, each of them smaller than the tiniest fly. She had made it to the hive.

Her feet found the ground, and she released her grip on the girders and turned. Several shapes, completely covered in flies, were arranged around the chamber's inner perimeter. She looked from one of them to the next. Her eyes landed on one of the shapes and her throat constricted. It was roughly the shape of a human, sitting with crossed legs.

It was possible that this was just a mass of flies in the shape of a human, a trick she had seen the creatures do when they'd mimicked Eagleton's form and movements. She took a deep breath and stepped closer, holding the orb out to get a better look. As she did this, the swarm's humming began to grow louder, as if the hive were becoming agitated. At the same time, the flies in human form began to disperse, fleeing from the orb.

The shape grew smaller as the flies scattered. Skin began to appear, first only patches and then entire body parts—a forehead, a nose, a set of eyes. Desmond.

Infinity felt like she couldn't breathe.

Desmond's eyes fluttered open. He squinted at the glowing orb, and then his eyes found hers. He smiled. "Infinity, I'm so glad you're here." Then he frowned. "You're disturbing the hive with that light. You need to take it away."

Infinity forced herself to exhale. "Your face was covered with those things. How could you breathe?"

His frown deepened. "You haven't talked to the hive yet? You're not here as a friend, are you?"

"I'm here as *your* friend. I want you to come with me."

He unfolded his legs and got to his feet. He gazed at her for a moment, turned to glance at the massive black swarm, and then turned back to her. "Something is wrong. The hive should have already talked to you."

"I don't want the hive to talk to me. I'm not going to allow it to."

His brows furrowed in confusion. "But you need to understand. The hive will talk to you and help you understand." He took a step closer. "Give me that light."

She pulled the orb back out of his reach. "I want you to see something." She stepped around him, approached the black column of flies, and thrust the orb to within inches of the swarm. The column responded by shifting away, revealing a framework of girders beneath. Their buzzing became even louder.

"You're disturbing them!" Desmond said, appearing to be genuinely upset.

"Yes," she said. "And I'm going to do a lot more than disturb them if you don't come with me right now." She held up the orb. "I'll drive them out of this mound. They wouldn't like that, would they? They might even die."

Desmond's eyes widened, as though he were shocked that she could even say such a thing. He held out a hand, palm down, as if to calm her. "You don't understand, Infinity. They don't intend to hurt us."

Infinity growled in frustration. "I don't give a shit what they intend! They've taken control of your mind. That's not okay."

Infinity saw movement to her left, and she turned. The other shapes, previously covered in flies, were now emerging as the flies dispersed. An arm became visible on one of them, and then a face. It was Emily Sanchez, blinking and taking in the scene around her.

Infinity's attention shifted to the other emerging shapes. There were four, all of them apparently creatures of the same species, insect-like animals the size of cocker spaniels. Now completely uncovered, the creatures all got to their feet and began turning in circles, as if scanning their surroundings. One by one, they all stopped as they faced Infinity. They each had four long legs with climbing hooks for feet. Below the head were two arm-like appendages with pincers for grasping. The head resembled a hardhat and was held above the body by a thin neck. Any bug this size would be startling, but otherwise there was nothing particularly threatening about the appearance of these animals. They made Infinity think of delicate shrimp that fed on tiny specks of food. But she wasn't going to bet on them being harmless. For all she knew, these things could be deadly.

Emily spoke up. "I'm surprised to see you here, Infinity. I thought you'd have to be dragged kicking and screaming."

"Listen to me carefully," Infinity said. "You're both coming with me. We're going back to Mossview." She paused, unsure about whether it was time to escalate the situation. "You both seem very fond of this hive. I'm betting you'd be willing to do whatever it takes to prevent the hive's death."

Emily suddenly stepped toward her menacingly. "Give me that light!"

Infinity dodged her and rushed over to the column of flies. She held out the orb, and the swarm went into a frenzy trying to move away. "Gideon!" she shouted. "Can you hear me?"

"I hear you." His voice was faint over the swarm's droning.

"Get that fire ready! Let me know when you're ready to torch the mound. If I don't respond, do it!"

"You got it, Infinity."

Desmond and Emily glanced at each other, their faces showing real alarm.

Emily shook her head. "Infinity, this is wrong. You can't be serious."

Infinity held up the orb, illuminating her own face. "Do I not look serious to you?"

Desmond stepped up to the swarm and shoved both his hands into the mass of flies. The swarm immediately covered his entire body except for his face. He then withdrew his hands and turned to Infinity. "She is threatening to burn the entire mound."

Infinity stared at him, puzzled.

Desmond spoke again, but this time his voice sounded different, more slurred. "We do not want her to burn the mound. We will not allow her to do this."

"I don't think you can stop her," he said, his voice sounding normal again. "She doesn't understand, and she is afraid. I know her very well, and I believe her when she says she will burn the mound."

While Desmond had been speaking, his gaze had gradually drifted down toward his feet, but now he snapped his head back up and looked directly at Infinity. "We do not want you to harm us. We want to talk to you instead."

"Listen," Infinity said. "You're not coming near me. If you

don't want me to burn your mound, you need to get the hell out of my friends' minds. Let them go with me back to Mossview. If you do that, I won't hurt you. If you don't do it, I'll have Gideon burn your mound right now. If you escape the mound before the fire kills you, I or one of my friends will burn the next mound you move into. And the one after that. And we'll kill all of the isopods that provide you with food."

For several long seconds, Desmond gazed at her with no expression. "We do not want you to do those things."

Infinity noticed the chamber wasn't as brightly illuminated as before. The anglerbeast's severed orb was dimming more rapidly now. "Then get out of the minds of my friends. I want to take them with me. Now!"

Desmond glanced down at the fading orb. "We will come to you soon, and we will talk to you. Then you will understand, and you will not hurt us."

"Goddammit, I'm not kidding. Gideon! You got that fire going yet?"

"It's ready," his voice replied faintly.

Infinity looked in the direction of Gideon's voice. She could see a flickering orange glow through the framework. "You see that?" she said to Desmond. "It doesn't matter what you do to me. If I don't leave this mound with my friends right now, Gideon is going to torch the whole damn place."

Desmond turned and gazed toward Gideon. "We do not want you to do that. It would kill you. And it would kill Desmond. And Emily. We want to talk to you instead."

Infinity felt a twinge of uncertainty. Was the hive actually concerned that the fire would kill her and the other humans? Or was it just pretending, as a form of self-preservation? "Why do you want to talk to us, anyway?"

"We like talking to you. You are different from all other creatures we have ever talked to. And so we want to understand you. Desmond talks to us in a different way. We especially like talking to him."

Infinity chewed her lip, considering this. Was it possible this was all the hive really wanted? Someone to talk to? She looked down at the orb in her hand. It was getting dimmer with each passing minute.

"Infinity, you okay in there?" Gideon shouted.

"Yes, but keep that fire ready," she replied. She then eyed Desmond. "I have an idea you might like. If you get out of Desmond's and Emily's minds right now and let them go with me, then I promise one of us will come back here to talk to you often. Every day if that's what you want. But you have to promise to talk to us without taking over our minds and trying to force us to stay here. We want to stay in our own colony, with our own kind. If at any point you try to make one of us stay here, others will come and burn your hive and kill your isopods. Does that sound like an agreeable arrangement to you?"

Desmond responded immediately. "Yes. Yes, yes, yes. We like that arrangement. We want to talk to Desmond often. To all of you."

Infinity decided to push her luck one step further. She had been pondering something since listening to Desmond, Lenny, and Xavier discuss the mutualistic relationship between the hive and the isopods. "I have one additional requirement for our arrangement." She paused.

Desmond continued staring at her with no expression, his entire body covered in a black cloak of flies except for his face.

Infinity swallowed. What she was about to ask could possibly determine the fate of the last human colony. "We know you do something to the isopods to make them safe. Predators won't go near them. I want you to make me and all my people safe from predators, too."

Desmond turned his head slightly to the side, as if he were listening for a distant sound. His eyes then flicked back to meet hers. "We like this arrangement. We will talk to one of you every day. You will not harm us. And predators will not harm you. This is a good arrangement."

Infinity let out a long breath, suddenly realizing she'd been holding it in. "So you'll release my friends now and let us go?"

"Yes, that is part of the arrangement. Each of you will have to come to our hive so that we can make you safe from predators. And you will have to return often."

Desmond abruptly blinked a few times, looking confused. The flies quickly lifted from his body and drifted like a wisp of smoke over to Emily, covering her shoulders and head, including her face. After several seconds they left her too and returned to the swarm's main mass.

"Well, that was one hell of a turn of events," Emily said.

Infinity stepped up to Desmond and looked him in the eyes. "Are you back?"

He extended a hand and placed it on her shoulder. She heard his words silently in her mind. "I was never really gone. But if you're asking if I'm willing to leave the hive now, I am."

***

As INFINITY CRAWLED down the slope of the hive's mound with Desmond and Emily, she spotted Gideon sitting beside the small fire he'd been nurturing. When he noticed them, he got to his feet and snuffed out the flames with his bare foot.

"Damn, Infinity, remind me never to underestimate you," he said.

"You don't know the half of it," she said as she and Desmond slid the last few yards to the ground.

Gideon picked up something from the ground and brought it over—Desmond's mandible weapon. He started to give it to Desmond, but then he paused and eyed Infinity, his face barely lit by the nearly-extinguished orb in her hand. "Is he in any shape to have this back?"

Infinity glanced at Desmond. "You going to use that thing on us?"

Desmond half-smiled. "Of course not. Eventually you're going to have to trust the hive, you know." He turned to Gideon and accepted the weapon. He then asked, "Were you really going to torch the mound?"

The guardsman shrugged. "Hadn't decided yet. Maybe."

Emily said, "You're going to be really glad you didn't."

Infinity tossed the dying orb to the ground and started walking. "Let's go home."

They made their way west, hugging the edges of framework hills as much as possible in case they needed quick access to shelter. Infinity had no idea when or how the hive intended to make them repellant to predators, but it didn't seem wise to assume they had already done so. Perhaps they didn't even intend to.

"Do you think the hive is capable of lying?" she asked the others as they walked.

"No," Desmond replied almost immediately. "I know it will be hard for you to believe, but the hive is oblivious to the concepts of malice or deceit. And although it's probably more intelligent than you think, it's also extremely isolated. The hive may be made up of billions of individuals, but the collective intelligence is only one mind. There are other hives, and some of them aren't all that far away, but there is no way for them to interact with each other. The only time any of them leave their mound is when the hive gets too large and its population splits. Some of them fly off to settle in another mound, where they gradually gain awareness as a juvenile collective intelligence with the mind of a child. Each hive learns to think and survive on its own. As a result, all the hives presumably have different personalities and strategies for accomplishing things."

Infinity realized this could explain the absence of isopods surrounding the hive she and Gideon had encountered. "How could you possibly know all this?" she asked.

"They taught us," Emily said.

Desmond nodded. "You'll see, the first time you talk to the hive." He paused. "You do intend to talk to the hive, right? It was the deal you made."

She considered this. Her gut instinct was telling her she should torch the hive and be done with it. But Desmond seemed so convinced. And the hive seemed to have kept its promise to release his mind. Besides, the arrangement she'd made with the hive was intriguing, not to mention tactically beneficial. "Yes, I intend to, as long as I continue to feel the hive isn't a threat."

"What about when the hives fly up out of their mounds in the morning?" Gideon asked. "You said they only leave the mound when they split off into new hives. Don't they leave the hive every morning?"

"I didn't have a chance to learn about that," Desmond said.

"Nor did I," Emily added.

"Infinity," Desmond said, "you made a reasonable arrangement with the hive. But you were actually thinking very small."

Infinity bristled. "What's that supposed to mean?"

"It's not your fault, you couldn't have known. But this particular hive is capable of providing more than what you asked for. Very much more."

She looked over at him. His pale face bobbed up and down in the darkness like a glowing orb on a walking anglerbeast.

"Damn, would you look at that," Gideon said.

They all followed his gaze. Mossview was only a hundred yards away, to the northwest. A warm glow of firelight was visible in its center. A column of smoke was gently rising from its peak against a backdrop of rocky hillside. In the starry sky above were familiar constellations, including the Big Dipper.

Desmond grasped Infinity's hand. "I was happy when I was with the hive, even though you may not understand why. But this... this is home."

14

____

COLLECTIVE

Four Days Later

Desmond smiled as he watched Lenny's face. "Whenever you're ready, just hold one of your hands out."

Lenny shook his head slightly. "Nope. Nope, nope, nope, nope. Not ready now, ain't never going to be ready."

"You want to spend the rest of your life hiding from tiger beetles? Man up and get it over with. If Isabelle could do it, I'm sure you can too."

That did the trick. Lenny closed his eyes and mumbled something incoherent. Then he extended a hand until his fingers entered the black, swirling swarm. The flies swept up his arm and onto the rest of his body, covering every part of him but his face. His mouth opened briefly in protest, but then he relaxed.

Desmond smiled again and turned away. The process would go smoothly, just as it had with Richard, Poppy, and Isabelle. He had brought one person with him to meet the hive on each of his daily visits. So far, no one had completely freaked out, and the hive hadn't violated its agreement to not take over their minds. Not only that, but the predator repellent had proven to be effective on more than one occasion.

Unfortunately, the repellent wasn't permanent. It was actually nothing more than a chemical applied to the humans' skin and would eventually wash off. It had occurred to Desmond that the hive may have arranged it this way on purpose. The collective intelligence seemed intent on ensuring daily human visits, and what better way to ensure the humans would keep coming back?

The success of the arrangement so far had not yet diminished Infinity's reluctance to trust the hive. No big surprise there. She was currently waiting outside the hive mound, as she had each time another colonist had been brought here to meet the hive. She intended to torch the mound if the hive tried to renege on their arrangement.

Desmond scanned the mound's central chamber until he spotted one of the four thirty-pound arthropods that were permanent residents here. The creatures seemed to serve the purpose of cleaning up by removing debris. Which was why Desmond had named them *house elves*. For the last two days, the house elves had been busy removing every scrap of dead moss from the mound's floor and depositing it in another framework hill hundreds of yards away. The hive had recently become concerned, for good reason, that their mound was vulnerable to fire. Desmond was certain the hive did not intend to abandon their arrangement, but he hadn't yet told Infinity about the house elves' current efforts, for fear of what she might do. She was simply not predisposed to trusting anyone or anything.

Desmond glanced back at Lenny, who now had his eyes closed. It would be at least another fifteen minutes before the hive was finished with him, so Desmond stepped over to the heart of the hive and extended a hand. Seconds later, the minuscule creatures had covered him and established a connection with his thoughts.

Although the flies were proficient at projecting detailed visual scenarios into his mind, they were apparently incapable of projecting simple words and sentences in this way. They would always speak by physically controlling Desmond's mouth. To simplify things, Desmond chose to project his words mentally.

"We are happy you have come to talk to us again, Desmond," his mouth said. "We have been waiting for you."

He smiled in response. Then he relaxed his face, which had seemed to make it easier for the hive to speak through his mouth. "Well, I have been busy with other tasks," he projected silently. "Our human colony is just getting started. You would be surprised at how many problems we have to solve."

"It must be difficult for you, with each of your minds functioning independently of all the others. It is a wonder you can solve any problems at all. Tell us how you manage this, please."

Desmond thought for a moment before answering. "Sometimes we discuss matters between ourselves, coming up with solutions that everyone can agree on. And sometimes it works better if we just designate a leader. The leader hears everyone's opinions and then makes a decision, and everyone goes along with that decision, even if some of them don't agree with it."

"Such a way of doing things is confusing," the hive said with Desmond's mouth. "You should consider forming one hive mind."

Desmond smiled again, although he was aware the gesture temporarily wrested control of his facial muscles from the hive. "There are only eighteen of us," he said silently, "whereas your population numbers in the billions. At least. You are better equipped for this collective intelligence thing. Besides, we have eighteen minds that can think about problems in eighteen different ways. You have only one mind."

"This is true," the hive said.

After a few seconds, Desmond said, "There are many other hives out there. We've seen some of them. Perhaps if you communicated with them, you could solve problems together like we do."

"Yes, we are aware that there are other hives. We would like to talk to them. But they are too far away. We cannot all leave our hive, as that would require that we put too much distance between our individual bodies. Leaving our hive would destroy our mind. And since we cannot leave, we like talking to you. You come into our hive, and you talk to us in a way that is different from all the other creatures we have talked to. We are happy you are here."

"Are the other hives like you? Do they also long for someone to talk to?"

"We do not know what the other hives are like. They are too far."

The conversation continued for several more minutes until Desmond's mouth abruptly said, "We like talking to your friend, Lenny, but we have finished our treatment. He will now be safe from predators. Because we like our arrangement."

The flies began leaving Lenny's body. Seconds later he opened his eyes. He blinked a few times and scanned his surroundings until he found Desmond. "Brother, in a million freaking years, I never would have imagined I'd ever experience something like that. What a rip-snortin' mind-fuck."

"Infinity, you *have* to do this!" Lenny said as he and Desmond slid down the last few yards of the slope. "I know you're not keen on it, but damn!"

Infinity got to her feet. "Still sounds like brainwashing to me. I won't do it until everyone else has. And even then I won't unless one of you swears you'll stand guard and be ready to torch the mound at my command."

Desmond glanced at the pile of dead moss and the fire-starting tools at her feet. He decided it was time to fill her in on the hive's recent activities. "Um, about that. Just so you know, the hive has been taking measures to make sure you can't burn their mound. The house elves are removing all the combustible material and transporting it to another mound. They'll probably complete the task within another day or so."

She glared at him. "How long have you known about this?"

He sighed and tried to form a sheepish grin. "I didn't want to alarm you."

She continued glaring at him a few more seconds. Finally, a growl erupted from her throat as she kicked the pile of dead moss. "I don't know what the hell you've done to me. There was a time when I would have beaten someone senseless for hiding something so important. But you... I can't even force myself to stay mad at you. Maybe the hive has given you the ability to control people's minds."

Desmond smiled for real this time. "If I could control your mind, you wouldn't be mad right now."

Her eyes narrowed. "Don't push it."

Lenny rubbed his hands together excitedly. "I know what it is. It's the fact that we all know there are only eighteen humans on this world. You both know you can't afford to be mad at each other. That's like, love, man."

Desmond watched Infinity's face. "It is," he said. "It's very much like love."

Finally, the edges of her mouth turned up slightly. "Let's go. We've got work to do." She turned and began leading the way west.

Desmond and Lenny followed.

"Me?" said Lenny. "I'm focusing my attentions on Isabelle. And, lucky for me, there aren't that many guys for me to compete with."

"What about Gideon?" Infinity said over her shoulder. "He'd be a hell of a catch."

Lenny remained silent for a moment. "Don't mess with my mind, Infinity. It's fragile."

Desmond and Infinity sat on the slope overlooking Mossview and the plain, the sun dropping behind the rocky hillside to their backs. Five colonists were still at work on the mound's peak, hoisting up one of the shell segments from the isopod they had killed the previous day. The plan was to tie it in place using cord Lenny and Xavier had made from the isopod's internal connective tissue. Removing the shell segments from the isopod and scraping them clean had been a labor-intensive job, but the colonists were turning out to be hard workers, likely motivated by the prospect of a dry, comfortable shelter. So far, they had only shingled an area about ten feet across. But the vast plain was home to a seemingly endless supply of isopods.

Chloe, Àurea, and Sarah had volunteered to work on the daunting problem of making clothing. With no plant fibers longer than a few inches, they had little choice but to use animal parts. Upon discovering the pliable, leathery skin that covered much of the isopods' underside, they had immediately declared this resource off limits for any other use but for making clothing. So far they hadn't created anything the colonists were willing to place in direct contact with their skin, but their efforts were ongoing.

Desmond looked at his palms. They were blistered from having spent several hours helping Gideon and Richard dig a latrine two hundred yards from Mossview. Poppy had convinced Desmond that his initial idea of depositing human waste in the stream to be carried away by the current had been ill-considered. For now, the latrine was nothing more than an open hole, but Richard had volunteered to take on the task of somehow building an outhouse around it, perhaps even with a seat. Like the clothing, the outhouse would likely have to be constructed from animal parts.

After Infinity had been sitting in comfortable silence with Desmond for several minutes, she said, "You washed yourself off in the river, didn't you?"

"Why? Do I stink?" He realized Infinity was looking to the north and followed her gaze. Two tiger beetles were making their way along the hillside. The predators were higher up the slope, but then they spotted the two humans and changed course. "One washing shouldn't diminish my repellent much," he said. "I think we'll be fine.'

"You *think*? That's not good enough. Should we run for the shelter or not?"

Desmond took a deep breath. The predators were about to cross the critical threshold beyond which they'd be too close to outrun. His repellent had already proven itself to be effective, but that had been before he'd bathed. "We don't need to run," he said firmly.

The predators kept coming. It was definitely too late to flee now. At fifty yards they began trotting, and then they were running. Desmond fought to stay calm, but his heart was pounding. He saw Infinity's muscles tense up.

"Dammit, you'd better be right," she muttered. She grabbed her girder weapon and got to her feet.

"I'm right!" Desmond replied. He didn't get up, but he felt himself gripping his mandible weapon more tightly.

The creatures skidded to a stop ten yards out, their clawed feet digging into the soil and scattering clumps of moss. They shook their heads, brandishing their mandibles.

Infinity stayed on her feet. She and Desmond watched the creatures pace back and forth until they finally gave up and continue on their way to the southwest.

"I trust the hive," he said.

She snorted. "Yeah, you've made that clear." She set her weapon down, shoved his legs apart with her foot, and then sat between them with her back against his chest. Together they gazed down at Mossview. A fire was already glowing from within the structure. The others were no doubt cooking a second meal of isopod meat. The first had been yesterday, and the meat had been decidedly better than mashed hubcap tissue.

"I actually think we may have a decent chance of surviving here for awhile," Infinity said softly. "Unless we get sick."

Desmond put his arms around her and intertwined his fingers over her belly. "I honestly don't think there's much chance of disease. Some of these creatures, like the isopods, are warm-blooded. But they're arthropods, not mammals. In fact, they're so different from the arthropods from home, they'd probably be classified in a whole new phylum. We may get minor bacterial infections in our wounds, but any disease pathogen adapted to the creatures of this world just wouldn't be capable of infecting our bodies."

"Famous last words," she said.

"Well, either way, we have no soap, no antibiotics, and definitely no bio-suits. There's no point in worrying about something we can't control."

"Everything can be controlled. We just haven't figured out how yet."

He kissed her on the head above her right ear. The bristles of hair that were already covering her scalp tickled his lips. Her fingers tapped his knee rhythmically, and he could tell she was still anxious about something. He waited, watching the faint fire in Mossview as it glowed like a beacon in the encroaching darkness.

Finally she spoke. "There's something I need to tell you." She gently disentangled his right hand from his left and moved his fingers to a spot on her belly. "You feel these scars?"

He ran a finger lightly over her skin, feeling the slight ridges. "Yeah. You have three of them there. You've never told me what they're from."

"They're from a knife. It happened a long time ago, but... well, there's a good chance I can't have babies."

This was the last thing he had expected her to say. It took him a moment to even process her words. He was acutely aware that he needed to choose his next words carefully. He cleared his throat. "Did a doctor tell you that? Or are you making an assumption?"

"A doctor examined it when it happened. I was sixteen. There was damage to my cervix."

"You were in a knife fight at sixteen?"

She stared out over the plain without answering.

Desmond inhaled deeply. "In case you were afraid that this news would disappoint me, it doesn't. It's not your job to have babies." He pulled his hand from under hers and started counting off with his fingers. "We've got Isabelle, Celia, Poppy, Àurea, Sarah, and Emily. And there's even Chloe and President Millwright. They seem healthy enough, despite their age. The human species isn't going to go extinct because of your knife wounds." Desmond then regretted making this last statement. He knew Infinity already felt at least partly responsible for the deaths of eight billion people. He decided to shut up, for fear of making things worse.

"There were supposed to be 720 in this colony," she said.

"Yeah, well, it's hard enough keeping eighteen out of trouble."

She let a brief laugh escape.

Desmond wrapped his arms around her waist again. "Should we head back before the others start to worry?"

She caressed his knee. "Nope. I told Xavier and Lenny we'd be out late. In fact, I told them we'd probably spend the night up here."

Desmond felt his pulse quicken. "Seriously?"

"When I saw you bathing in the river, I decided to bathe too. Why do you suppose I did that?"

He smiled and pulled her closer. "But... sleeping out here in the open?"

She turned around and pushed him back onto the soft moss. "It's our first night alone on this world. How much sleeping do you expect we'll do?"

***

DESMOND AWOKE to a hand gently shaking his shoulder.

"You're missing the sunrise," Infinity whispered.

He opened his eyes. She was sitting up beside him, elbows on her knees, staring out to the east. He rubbed his eyelids to clear them as he sat up. "Unbelievable. There's not even a chill in the air. This world is growing on me more every day."

Infinity pointed to the northeast. "Take a look at that."

It took Desmond a moment to realize what she was pointing at. As usual, he could see the large river miles away, sparkling in the light of the rising sun. Then he noticed that the ground on their side of the river was gray instead of its usual green. He squinted. The gray color was actually a herd of animals, steadily moving from west to east, parallel to the river. The herd was incomprehensibly vast, at least two or three miles wide and stretching out along the river for as far as Desmond could see to the east and west.

"Do you think they're isopods?" Infinity asked.

"I can't tell. They're large—there's no doubt about that. I can make out individuals even from this distance."

She took his hand and squeezed it. "I've been to a lot of alternate versions of Earth, but this might be the most beautiful sight I've ever seen."

"I wish I could have gone with you to all those worlds."

"No you don't. You've been on enough excursions to know that most of them are just different versions of hell."

Desmond gazed at the massive herd as it moved east. "I wonder if there are other species here that have evolved collective intelligence. Like that herd, for example."

"God, I hope not."

Desmond noticed a smoke-like column rising from a framework mound almost directly in his line of sight to the rising sun—the first hive to emerge for the morning ritual. He pointed it out to Infinity and said, "I've finally learned from the hive why they and the other hives do that every morning."

She pointed to a second smoky column several miles to the south. "Let me guess. It's their morning workout."

He smiled. "That might actually be part of it. But it's more complex than that. First you have to understand that each hive is one mind, and each of those minds has existed in isolation for a really, really long time. I'm talking millennia. They have each developed to intellectual maturity in their own way. I don't know much about the other hives, but our hive is intelligent and inquisitive. I can only assume the others are as well. They can't disperse from their mounds without disabling their own collective intelligence. So they exist in isolation, year after year after year. Imagine what that must be like. The hive regularly probes the minds of other native creatures, but none of those have been capable of sophisticated thought."

"And then we came along," Infinity said.

He nodded. "Originally I thought, like you said, that the morning ritual served a purpose related to exercise. Or maybe thermoregulation of the hive, or acquisition of oxygen. But the truth is more fascinating. We already know the creatures act as a collective intelligence, but they also have at least one *physical* function that is collective as well, a concept that still boggles my mind. As it turns out, each individual fly has a rudimentary eye, capable only of seeing rough shapes and discerning intensity of light. But together, with millions of flies looking in the same direction, they have collective vision. Apparently the hive mind can see considerable detail, even at a distance."

Infinity shook her head. "You've got to be kidding."

"It's true. Like I said before, I don't think the hive even knows how to lie. But here's the kicker. The morning ritual— flying high over the hive—is their small way of making contact with other hives. They can never go out and visit another hive or truly have a conversation with them. But this ritual is their way of saying, 'Hello, we exist, and we see that you exist, too.'"

Infinity stared out over the plain without speaking.

Desmond now counted eight hive plumes, each of them churning and spiraling, their collective movements looking almost playful. They were beautiful, despite being a symptom of profound and utter loneliness.

After at least a minute of silence, Infinity said, "I'll do it—I'll take my turn today. I think I'm ready to meet the hive."

15

———————

EXISTENCE

NINETEEN MONTHS Later - April 9

INFINITY PAUSED her story to think. After a moment, she resumed. "So, Dorothy was frightened, and she tried to run. But the flying monkeys were too fast. They caught up to her and surrounded her, and they kept shrieking and laughing at her. Dorothy knew her friends were hiding. They wouldn't be able to help her. She looked at the nearest monkey, which was taller than all the others. He was their leader. She decided her best bet was to take him out first. She said, 'I'm afraid of lions, and tigers, and bears, but I'm not afraid of you!' She pulled the tin man's axe from where she'd hidden it in her dress, and the monkey jumped back in surprise. She swung it mightily, slicing the monkey's head cleanly from his shoulders. She then took out seven more flying monkeys without breaking a sweat. The axe, soaked in monkey blood, was a blur of motion as she swung it with the expertise she'd gained from her years of training. But there were just too many of them. The monkeys eventually overwhelmed her and carried her away kicking and screaming. They flew straight to the witch's castle."

Infinity decided to stop there. "That's it for today's episode." She then relaxed her mouth to make it easier for the hive to take control.

"We like your story," her mouth said. "We want you to tell the next episode now, please."

She smiled. "You always want the next episode now. But I have other things I need to do today. I'll try to come tomorrow. If I don't make it, don't get worried. I'll come back soon." She started to get to her feet but then paused. "By the way, Grimhold Hive asked me to tell you they really enjoyed my Winnie the Pooh story. They recommend you request it next. Also, they have a house elf they'd like to give you. It would be a gift—a gesture of friendship. Sort of. They did want me to ask what you might do for them in return. Since you don't have house elves here, I'd recommend you accept the offer. House elves can be damn handy to have around. They do smell, but I doubt you'll care about that."

"Yes, we want the Winnie the Pooh story," her mouth said. "And we will accept the house elf. Perhaps we can send Grimhold Hive some skitterbugs in return."

Infinity shuddered. She still hated skitterbugs, even though the hundreds of them living in this mound with Aerafall Hive had never tried to harm her. "I'll let them know," she said. "I'll even lead the skitterbugs there, as long as the damn things keep their distance."

"Do you have any news from Goggleglen, Laghollow, or Duskmere?"

"Not today," Infinity said as she got to her feet. "I haven't had a chance to visit the other hives in a while." Infinity and the colonists had created alliances with five hives in total, and

Desmond, Lenny, and Xavier had insisted on giving each one a stupid name like Goggleglen. Apparently these names came from fantasy books. Infinity would have preferred giving them names that were easier to remember, like Hive One and Hive Two.

"Thank you for coming to talk," Aerafall Hive said through Infinity's mouth. "Please come again tomorrow."

"I'll try." Infinity held her arms out to make it easier for the flies to disperse and return to the main hive heart a few yards away. She took a moment to carefully comb her fingers through her hair to work out any remaining flies. Her hair was now about ten inches long, and sometimes it drove her crazy. It was always getting tangled and blocking her vision. One of these days she was going to hack it all off with a girder shard. She took a moment to gently shake the straggler flies from her tunic and shorts. Both articles of clothing had been made by weaving together thin strips of isopod belly leather. The leather first had to be softened by grinding it between stones, but then it could be used to produce durable and reasonably comfortable material.

Desmond and Jagger were waiting for her outside the hive's mound. Jagger was a creature about the size of an isopod but with six legs built for speed and power. The creature had been a gift from Laghollow Hive. Jagger looked fierce at first glance, but like the isopods, it was a moss grazer and scavenger. And Laghollow Hive had somehow made it as docile as a saddle horse. Because the creature's abdomen vaguely resembled that of a lobster, and because it was willing to allow the colonists to ride on its back, Lenny had given the species the name *lobstersteed*.

As Infinity descended the mound, Desmond looked up from the shard of isopod bone he had been sharpening against a stone gripped between his feet. His hair, also now about ten inches long, was tied back in a ponytail with gut cord. If Infinity squinted slightly, he looked similar to the Desmond she'd first met nearly two years ago. But back then he'd been soft, maybe even a bit pudgy. Now he was lean, his features hardened by many months of hard work and protein-rich food. Infinity would never admit it out loud, but sometimes when he turned to look at her, it nearly took her breath away. This was one of those moments.

He got to his feet and put the bone shard in one of the pockets of his tunic. "We're going to be late," he said matter-of-factly, breaking the spell of the moment for Infinity.

She put one foot on the knee of Jagger's foremost left leg and used it to hoist herself onto the creature's broad back just behind its head. "We already know what the announcement's going to be. Sarah is pregnant again."

He frowned in an exaggerated way, letting her know he wasn't happy she was forcing him to sit behind her. Too bad—first one on gets first choice. He climbed on and arranged himself behind her. Infinity leaned forward and nudged Jagger's head to the left with her hand, and the creature turned. She then pushed directly on the back of its head, and it took off walking in the direction of Mossview.

"Maybe Sarah *is* pregnant," Desmond said, his mouth now inches from her ear. "But that doesn't mean we should show up late."

Infinity pushed harder on Jagger's head to speed the creature up. She then smiled to herself. Sometimes she and Desmond sounded like an old married couple. And when they did, she felt strangely content.

As THEY NEARED MOSSVIEW, Infinity realized everyone was already inside. She cursed silently. Desmond had been right—they were late.

Mossview was now entirely shingled in isopod shell segments, except for a rain-proof vent at the peak for smoke to escape. Evenly spaced around the perimeter of the dome were thirty-two windows, each about fifteen inches by six inches. Instead of glass, these windows were covered with the transparent wings of an eagle-sized animal Xavier had named, *dragonfly*. Aside from their wings, though, these creatures really looked nothing like dragonflies.

Infinity guided Jagger between two livestock pens made from framework girders. The pen on the right held seven young isopods. The smaller ones had proven to be the easiest to separate from their herds. The pen on the left contained over a hundred *hermit crabs*. Like their namesakes, these arthropods each had a spiral shell they could retreat into when threatened. But unlike the shells of true hermit crabs, these shells were actually living parts of the creatures' forty-pound bodies. The shells were made of loose segments, allowing the hermit crabs to compress them to a smaller diameter in order to crawl through tight spaces in the framework hills. The creatures fed on smaller arthropods living in the dead moss at the bottoms of the mounds, so keeping this herd fed was just a matter of hauling loads of dead moss from nearby hills. After this moss had been picked clean by the hermit crabs, it could then be burned as fuel. Due to their mild taste, Hermit crabs had become the colony's favorite food source.

Infinity and Desmond dismounted, and she tied Jagger's lead to a girder post. Desmond dragged a recently-harvested, seven-foot-long isopod shell segment over and deposited it beside Jagger. The lobstersteed immediately began scraping off fragments of soft tissue that were still clinging to the shell, not only feeding itself but also picking the shell clean enough to be used as construction material.

The two humans entered Mossview's main doorway, which now was a large opening at ground level, and walked through a narrow hallway to the central chamber. Segments of isopod shell had served to wall off smaller rooms within the mound. Situated around the central chamber were living areas—fondly referred to as apartments—for each family or individual. Actually, Gideon was now the only colonist who was not paired up with someone.

When Infinity and Desmond entered the chamber, the others were already seated in a circle around the three main fire pits, where bowls of meat stew were steaming. Lenny pointed and said, "Late! Late, late, late."

The others joined in, continuing the chant until Infinity raised both hands. "Yeah, we're late. Give me the damn mossmead."

Celia carefully picked up a basketball-sized bladder filled with liquid, waited for Infinity and Desmond to sit down, and then placed it on the ground between them.

Desmond started to pull the bladder toward himself.

Infinity pushed his hand away. "No, it's my fault we're late. I'll do it." She hefted the bladder and set it between her knees. The bag's surface was tight from internal gas pressure, but that didn't guarantee the mossmead was good. She untied the cord that held the bladder shut, and a hiss of gas hit her in the face. She frowned and looked around the room at the others, who were watching anxiously.

"Crap, it's bad," Xavier said.

Infinity picked up the bladder, poured enough liquid into her mouth that it flowed down her chin, and then smiled.

"Yes!" Xavier exclaimed, prompting laughter and cheers all around.

Infinity passed the mossmead to Desmond, who took a sizable swig and then passed it on. Mossmead had originally been Richard's creation. Its ingredients were simple: water, isopod nectar, and the tiny, pod-like structures—which Desmond called sporophytes—that grew on a specific variety of moss found near the top of the rocky hillside. About five out of every six bladders of the stuff would ferment properly, although no one had any idea what type of yeast or other microorganism was responsible for the fermentation. However, those occasional bags that didn't ferment properly were extremely unpleasant to open, which was why whoever was last to any special gathering was given the honor of opening the bladder.

As the mossmead made its first round, passing from colonist to colonist, the alcohol from Infinity's first and only swallow began tingling through her body, and she allowed herself to relax. She gazed around at her friends, still amazed at how they had adapted to this world. Except for Gideon, the colonists had all formed partnerships and family groups.

Lenny and Isabelle had hit it off from the beginning. At this moment, the two were sitting side-by-side. Each of them had a finger extended in front of them, and Daisy was gripping their fingers in her tiny hands, bouncing up and down with her chubby legs. Daisy, now ten months old, wasn't quite ready to walk, but she was getting pretty damn good at bouncing. It was rumored that Isabelle might be pregnant again, but everyone seemed content waiting for an official announcement gathering, which, like today's gathering, would no doubt involve merriment and a bladder of mossmead.

Xavier had paired up with Celia, who was now about six months pregnant. Celia was currently on her knees, making baby sounds at Daisy, and as usual the woman was wearing a backless tunic. Once, Infinity had asked her why she always kept her back exposed, and Celia had explained that she wanted the nine hundred tattoos—the supposed key to bridging technology —to be a perpetual reminder to the colonists never to give up hope that they might someday be rescued from this world. She and Xavier used to go on weekly treks to the bridge-in site. These had eventually become monthly treks, and now it had been three months since anyone had bothered to go there.

Reece Eagleton and Chloe had become partners. Although Chloe was in her late forties, she was now about eight months pregnant. Richard, their OBGYN doctor, had expressed concern about Chloe being pregnant at her age, but he was cautiously optimistic.

Richard had paired up with Poppy, although there had been no announcement yet of a pregnancy there.

The two guardsmen, Emily and Steven, were the only new couple who had insisted on having an actual wedding ceremony, which had been officiated by Hayley Millwright. Emily had given birth to a baby boy six months ago, but the child had mysteriously died five days later.

Hayley and Alexander Millwright seemed happy. As they had once promised to do, they had become essential to the colony, particularly in matters regarding food preparation and the inventing of palatable recipes. Hayley had frequently expressed how thankful she was to be in a role that had nothing to to do with politics or leadership. Alexander's leg had been amputated at the knee. But he had survived the process, thanks to the four doctors and an ample supply of isopod saliva. He now got around surprisingly well. In fact, he had become proficient at crawling through framework mounds fast enough to catch hermit crabs.

Today's gathering had been called by Àurea, Sarah, and Tyrone. These three, along with Sarah's six-month-old boy Brooks, made up the colony's most unusual family. The family had started when Àurea and Sarah decided they wanted a child. They had asked Tyrone to impregnate Sarah, and he'd been more than happy to help. This had led to Tyrone becoming part of their family, and he clearly cared deeply for both Sarah and Àurea. By the time Brooks was born, Tyrone had expanded an apartment so all four of them could live together.

The mossmead started its fourth round, and soon after, the bladder was empty. This was met with groans and half-hearted attempts to blame one colonist or another for having drank more than their share.

Sarah clacked two girder pieces together to quiet the laughter and chatter. "Before we begin eating," she said, "I want to thank you all for attending this gathering. I suppose you're waiting for our big announcement. I know... you think you already know what we're going to announce. But if you've been watching carefully, then you noticed that I happily took a drink of mossmead. Àurea, on the other hand, did not."

A chorus of surprise immediately arose, interspersed with a few comments like, "I knew it!"

Lenny tossed a wadded-up chunk of dead moss at Tyrone. "You swashbuckling Casanova! Nine women exist on this world, and you've impregnated two of them."

Amidst the groans of admonishment aimed at Lenny, Infinity discreetly watched Gideon's reaction. She had often wondered if he resented being the only colonist living alone. He was smiling, having a good time, by all outward appearances.

Gradually, the laughter and teasing quieted down as Hayley and Alexander began serving generous portions of hermit crab meat.

As Infinity was waiting for her serving, she heard a sound drifting in from outside. She tilted her head to listen. The sound had stopped, but then it came again, distant and barely audible. She looked at Desmond.

He was frowning, obviously hearing it too.

"Everyone shut up!" Infinity ordered.

The chamber became silent except for the soft babbling of Daisy and Brooks.

The sound came again, and Infinity's pulse quickened. It sounded like a voice. She jumped to her feet, ran for the main doorway, and emerged into the afternoon sunlight. The others poured out behind her, and they all stopped to listen.

The sound came again, distorted and echoing like a massive loudspeaker in the distance. "Colonists. If you can hear this, come to our location." Several seconds of silence followed. "Colonists. If you can hear this, come to our location."

The words repeated, over and over.

Infinity and Desmond approached the bridge-in site, having pushed Jagger relentlessly to cover the three-mile stretch in record time. They had left the others behind to decide who would follow on foot. By the time they had covered half the distance from Mossview, it had become clear the recorded, amplified voice was that of Armando Doyle.

As they drew near the voice's source, they stayed behind a framework hill in case the situation turned out to be threatening. Infinity dismounted, her thoughts swirling, and she felt as if she were in a surreal dream. Desmond tied Jagger to the framework mound, which was the same mound where they'd been attacked by skitterbugs that first day so many months ago.

They crept around the mound and peeked out at the bridge-in site. What they saw made Infinity wonder if she'd lost her mind.

At least a dozen men stood in a defensive circle around a cluster of objects that must have included the loudspeaker. The men were fully outfitted in black fatigues, and they were holding weapons of some kind. They were obviously military. Beside each man was a dog-sized creature that appeared to have no hair. Lying in broken heaps near the group of men and animals were two dead tiger beetles, proof that the weapons the men held were functional and deadly.

"How did they get here with clothing?" Desmond whispered near Infinity's ear. "And gear? It's impossible!"

Infinity shook her head, baffled. This *was* impossible. The bridging technology didn't allow for it.

Behind the perimeter of armed men, several people moved. Infinity watched as one of them stepped out between two of the soldiers and stood there staring directly at her and Desmond.

"Hello!" the man called out. "Colonists?"

Infinity blinked and muttered something to herself, not even aware of what she'd said. She stepped away from the mound into full view.

Desmond grabbed her elbow. "Maybe we should be careful."

"Infinity, is that you?" the man called.

"That's Armando Doyle," Infinity said. She stepped cautiously toward the newcomers.

"It's them," Armando said to the soldiers behind him. "Please lower your weapons."

The men complied, and this was enough for Infinity. She grabbed Desmond's hand, dragging him along with her as she ran toward Armando.

"I'll be damned!" Armando said. "You really are alive." He

turned to the men again. "It's Infinity and Desmond. We've found them!"

Seconds later Infinity and Armando were standing face to face.

Armando stared. "God almighty, Infinity. I hardly recognize you."

Before she could stop herself, Infinity lunged forward and threw her arms around Armando—partly because she needed proof that he was real. After embracing him for several seconds, she stepped back and gazed into his eyes. "How in the hell is this possible?"

He smiled, turned slightly, and patted his own back, apparently alluding to the nine hundred symbols tattooed beneath his shirt. "Turns out the key to bridging technology Desmond brought back is the real deal. You're going to be amazed at what we can now do. When you bridged out over a year and a half ago, the bridging device had been damaged. It malfunctioned, and we had no idea where it sent you. The SafeTrek facility was literally falling apart around us, but we were able to identify the problem and correct it, resetting the device to bridge to the original target world with a twenty-year divergence. We managed to bridge out one group, of which I was a member. But we must have done it just in time because the next group never did arrive on our destination world."

Armando gestured toward another man who had emerged from the circle of soldiers and was now gazing at Infinity and Desmond intently. "This is Dr. Kyle Fornas, a physicist from our new home world. And these good men," he nodded to the soldiers, "are highly-qualified Marines who volunteered to help us with our endeavor."

"Your endeavor?" Desmond asked, speaking up for the first time.

Armando appraised him. "It is wonderful to see you alive, Desmond. Our endeavor is the reason we are here." He looked over Infinity's shoulder into the distance. "Are the others alive as well? Celia? President Millwright? Poppy?"

"Yes, they're fine," Infinity said. "We lost two of our people within days of arriving here—William Dixon, an historian, and Alfie Lewis, a guardsman. But the rest of us are alive. In fact, we have two babies, with more on the way."

Armando's eyes widened, and he glanced down at Infinity's belly.

"No, not me," she said. "Several of the others."

"About your endeavor...." Desmond reminded him.

"Yes, yes. Well, to our great relief, we determined that the people of our destination world had not yet discovered the Outlanders' radio signal. Therefore they had not created bridging devices, and hence they had also not yet destroyed their Earth. We were lucky—they accepted us, and they were intrigued by our story. With our guidance, and with great caution, they pinpointed the Outlanders' signal. For months we puzzled over the key and how it could be used to reveal additional information hidden in the radio signal. Finally, after a breakthrough, we were able to use the key to unlock functions of the bridging technology we had previously thought to be impossible. Most importantly, we were able to create a bridging device that does *not* produce planet-destroying particles. We accomplished this seven months ago."

The weight of this statement hit Infinity like a bare fist. She and the other bridgers had killed every living thing on Earth. And all the while there had been a way to bridge without causing such an unthinkable tragedy. For whatever reason, the goddamn Outlanders had hidden this safety feature, apparently deciding it should only be available to certain civilizations.

"Since then," Armando continued, "we've stumbled upon many additional functions. We learned how to tweak the bridging device so that it will allow us to remain on a destination world for longer than thirty-six hours. Or shorter, if desired. Still, we were unable to overcome the basic limitation of bridging only living tissue. But we gained access to vast information on how to create bridgeable objects, including clothing, weapons, and the sound amplification device we used to alert you to our arrival." He turned and gestured toward the Marines.

Infinity looked closer at the men's weapons. The devices had the basic shape of rifles, but they were otherwise unlike any guns she had ever seen. "Those are alive?" she asked.

"Yes, more or less. And the creatures accompanying these fine Marines are also specially-designed weapons."

The dog-sized creatures were hairless and looked like they were made of muscle and tendon fused to pieces of white plastic. If they hadn't been visibly breathing, she would have assumed they were some type of advanced robots.

"And ultimately," Armando said, "we were able to use the new bridging device to pinpoint the specific alternate universes our previous devices had targeted as destinations. It turns out that every bridging excursion, in every universe, leaves a signature marker that is catalogued and then is accessible through technology we now possess. Almost miraculously, out of infinite possible universes, with infinite possible divergence points, we were able to zero in on this particular world, the second-to-the-last destination world targeted by a bridging device on our version of Earth. And here we are. We're here to rescue you, to take you back with us."

Infinity glanced at Desmond. He was frowning.

She turned back to Armando. "This is amazing. In fact, it's

overwhelming. But we've made a pretty good life here. I suspect that many of us will prefer to stay."

Armando shot her a puzzled look but then relaxed and smiled. "It's an immense relief for me that you don't need saving. I've been agonizing over your fate all these months. And of course we will respect your colonists' wishes. But before you make a decision, know that there is an additional reason I'm here. Whether the rest of your colony chooses to stay or not, I need the two of you to come with me. I intend to rescue each of the colonies we so desperately bridged to dangerous and unknown worlds."

Infinity stared at him. "You're kidding. You want us to go back to the world of thirdlings and orcs? To the world of mongrels?"

"Yes, but that's just the beginning. We have determined that, in the final days of our Earth's existence, twelve colonies—or portions of colonies—were bridged out in humanity's attempts to save the human species. Twelve colonies, bridged out by the seven bridging facilities around the world. Many of them may be suffering as we speak, dying off due to starvation or other threats. Now that we know how to get to them, we have the opportunity to save them, and I need your help. I understand that you may have created a good life here for yourselves and your colony. But please—I'm begging you to come with me."

LATER THAT EVENING, Infinity and Desmond sat upon the peak of the framework mound that was nearest to Mossview, watching the sun drop behind the rocky hillside. This particular mound was often occupied by a swarm of skitterbugs, but the colonists no longer had to worry about being attacked—Grimhold Hive had continued to honor their original agreement, reapplying predator repellent each time the humans visited them.

A dark figure—Gideon, based on the confident stride—crossed the field of moss below and then expertly climbed the slope. Without saying a word, he sat down on the girders next to Infinity and Desmond and stared out at the view. Infinity could tell he had something important to say but decided to let him get to it in his own time.

He finally spoke. "A lot of talking going on down there." He was referring to the conversations of the other colonists, who were now faced with the decision to stay or go. Armando and his entourage had bridged home, with the understanding that they would bridge back to this world at noon tomorrow. Those colonists who wanted to leave needed to be at the bridge-in site at that time.

"Any firm decisions?" Desmond asked.

Gideon picked a chunk of moss from the framework and tossed it toward Mossview. "Pretty much unanimous. They all want to stay. Especially the Millwrights, who have no interest in going back to any kind of public life. I guess there's something to be said for being the founders of a new civilization. They're all proud of what we've accomplished." After tossing another moss chunk, he turned his eyes to them. "Don't feel bad about leaving. We all understand why it's important. You've done a hell of a job here. This existence," he waved his hand toward Mossview, "is because of you."

Infinity squinted at him. "So you're all staying?"

"Eagleton and Chloe want to go, but just long enough for Chloe to deliver her baby in a real hospital. They say they'll come back after that, if the powers-that-be allow it."

"And you?" she asked.

He blew a puff of air through his nose and then nodded slightly. "I'm coming with you two. If you want my help, that is."

"We absolutely want your help," Desmond said.

Infinity just nodded.

Gideon turned back to gaze at the setting sun for a moment. Then he got up. "Alright then." He descended the slope and began trekking back across the moss.

Infinity moved closer to Desmond until she was pressed against his side. As she watched the hill's shadow creep over Mossview and the livestock pens, she slipped a hand beneath her tunic and ran her fingers over the three scars on her belly.

That's right—*Bridgers* continues. Infinity and Desmond have even greater challenges ahead.

Be sure to check out the next book in the series, ***Bridgers 5: The Trial of Extinction***.

And be sure to pick up the series prequel, ***INFINITY: A Bridger's Origin***. This is the book readers have been asking for—the story of how Infinity became a bridger!

And you're also going to want to check out my ***Diffusion series***, my ***Across Horizons series***, and my ***Fused series***.

Bridgers 5: The Trial of Extinction

Annihilation has a way of following some people.

Infinity and Desmond are bridgers, sworn to protect travelers to alternate versions of Earth. But now their own Earth has been destroyed, and they have a new task—protecting a small community of fellow refugees who managed to escape to a world teeming with giant arthropods. Stranded there, they've gradually managed to etch out a fulfilling existence. But it seems nothing good can ever last.

Infinity and Desmond's hopes of living out their lives in peace are shattered when their old friend Armando inexplicably bridges to their world. Armando's arrival triggers a devastating series of events and forces the bridgers and their fellow refugees to leave their new home. After narrowly escaping, they find themselves entangled in a cruel game, a trial to decide humankind's worth. The rules of the game are unclear, but the stakes are high—the annihilation of billions of people.

Caught up in an impossible dilemma, on a world populated by extraordinary sentient creatures, Infinity and Desmond discover the limits of what they are willing to do for their species —and for each other.

AUTHOR'S NOTES

Some of you may have questions. So I have decided to offer my thoughts on a few things related to **Bridgers 4: The Mind of Many**. These topics are in no particular order, and they may not even be important to most people. But I like to contemplate things like this.

Is it really possible that the earth could implode? This series is based on the destruction of Infinity and Desmond's version of Earth. This is a result of humans using seven bridging devices that have been constructed around the world, including the one at SafeTrek. Unbeknownst to humans, the bridging devices have been emitting a previously-unknown particle. This particle is heavy and therefore drifts down through the Earth's crust and settles at the Earth's core, the planet's center of gravity. Unfortunately, these particles have a peculiar property: they make every other particle they touch disappear (actually, the substances get bridged to some unknown alternate universe). The result is that, over a period of time, these particles have reduced the mass of the Earth's core. More bridging excursions have resulted in more of these particles, which have resulted in more of the Earth's core disappearing. Eventually, over several years, this began to have an effect on the entire planet. And ultimately, it will result in complete destruction.

The particles created by the bridging devices are obviously fictional (at least I hope they are). And the effects of diminishing the Earth's core can only be based upon speculation. But... people much smarter than me actually *have* speculated about this. If the Earth's core were somehow diminished, one of the first things you could expect to see is unusual and widespread northern lights (aurora borealis). Under normal circumstances, auroras occur near the north and south poles. This is because when the charged particles in the solar wind approach Earth, they are drawn to the magnetic north and south poles, where they interact with atoms and molecules of oxygen, nitrogen and other elements, resulting in a dazzling display of lights in the sky. But the earth's magnetic field is created by the swirling molten metals in the earth's core. If the earth's core is destroyed, so is the earth's magnetic field. So you would start to see auroras all over the earth, not just near the poles. That's why Infinity and Desmond have been seeing auroras even at SafeTrek, which is in Missouri.

You would also expect to experience widespread violent storms (like the super tornadoes in Chapter 1) and widespread earthquakes. As the earth's core gets smaller and smaller, these would become more common and more severe. Eventually, due to the pull of gravity, you would experience the mother of all earthquakes as the earth's crust collapses and falls inward to fill the empty space left behind by the missing core. As you can imagine, no living things would survive this.

Why did Infinity and Desmond's version of Earth implode while other versions didn't? The humans on Infinity's version of Earth discovered the radio signal from the extraterrestrial civilization known as the Outlanders, which included instructions for constructing bridging devices. The Outlanders at some point in the distant past decided that only certain civilizations should be allowed to exist. Specifically, those civilizations capable of figuring out that the radio signal included a hidden "key" to using the bridging devices without destroying their planet. Without this key, the resulting bridging devices would create the planet-killing particle. With the key, the bridging devices could be used without creating the particle and without harming the planet. Any civilization that discovers the radio signal but not the key would be tempted to construct and use bridging devices, resulting in the death of their civilization. Any civilization that discovers the signal *and* the key is deemed by the Outlanders to be worthy of existing.

There are an infinite number of alternate universes. In some of these, the Outlanders don't even exist. In others, the Outlanders exist but never did send out their signal. In others, the Outlanders exist and did send out their signal, but the humans on Earth have not yet discovered the signal. On some versions of Earth, the humans discovered the signal but wisely chose not to construct bridging devices. And on some versions of Earth, humans never even evolved in the first place, and therefore they didn't get the opportunity to discover the signal. With infinite universes, every scenario is possible.

What about other civilizations besides those on various versions of Earth? The Outlanders did not specifically target the Earth. They intended for the signal to go out to other civilizations in their universe, to destroy all civilizations that were becoming highly advanced but did not have a specific ability—the ability to decipher the hidden key. For whatever reason, the Outlanders believed that the ability to decipher this key was a good criterion for being allowed to exist. There is no way to know how many other civilizations, if any, have been destroyed, or will be destroyed in the future, by this cruel plan for "thinning the herd."

Is it possible that a version of Earth could become dominated by large arthropods? On our version of Earth, vertebrate animals evolved (fish, amphibians, reptiles, birds, and mammals). With an internal skeleton for support, vertebrate animals were able to grow to large sizes. But what if we have the opportunity to see a do-over of the last 550 million years? At 550 million years ago, the first primitive fish were starting to appear, but those didn't yet have a vertebral column (a backbone). So none of the more modern vertebrates had yet evolved. Also at that time, some of the first arthropods were showing up (such as trilobites). It could be argued that on our version of Earth, arthropods *are* actually the dominant life form. After all, it is estimated that there are 200 million insects for every human on Earth. For every pound of humans, there are 300 pounds of insects. And insects are not the only types of arthropods—the phylum also includes crustaceans, spiders, millipedes, centipedes, and more. But, the fact remains that the vertebrate animals were the ones to develop internal skeletons that allowed them to grow to a large size. Arthropods, on the other hand, are supported by their exoskeletons, which limits their size.

In the version of Earth featured in Bridgers 4, arthropods got the upper hand by developing internal skeletons (in addition to their exoskeletons). If this were to actually happen, there is no reason that arthropods couldn't have evolved to become the large and dominant creatures of the planet. In fact, in a scenario such as this, the large arthropods might eliminate all vertebrate animals altogether, resulting in no fish, amphibians, reptiles, birds, or mammals.

Is it possible that a version of Earth could be dominated by moss rather than trees, grasses, and other large plants? Again, if we had a do-over of the last 550 million years, this is certainly possible. First, it is important to understand the difference between vascular plants and nonvascular plants. Vascular plants have veins that carry water and nutrients from the soil to the upper parts of the plant. This allows vascular plants to grow very tall. Nonvascular plants do not have these veins, and therefore they cannot grow to more than a few inches because their water and nutrients cannot be carried any higher than that. Mosses are nonvascular plants, and they started appearing on Earth about 470 million years ago. Vascular plants, on the other hand, did not appear until about 50 million years later.

So the question is, in a do-over of the last 550 years, would it be possible that vascular plants never evolved? Yes, it would be. For one thing, the appearance of specific species or categories of living things (such as vascular plants) is not inevitable. Instead, it is the result of random events (random mutations, as well as random environmental events that make certain mutations beneficial). It is quite possible that, simply by chance, plants with veins may not have appeared. It is also possible that vascular plants may have appeared but did not thrive. In the world of Bridgers 4, vascular plants may have appeared, perhaps even multiple times, but they never did thrive because of the tendency of fires to destroy them. That world has a higher proportion of oxygen in its atmosphere (at least 23% oxygen, maybe more), which makes fires burn more easily.

What about an intelligent hive mind? Is it possible? This is perhaps the most speculative aspect of Bridgers 4. Maybe it's possible, maybe it's not. The concept comes from studies of large hives of ants, bees, and termites. Colonies of these insects (as opposed to the individuals) display remarkable qualities. For example, as a collective hive, honeybees ingest and digest food, maintain nutritional balance, circulate resources, exchange respiratory gases, regulate water content, control body temperature, and sense the environment. So, physiologically, it is easy to compare a hive to a larger creature. But mentally or cognitively? That's a different matter. Bee hives do make collective decisions about how to respond to the environment. But these decisions are collective because of visual cues they get from each other, pheromone signals from each other, and other cues passed between individuals. In order for true collective thought to take place, though, the individual bees would have to be connected the way neurons are connected. I can think of two ways this would work: the bees' nervous systems could be physically connected (not very practical), or the bees' nervous systems could be connected by telepathic means (telepathy is a fictional concept).

So, if you believe telepathic connections are possible, then the truly intelligent hive mind in Bridgers 4 is certainly possible. In the Bridgers series, we know telepathic connections are possible. After all, Desmond has the ability to project his thoughts telepathically to others through physical contact.

Why the title, The Mind of Many? This one should be obvious. It is simply a reference to the hive mind, which is made of many (billions) of individual winged arthropods. By the way, this title was selected after rejecting numerous others, including: *The Mind of Multitudes, The Power of Many, The Pres-*

ence of Mind, The Few and the Many, and *The Essence of Thought.*

Why did the characters refer to these creatures as flies? Because they didn't really know what else to call them. This world diverged from Infinity's version of Earth over 500 million years ago, and so it is possible (in fact, likely) that insects don't even exist there. And neither do millipedes, tiger beetles, and so on. Instead, the creatures of the Bridgers 4 world would actually belong to categories of creatures that are quite different than any on Infinity's version of Earth. In fact, they probably aren't even arthropods—they are probably so different from what we call arthropods that scientists would put them into an entirely different phylum. But, it is likely that some of these creatures have the same basic appearance as some we are familiar with (like a small, winged fly). So, wouldn't you have a tendency to give them names based on what they remind you of?

Is Infinity incapable of having children? That's a good question. When she was sixteen, she was stabbed three times in the abdomen (a scene depicted in Chapter 1 of Bridgers 3). At that time, the doctor told her that the blade had damaged her cervix. But to this day she has no definitive proof that she is incapable of bearing children. Perhaps a better question is, does she *want* to have children? Maybe soon we'll find out.

Are Infinity and Desmond really going to go back to the world of thirdlings and the world of mongrels? Well, that's what Armando would like them to do. And it makes sense, right? If they now have the capability to pinpoint the worlds where they have previously sent colonies of refugees, shouldn't they go rescue them? Or at least go and see if they are still alive? Infinity has said on several occasions that she wished that she could know whether or not she has really helped these colonies survive. So I would think she would at least want to check in on them. Of course, something could happen at any time to prevent such a mission. The multiverse is a dangerous place, after all.

Armando and several other humans managed to escape to a version of Earth with a divergence of only 20 years. Armando plans to rescue all the refugees and take them there. What is this new version of Earth like? Since it diverged from Infinity's version of Earth only 20 years ago, it is very similar. Up until 20 years ago, it was identical to Infinity's Earth. During the last 20 years, it has been on its own timeline. So you would expect some differences. Different politicians elected to office, for example. Infinity and Desmond are both older than twenty, so their other selves could exist there, and they might even meet them. Unless, of course, their other selves died during the last 20 years. Actually, if you think about it, a lot can happen in 20 years. It will be interesting to see what they find there.

Okay, what about the rather mind-bending concept of the possible existence of infinite parallel universes?

While there are certainly cosmologists who are skeptical of the concept, it is important to point out that multiple parallel universes is not a *theory*. Scientists did not simply come up with the idea using their imaginations. Instead, the concept is a mathematical consequence of our current theories in physics, particularly *quantum mechanics* and *string theory*.

If we assume that quantum mechanics and string theory are not completely wrong, then it is important for scientists to examine all of the mathematical consequences of those theories.

Even if those consequences (such as parallel universes) seem strange to us. This is often how science moves forward.

There are at least five plausible scientific theories that suggest the existence of multiple universes (the "multiverse"). My favorite of these is the concept of "daughter universes" suggested by the theory of quantum mechanics. Quantum mechanics describes things in terms of probabilities, rather than definite outcomes. The mathematics of quantum mechanics suggest that every possible outcome of every situation actually occurs—in its own separate universe.

Everything is made up of tiny particles, and what this "daughter universes" concept boils down to is that there could be infinite parallel universes, each of them differing by the position of only one particle.

The concept boggles the mind. But it certainly makes for a fun story.

ACKNOWLEDGMENTS

I am not capable of creating a book such as this on my own. I have the following people, among others, to thank for their assistance.

When it comes to editing, my son Micheal Smith is extremely talented, and his tireless and meticulous suggestions are invaluable. If you find a sentence or detail in the book that doesn't seem right, it is likely because I failed to implement one of his suggestions.

My wife Trish is always the first to read my work, and therefore she has the burden of seeing my stories in their roughest form. Thankfully, she kindly points out where things are a mess. Her suggestions are what get the editing process started. She also helps with various promotional efforts. And finally, she not only tolerates my obsession with writing, she actually encourages it.

I also owe thanks to those on my Advance Reviewer team. They were able to point out numerous typos and inconsistencies.

Finally, I am thankful to all the independent freelance designers out there who provide quality work for independent authors such as myself. Jake Caleb Clark (www.jcalebdesign.com) created the awesome cover for *Bridgers 4: The Mind of Many*.

ABOUT THE AUTHOR

Stan Smith has lived most of his life in the Midwest United States and currently resides with his wife Trish in a home nestled within an Ozark forest near Warsaw, Missouri. He writes adventure novels and short stories that have a generous sprinkling of science fiction. His novels and stories are about regular people who find themselves caught up in highly unusual situations. They are designed to stimulate your sense of wonder, get your heart pounding, and keep you reading late into the night, with minimal risk of exposure to spelling and punctuation errors. His books are for anyone who loves adventure, discovery, and mind-bending surprises.

Stan's Author Website
http://www.stancsmith.com

Feel free to email Stan at: stan@stancsmith.com
He loves hearing from readers and will answer every email.

3. Hostile Emergence

4. Binary Existence

Prequel: Genesis Sequence

The FUSED series

Prequel: Training Day

1. Rampage Ridge

2. Primordial Pit

Stand-alone Stories

Parthenium's Year